KINGDOM OF THE DEAD

OTHER BOOKS BY ANTHONY GIANGREGORIO

THE DEAD WATER SERIES
DEADWATER
DEADWATER: Expanded Edition
DEADRAIN
DEADCITY
DEADWAVE
DEAD HARVEST
DEAD UNION
DEAD VALLEY
DEAD TOWN
DEAD SALVATION
DEAD ARMY (coming soon)

ALSO BY THE AUTHOR
DEAD MOURNING: A ZOMBIE HORROR STORY
THE ZOMBIE IN THE BASEMENT (YOUNG ADULT)
THE MONSTER UNDER THE BED
DEADEND: A ZOMBIE NOVEL
DEAD TALES: SHORT STORIES TO DIE FOR
DEAD MOURNING: A ZOMBIE HORROR STORY
ROAD KILL: A ZOMBIE TALE
DEADFREEZE
DEADFALL
DEADRAGE
SOUL-EATER
THE DARK
RISE OF THE DEAD
DARK PLACES
BLOOD RAGE

KINGDOM OF THE DEAD

ANTHONY GIANGREGORIO

KINGDOM OF THE DEAD

ISBN   Softcover   ISBN 13: 978-1-935458-30-2
                          ISBN 10: 1-935458-30-2

This is a work of fiction. Names, characters, places and incidents either are the product of the author's imagination or are used fictitiously, and any resemblance to any actual persons, living or dead, events, or locales is entirely coincidental.

This book was printed in the United States of America.

For more info on obtaining additional copies of this book, contact:
www.livingdeadpress.com

Chapter 1

The helicopter hovered over the office complex, the pregnant woman in the pilot's seat gazing down at the zombies milling about on the roof. Their hands were upraised, fingers curling as if they could somehow pull the helicopter back to earth.

More than fifty bodies were now on the roof with more pouring through the skylight with each passing second. Francesca Jones stared at their undead, pale faces in horror.

It was strange, seeing the familiar mixed in with the truly macabre. There was a dentist's assistant on the roof; her once white uniform stained a mottled brown, her blonde curly hair, once shiny and beautiful, now a stringy mass of blood and gore. There was a man wearing a brown shirt and jeans, and in each of his hands he held a shotgun. One was Richard's, now dead and the other one belonged to Paul.

There was an old man, his beer belly hidden under his red and green sweater. His mouth was in the shape of a circle, and his dead eyes stared up at the underbelly of the helicopter.

Francesca felt the unborn baby kick and she glanced down at her stomach, her child moving in the womb, as if the child could sense its mother's emotions.

All this she took in at a glance. All these things were processed in her mind in an instant, in less time than it would take her heart to beat twice inside her chest.

She was pulled from her reverie by a man's voice. A deep bass filled with strength and confidence.

"Well, how much fuel do we have left in the tank?" Paul Washburn asked from behind her. He was breathing heavily, the mad dash from the roof of the office complex to the helicopter straining his energy to the max, covering his skin with a thin sheen of perspiration. His Mexican heritage was apparent to anyone who met him. Only minutes ago he'd had a small pistol to his head, but at the last second, when the ghouls were surrounding him, he'd realized he couldn't do it, that he didn't want to do it.

So he'd shot the first ghoul in the head and had then dashed for the skylight of the office, battling his way to the roof and the waiting helicopter above.

Sure, it would have been simpler to just squeeze the trigger, and he could have, if it would have served a purpose, but Paul was no coward and killing himself would have been the coward's way out.

And there was still a chance, however slim, that he would live to see the next day. Francesca checked the fuel gauge at Paul's question and she frowned deeply.

"Not much at all, barely a quarter of a tank," she said.

Paul nodded grimly. "Okay, let's get going and see what's out there."

She flicked her head ever so slightly and then banked the helicopter to the right, soaring away from the office complex and into the rising sun that was even now dawning on a new day.

She gazed down to the parking lot one last time, seeing the large bread trucks blocking the office complex's doors and the blood and gore splattering the front grilles. As she flew through the air, she saw the loading dock, now opened and exposed to the open air. The zombies were wandering about, some with shattered limbs and large pieces of their bodies missing. There had to be hundreds of them down there, all wandering aimlessly, all seeming to be bowing at the church of employment as they waited to enter the office building like churchgoers arriving for Sunday mass.

Intertwined with the undead were some new recruits; a roving military gang of men and women that had attacked the office complex hours ago. It seemed they had suffered many casualties, too, not a few of them thanks to Paul.

But the two weary people in the helicopter had suffered casualties of their own, and recently.

For one thing, Shaun, Francesca's lover, the original pilot of the stolen helicopter, and the father of her unborn baby, had been killed. And worst of all, he had returned later as one of the walking dead. It was he that had led the horde of zombies right to their front door, so to speak, as some residual memory of his former life had directed him back to Francesca. That's what she wanted to think, though she had a feeling memory had nothing to do with it and it had been simple instinct.

It was Paul who had shot Shaun in the right eye, the back of the dead man's skull exploding onto the rear wall of what was once their sanctuary, their living quarters on the fifth floor of the empty complex for more than five and a half months.

Down below, near the south side doors, was the large bread truck where Richard had been attacked and bitten when he had gone out in search of other survivors; the moment in time forever trapped in her mind.

Richard had been Shaun's friend and she had known him by association. He had been a free-spirited, second generation German man with bright red hair and freckles, who was always cheerful. He was the polar opposite of Paul, who was a tall, dour, Mexican man with a firm jaw and piercing black eyes.

Richard had been infected from the bite and had died days later, returning as one of the undead. Paul had put him down for good, and had buried him in the small garden in the middle of the small food court on the first floor. His dog tags were the only thing marking the grave, a grave the zombies were even now probably walking on; their lack of respect in death no excuse in Francesca's eyes.

The office complex was quickly fading away to be lost behind her and she couldn't help but feel a pang of loss. The office building had been her home for almost six months and she was leaving a good friend there as well as her lost lover.

She had told herself they couldn't stay at the complex forever, but as the world had crumbled apart, she, Paul and Shaun had lived in solitude, pining away the days as the undead slowly dominated the planet.

As she adjusted the controls on the helicopter and evened out the aircraft, she wondered what they would find now that they were on the move again. The television and radio broadcasts had cut out months ago, and other than the rogue military personnel attacking the office complex, they'd had no contact with other human beings.

It was as if they were the last people alive on Earth.

Apparently it would not be the meek who inherited the Earth, but the walking dead.

She shook her head to clear it, still trying to accept her new reality even after all this time.

The dead were walking and eating the flesh of the living, and any recently deceased bodies were rising to walk the land as ghouls, now hungry for the taste of human flesh. It was so bizarre, like one of those old 1960's horror movies with Bela Lugosi she had seen when she was a teenager.

The baby kicked again inside her, causing her to gasp in surprise.

"You okay?" Paul asked from behind her.

She nodded, her brown hair flowing about her ivory-toned face. She was a beautiful woman, with striking features and deep brown eyes that any man would find attractive. And even now, when she was as big as a whale, or so she thought, her skin glowed with motherhood.

She had come so far in her own personal development since the world had collapsed and the dead began to walk. Before she had been an intern at a local television station, and now she was Francesca Jones, zombie hunter and helicopter pilot.

Thinking of the helicopter made her think of Shaun. He had taught her how to fly when she had been adamant about learning. She'd had the foresight to realize if something had happened to him, they would all be trapped in the office complex with no way to escape so she had learned to fly with textbooks and Shaun's help.

So now she was flying, the controls feeling comfortable in her hands despite her nervousness as a novice pilot. She knew she could do this, and the practice she had would assure it.

"I'm fine, Paul, he just kicked again," she told him with a grin.

"Oh, yeah? How do you know it's a boy?"

She shrugged slightly. "I just do, call it mother's intuition."

He didn't reply. Paul was a quiet man, taciturn to the point of being mute. He never said three words when two would suffice.

"We need fuel," he said calmly, his Mexican accent barely noticable. "And that baby's gotta be almost here. We'll need to find someplace safe where you can deliver it safely."

"Yes, Paul, I've been thinking about that, too, but I haven't wanted to bring it up," she said.

He grunted in reply.

She banked the helicopter over a small neighborhood, the once pristine urban setting now resembling something from a third world country.

Where once majestic homes had stood, now there were burnt out husks and wrecked motor vehicles. Manicured lawns of the past were now three feet high, the tall reeds falling over from their own weight. Dark maroon spots could be seen painting the street with a kaleidoscope of shapes, the residue of some past carnage.

And then she saw them, as she knew she would.

The undead appeared, shambling from cover at the sounds of the helicopter. They crawled out from under wrecked cars and stumbled out of destroyed homes and gazed up to the sky with milk-white, dead eyes. Rigid hands with bent and warped fingers reached upward to the sky, as if they could pluck the helicopter out of the air and crush it to their rotting chests.

And rotting they were.

After more than six months of moving across the land, the zombies had begun to decay, their flesh sloughing off their bones like old porridge. Faces were gaunt, lips pulled back so that blackened gums could be seen, teeth stained with blood from past feedings. Foreheads were now more pronounced and many of the male ghouls had light beards, their skin shrinking, allowing the follicles to protrude more. Some had gaping wounds on their bodies, maggots squirming inside like a thousand jumping beans as they fed on the decaying flesh.

Rats scurried about the streets and between the zombie's feet, nipping at pieces of tissue to quickly dart away to hide under a dented, blackened car with their prize.

A 1970 Chevy Nova, only nine years old to the day, was now a home to a large family of rodents, the rats prospering like never before.

A few housecats, now turned feral, prowled the edges of the streets, searching for an unwary rat to make dinner, but they had to be cautious. Though the undead preferred human meat, they would settle for feline. Not to mention the cats had to watch out for wild dogs. Man's best friend was now his enemy, the canines wary of the undead and humans alike. They had turned into true carnivores and would kill and eat a cat at a moment's notice if the opportunity arose.

And then the zombies began to moan, long and loud, the song of the dead rising to the helicopter and overriding the noise of the rotors.

"They look hungry," Paul stated as he gazed down to the street below.

Francesca didn't answer, there was no need.

As she studied the dead and the neighborhood below, she realized there were no living people like her and Paul, only the dead and the animals.

Could she and Paul really be the only remaining humans?

Though fantastic, it was possible. But then she thought of the military faction that attacked them and knew that wasn't the case.

No, there were still people out there, hiding, trying to survive, and there were others, who had become predators, preying on the week because they now could.

She glanced over her shoulder to see Paul. He was biting his lip as he watched the undead below, but then the helicopter flew on, leaving the dilapidated neighborhood behind.

"We need to go somewhere, Paul, do you have any ideas?"

He nodded ever so slightly, as there was no need for a full one. That was Paul, reserved to the last.

She waited for more than a minute for a reply and then she turned and glanced over her shoulder so she could see his dark eyes.

"Well?"

"The city, Francesca, we need to go back to the city. But not Philly. We know what it's like there. I say we try for Pittsburgh.

Maybe it's better there. Maybe it's not so bad. I had friends in Pittsburgh, so I used to go there a lot on the weekends. I know my way around."

She blinked at his answer, wondering if she had misheard him over the roar of the rotors. But with his face set in stone, she knew she'd heard him correctly.

"But that's crazy. Pittsburgh will be full of them, too. Shaun and Richard said to go north. Maybe we should just try to..."

He cut her off with a chop of his right hand, the gesture stating his decision was final.

"No, Francesca, we can't. You just said we're low on fuel. Anything north is too far from here, we'll never make it. No, our only chance is to get to a city and land on one of the high-rises. They have refueling stations on some of the high-rises for the fat cats that own helicopters. Hey, wait a second. I got a better idea than that one. How 'bout a hospital?"

"A hospital?" she asked, repeating his words.

"Yeah, Mercy Hospital or maybe the children's one, whatever looks the safest. But it has to be one with a helipad."

"But, Paul..." she said, and then stopped.

He nodded, his eyes softening. "I know, Francesca, but it's our only option. We've got to try. We'll need the medical supplies at the hospital for your baby when it comes and they might still have some fuel in their tanks if they have a refueling station on the roof." He reached out and touched her shoulder. "It's our only chance."

She stared at him for another three seconds, thinking, sucking her lower lip in thought, and finally she nodded.

"Okay, we'll try Pittsburgh, I just hope you're right about this," she said and banked the helicopter in the direction of downtown Pittsburgh.

"Yeah," Paul said under his breath. "Me, too."

Chapter 2

A gore-covered moving van slowed as it approached Haverhill's Supermarket on Fourth Ave. on the north side of Pittsburgh. All around the van, littering the streets, were abandoned cars with opened doors and shattered windows. Many had dark maroon stains on them, as if some mad painter had run around the city painting cars. Trash was everywhere, blowing about like tumbleweeds, collecting in every nook and crevice of the once great city of steel.

In front of the van, a brand new, cherry red, 1978 Chevrolet Camaro slowed down and pulled to the other side of the street until the car was alongside the van. In the driver's seat of the Camaro sat a young man in his early twenties, with long black hair and freckles. His name was Dale Evans and he was on point for the foraging party.

Until six months ago, he had worked at an electronics store, hocking stereos and GE televisions to suckers. But not anymore. Now he was just one of the sixty-five survivors trying to eke out a living in downtown Pittsburgh.

The passenger side window of the van rolled down and a man in his late forties gazed down at the Camaro, Dale grinning up at the man.

Frank Pearson stared at Dale with a cold intensity that wiped the smile from Dale's face like a hurricane to a feather.

"Stay sharp, Dale, there were reports that Carver's in the area, at least that was what the last search party said," Frank said flatly. There was no time for games now that they were away from the safe haven of their enclave. When they were safe inside the City County Building, he was a friendly man and would always have a nice thing to say to you with an accompanying smile, but now, when he was out in the city, where the undead were everywhere, he was all business.

He had to be, it was the only way to stay alive and to also keep the sixty-plus people who had come to see him as their leader safe.

"No, problem, Frank, we got this," Dale said as he slapped the leg of the woman sitting next to him in the Camaro. Lucy Walters only nodded, her assault rifle in her hands, ready if needed.

A shot rang out, followed by two more, and Frank glanced behind him to see three zombies drop to the streets. On the roof of the van, strapped there safely with rope, was his second in command, Don Falocci.

Don had served in the army for five years, had done a tour in Vietnam, and knew how to handle a firearm. He was one of the reasons they were all still alive. Before the dead began to walk, Frank had never held a firearm before, but now, his Glock 9mm felt like an extension of his body.

The Glock 17 was a prototype for the Austrian Army. It wasn't due to be released for actual use for another year or more. He had found it in a gun shop hidden in a safe. He had been in luck and before the owner had been killed and had turned into a zombie, he had left the safe open, thus allowing Frank and his men to pillage the safe and gun store for weapons and ammunition.

The Glock was a semi-automatic pistol with a polymer made casing, the first of its kind, and used a modified Browning breach. His had a fixed sight, but the weapon could also have an adjustable or night sight. It was manufactured in a flat black finish and carried a magazine of 17, but could also use an extended clip of 19 rounds, all 9mm. The gun had three safeties, one external and two internal. The external was located on the trigger, and the internal ones, one in the firing pin and the other to prevent accidental discharge if the weapon was dropped, would be disengaged whenever the trigger was depressed. With these three safeties, it was one of the safest weapons for a soldier to handle. Added to the Glock was a nine-inch Bowie knife that was strapped to his right hip. The knife felt like a third arm to him and was always there if he needed it, and he had, on one too many occasions.

Frank turned to the driver, a woman in her mid-fifties. She looked like a truck driver and that's what she was, at least in her former life. Maggie Collins was looking in her driver's door mirror, wondering where all the ghouls were that were being shot, when a pale, rotting face suddenly slapped against her window, making her almost crap her pants. She let out a yell, her foot leaving the brake, and the van bucked for a moment. The sound of something heavy dropping onto the roof came into the cab and Frank knew what had happened instantly. Maggie had bucked the van and Don had lost his footing and had fallen to the roof. He could only hope the man was okay as he sure couldn't check on him right now.

Meanwhile, the zombie was still pounding on the window and no sooner did the face appear than it disappeared. Maggie let out a sigh of relief. That is, until the zombie's hand appeared again, but this time holding an old piece of metal, an alternator or a compressor from one of the wrecked cars lining the street.

Before Maggie knew what was happening, her window shattered, the metal object dropping into the cab and falling on her lap. The heavy object struck her kneecap and she let out a howl of pain. But her screech was soon changed to one of panic when the ghoul reached inside the cab and grabbed her by her fiery red hair. Her head was yanked back and Maggie suddenly found herself fighting for her life as the ghoul attempted to sink its fetid teeth into her left ear.

A gunshot sounded inside the cab, causing both Maggie and Frank to wince. The ghoul's head exploded into a hundred bone fragments, and brain matter splattered across the inside of the cab. Maggie screamed again and Frank looked left and right, not knowing what was happening. Then he looked to his right and saw Lucy standing on the hood of the Camaro, her assault rifle in her hands. The barrel had a wisp of smoke drifting from it and the woman had a wide grin plastered on her face.

"You guys all right?" she asked as she scanned the area around her for more ghouls. She knew that gunshot and the ones Don had fired would attract every zombie in a half-mile radius. They would have to move and soon or risk becoming surrounded.

Frank didn't answer for a moment, still stunned by the violence only inches from him, but as he reached over to Maggie, the woman nodded she was fine. She reached for a few tissues on the dashboard and began trying to clean herself up, the blood and gore covering her from head to belt buckle.

Frank nodded slowly. "Yeah, Lucy, we're fine. Thanks, that was some damn fine shooting."

She merely shrugged. "Yeah, I guess." With a flick of her light-brown hair, she hopped down to the ground and climbed back into the Camaro, Dale clapping the entire time at her great shot.

Don tapped on the roof, notifying them in the cab he was all right, and just in time as more than a hundred ghouls appeared from the end of the street, with more coming from the other direction, as well. The undead were awake and were searching for the disturbance of the gunshots. It was dawn in Pittsburgh and Frank had found the best time to forage for food and supplies was when the sun was just breaking the horizon. He didn't know why, but for just that few hours, before the sun was entirely in the sky, the zombies seemed a little slower, more apathetic.

"Okay, guys, let's move out. Maggie, you can clean yourself up later while the rest of us are inside the supermarket. Right now we need to get going."

She tossed a few dark, blood-red tissues out the shattered window and then glanced in her mirror again, then out the front windshield.

"Shit, Frank, you don't have to tell me twice," she said as she slammed the transmission in drive, tooted the horn to warn Don she was moving, and proceeded to drive.

Dale waited for Maggie to leave, knowing he would now ride as backup. The moving van was the vehicle to go first as the added weight of the larger truck would easily plow through the crowd of zombies heading towards them.

All walks of life were represented in the undead crowd as well as all colors and sizes. There was a policeman with his riot helmet still intact, the strap that went under his chin to keep his helmet on now absorbed into his skin, pus and yellow ooze dripping down his neck. There was a doctor, complete with stained white coat and a stethoscope still hanging from his neck, and a mother with hair curlers and wearing a plaid nightgown. A business man, wearing a thousand dollar suit and custom Gucci shoes shambled at the head of the pack, his suit now covered with gore and mold. His face, once perfectly shaved, was covered in stubble, a large chunk of flesh now missing from the right cheek, and his once manicured nails were now broken or missing altogether. His hundred dollar haircut was ruined, the hair a tangled mess of gore and filth.

And the last two zombies to round out the melting pot was a Catholic priest and a Protestant reverend, both dead men now working together in death.

"Gun it, Maggie, send them back to Hell," Frank growled as he held on to the dashboard, careful to keep his hand out of the worst of the gore.

"You got it, Frank," she replied and stepped on the gas, the van surging forward.

The ghouls never slowed, never so much as moved an inch out of the way. Their dead brains knew nothing of self-preservation, and as Maggie drove through the center of the crowd, bodies and severed limbs went flying in all directions, the walking dead becoming churned up rotten meat in the tire wells of the van. The front grille of the van became choked with bone and tissue, gobbets of dripping black ichor covering the entire metal mesh. Behind the van, the Camaro drove over the twitching corpses, Dale frowning at the thought of his baby getting blood all over her.

The Camaro had a custom finish and wheels with a killer stereo. Dale had found the car in a garage on the outskirts of the city and had claimed it as his own. He had personally plucked the keys from the half-eaten male corpse that was still in the driveway, the keys having fallen from the dead hands. The slaughtered man had had a massive hole in his head, which explained why, when he'd died, he had stayed that way. The van plowed through the horde of undead like they were nothing but paper mache, sending the bodies spilling every which way. In less than fifteen seconds, the van was through the worst of them and the Camaro was right behind. The front, right tire of the Camaro drove over a head, the skull splitting like a ripe watermelon, brains squishing into the tire well. Immediately the odor of rot permeated the car and Dale swore deeply, knowing what a bitch it would be to clean his baby once they returned to the enclave.

Then the convoy of two was through the zombies and turning the corner onto Cherry Way, the supermarket only a few streets away.

"You think we'll get in and out without running into them?" Maggie asked Frank casually. Her free hand was still wiping brown goo from her face; her hand flicking the stuff out the window like it was pudding.

"Don't know, but I know if we do, we'll be ready for him and his cutthroat bastards," Frank said as he placed his free hand on the cold grip of his Glock.

"Far as I know, no one's touched this place yet. It's pristine. All the front windows are intact and the loading dock is still secure. At least that's what our scout said when he reported back last night. It looks like we'll be the first here; lucky, huh?"

Maggie only grunted in reply, her scarlet hair flowing around her head. She was still pretty for her age, though the crows' feet and wrinkle lines were slowly entrenching deeper over her visage.

She concentrated on driving, the street treacherous and full of abandoned cars. More than once she had to use the van like a plow, pushing the cars out the way, the flat tires on the wrecks protesting the entire time. There was one time when a green Dodge Dart blocked the road and she had to push so hard with the van, the car rolled over and then spun on its hood.

Frank glanced over his shoulder, his eyes taking in the rear of the moving van. Inside the cargo hold of the van were a half dozen men and women, the rest of his foraging team. He figured they were probably nervous and wondering what was going on, but for now they would have to wait for an answer. The reply would be found soon enough when the convoy reached the supermarket. And as Maggie stepped on the gas, the right side of the van crashing into an old wreck of a station wagon, she knew they would have their answer soon enough.

Once they reached the supermarket, they would clear the area of zombies, and then enter through the front doors to raid the store while a few of them stood guard. If all went as planned, they would be in and out and back on the road in less than an hour.

And best of all, he had beaten that bastard Carver to the prize.

If there was only enough food in the city to keep one enclave alive until help finally came, then he would make damn sure it was his enclave that received it.

Chapter 3

Ben Carver, or just Carver to his friends and enemies, slowed the beat-up Ford pickup truck at the rear loading dock to Haverhill's Supermarket as the two other battered and worn cars did the same behind him. The front of the Ford was a mess of blood, bone, and gobbets of dried flesh and tissue; residue from the zombies the truck had bowled over within the last hour.

There were a few zombies in the area, but it had been easy pickings to take them out. The brain dead idiots were helpless against him, his men and their superior firepower of automatic weapons.

Carver was the leader of another ragtag band of survivors. His small enclave was fifty strong, and they were the hardest, coldest sons of bitches you'd ever want to meet. Almost all of them had been on the wrong side of the law when the dead began to walk and a few had been locked up in the county jail. But when the world collapsed in on itself, it had been very easy, too easy actually, to escape from lockup. Which was what Carver had done. He had been in jail for the weekend on a count of assault with a deadly weapon.

And it was all true. If a few bystanders hadn't managed to pull him off the man he had beaten half to death, he would have finished the other half and sent the prick straight to Hell.

No one called him a pussy. At least not if they wanted to live after uttering the remark.

Out of all the coldhearts in his group, he was the leader, because he was the meanest bastard you would ever want to meet. Already, since he had taken charge, he'd had to kill three men who had attempted to usurp his power. All three were now either inside the guts of the zombies or were the walking dead themselves. Carver didn't know or care, as he had sent them packing with broken arms, caved in chests, and faces that looked like blueberries with spots of black on them, thanks to the pounding they had received.

Placing the truck in park, he hopped out of the driver's seat, his leather cowboy boots flashing in the morning sun. He had taken them off a ghoul who had attacked him and his crew, and as the boots weren't damaged in any way, he had decided to claim them for his own.

A zombie stumbled out from behind a nearby dumpster near the loading dock doors and Carver was already in motion, the rest of his men caught flatfooted.

Deciding he wouldn't mind getting his hands dirty, he pulled the policeman's nightstick hanging from his waist and brought it up in an overhand blow that had the nightstick embedding itself three inches into the ghoul's forehead.

The zombie stopped for an instant, but the blow wasn't a killing blow and it reached its hands out to grab Carver's arm. He slapped the hands away, yanked the nightstick from the head with gore flying off the tip, spun the weapon around, and then jammed it straight into the ghoul's right eye.

Ocular fluid squirted out the side of the nightstick as it slowly slid through the eye socket, the sides grating on bone, and continued until it had penetrated the rotting brain of the zombie. With a twist of his wrist, he made the tip of the weapon spin, mashing the brain into porridge. The zombie stopped moving then, and slumped to the ground. Carver placed his foot on the corpse's chest and pulled, the nightstick coming loose with a sucking sound.

He wiped the tip on the filthy clothes of the ghoul and then turned to his men who were watching silently.

"What the fuck are you idiots looking at? This isn't a goddamn Broadway show! Get your asses into a skirmish line and guard our backs!"

As one unit, the crew did as ordered. All but one, that is.

Lynn Hopkins waited by the Ford, her arms crossed in front of her, a .38 S&W revolver on her hip, worn Old West style. Her long blonde hair glistened in the sun and her shapely figure would have any red-blooded man drooling like a fool.

Carver took two steps towards her and grinned lazily.

"What the fuck are you looking at, bitch?"

She didn't answer at first; instead letting her eyes roam over the man she had taken as her lover. Carver was a big man, six-three easy, and he was made of hard planes and sharp angles. He resembled a slab of granite a sculpturer had carved using a dull hatchet. But he did more than resemble that piece of rock. He was hard, all of him, hands, feet, body, all rock hard muscle of steel under his clothing. Lynn knew this intimately and she felt a tingle down below in her nether regions as she thought about those rippling muscles holding her, on top of her.

No, she needed to stay focused. They were in danger here. Zombies were everywhere and they had been in luck so far that only a few had arrived.

"I'm looking at the meanest asshole this side of Pittsburg, that's what," she purred with a sly grin.

Carver chuckled at that and moved closer to her. Her red lips were so tempting, he couldn't refuse them, so he kissed her then, a passionate kissed that lasted an instance, but seemed to linger a lifetime.

"Hey, Carver, we got the loading dock open!" a voice called from his side. Carver turned to see one of his men, David O'Hara waving to him. O'Hara was an older man in his late sixties, but he was in shape and was tougher than most of the younger men in his crew. The man wore a black motorcycle jacket covered in chains and his biker's emblem was worn proudly on the back of the jacket. Now he was the only one left, the rest of his gang either dead for good or zombies.

Carver relied on him as a kind of second-in-command, though he kept it loose. If the men like the ones he ruled were too close to power, it wouldn't be long before they wanted it all.

And though Carver wasn't afraid of man, beast, or zombie, he was no fool, and preferred to limit his challenges where he could.

He stepped away from Lynn and rubbed his lips, relishing the taste of her.

"Come on, baby, let's go get some shit. We're low on everything back home. That bastard Pearson has been getting too much shit ahead of us. It's time we got the loot first for a change."

"So let's go, times a wastin'," she grinned and moved away, strolling to the loading doors like she was enjoying a walk in the park. Carver watched her leave, admiring the curve of her hips and thin waist. The gun on her hip only made her sexier, like a hotrod with a hot chick in a bikini lying on the hood.

With a quick glance over his shoulder to make sure his men were on guard and alert, he followed her to the loading dock, his eyes on her swaying buttocks.

It looked like they had reached the supermarket first and would be able to pick it clean. And all that asshole Pearson would find is empty shelves and a few boxes of dish detergent.

"Well, what's up, we good?" Carver asked O'Hara as he stepped next to the older man.

The biker nodded, signifying that, yes, they were good. The doors were up and the loading dock was exposed to the daylight. Inside, three bodies were spread out on the cement floor, their heads caved in, brains and blood spread out by the cracked skulls. The three ghouls had been inside when the doors were opened by the men and they had taken them down easily. It was only when the dead had numbers behind them that they were truly a danger.

The rest of the dock was empty, only a few discarded cardboard boxes and some milk crates strewn across the floor.

Three men were by the double doors that would lead into the supermarket itself. A man stood with a sawed-off shotgun, his long black hair hanging behind him, the upper half tied into a ponytail.

Carver nodded to this man, gesturing with his rifle.

"We good, Fred?"

Fred Sherman nodded they were. He was a skinny man in his mid-thirties; his thin glasses and long black hair making him look like a hippy. But if a hippy believed in peace and love, Sherman believed in shoot 'em all and let God sort 'em out.

Finally they would beat Pearson and his assholes to the punch and would get to ransack the supermarket for everything they could carry. The two enclaves had been battling for supremacy of what was left of downtown Pittsburgh for more than three months. With the world gone to shit, there were no more trucks bringing food into the city. After all the fires, many of the grocery stores and supermarkets had been damaged to the point only some rare finds of canned goods were still edible. Of course anything frozen, fresh or perishable was nothing but mush and maggots.

At one time, Frank Pearson had offered to combine the two enclaves, stating that the remaining living humans needed to work together, but after Carver had stated his ground rules, mainly that he would be in charge of everyone, Pearson had told him no.

And so the two enclaves were at constant odds with one another as they fought over the remaining resources inside the city. And if the ghouls weren't enough to worry about, then the raging gun battles with the last survivors in Pittsburgh was a constant threat.

But at least this time his men had beat the old bastard to the target.

Just yesterday he hadn't known this supermarket was still standing, but one of his scouts had reported back with the good news. The loading dock was locked and the front windows were still intact. The supermarket was untouched.

Now more valuable than gold, what was lining the shelves of the supermarket would feed his people for months, maybe longer. All the canned goods, bags of potato chips, bottles of juice and soda, crackers, cake mixes, flour and sugar, cooking oil, dried pasta, beer and hard alcohol, and cookies were a lucky find. And the batteries, hell, they always needed batteries, not wanting to waste their precious gas reserves for the generator, which was already low on fuel; that being just one more thing he had to worry about.

But he had won, finally, and this time Pearson would be the loser.

Carver grinned widely in victory.

"All right, boys, let's go shopping and we're gonna have to come back with a bigger truck."

With grunts of agreement, the scavenging party entered the supermarket through the back entrance.

Chapter 4

The gray and white helicopter hovered over the outskirts of Pittsburgh, just to the side of the Liberty Bridge. Below, the Monongahela River flowed, the choppy water filled with dead bodies and refuse from the carnage that had befallen the city months ago. Overturned boats and even a few cars floated near the shore. The bridge itself had many spots where the sides had been fractured, cars spinning out of control to crash into the frigid water below.

Interstate 376 was a parking lot of abandoned cars and trucks. If they had been driving, Francesca and Paul would have been stopped cold in their tracks, only the helicopter saving them from certain death.

Paul leaned forward in his seat, eyeing the terrain below. Interspersed amongst the cars on the highway, dozens of walking corpses could be seen in the bright sunshine. The sun was now up and the horizon was clear, only a few cumulous clouds to mar the otherwise perfect sky.

"Look at them down there," he said, gesturing with his chin. "They just walk around with nothing to do. I don't even want to think what it would be like if we were down there with them."

"Then don't, Paul. We're not down there and hopefully we won't end up there." She pointed to the right, toward downtown. "We should be near the medical center shortly. I thought I'd try for the Children's Hospital first."

"What about Allegheny or Mercy? They're just as close," Paul suggested.

Francesca shook her head and then nodded almost immediately after. "Yes, I know, but I've been to the Children's before, so I know it a little bit. The station did a story there about one of their clinics, I'm gonna try there first."

Paul frowned, not used to being overruled. In the time they had spent in the complex, Shaun and Richard had always deferred to him. Paul was a natural leader and the others had sensed that in him and so had let him take charge. But she was the pilot so he really had no choice in the matter.

"All right then, go 'head and get us there before we run out of fuel."

The helicopter banked to the right and she moved the control stick. She was proud of herself as she leveled out the aircraft, making sure she pressed the pedals the way Shaun had taught her to adjust pitch and angle. He would be so proud of her if he was here with her right now. But then she felt the baby kick and she reached down with her free hand, caressing her stomach.

Shaun was still here, in a small way.

As they flew over the city, Paul stared at the streets and buildings below. As a cop, he knew the city like the back of his hand and was amazed at how much of it he barely recognized now. Not only had parts of the city been burned, but it looked like some of the structures had exploded, possibly from gas mains. They flew over 2nd Avenue and he gazed down at the wreckage that was once the Public Works Building. The building was now nothing but rubble, large chunks of concrete scattered around the area like a massive hand had squished the building flat in a fit of rage. Even here, there were shambling forms moving about, pale faces that looked up to the sky as the helicopter soared overhead. A few tried to follow the helicopter, but soon lost it when it flew over nearby buildings.

Once the aircraft was gone, the zombies began doing nothing, merely moving about aimlessly. A few picked up pieces of wrinkled and torn paper drifting along the street. Yellowing picnic permits, battlefield permits and land records were scattered everywhere, the explosion that had taken down the Public Works Building throwing debris high into the air.

Francesca tried not to look down too much as what she saw sent a chill through her very soul. She hadn't realized how truly bad it was while she had been living safely in the office complex. Now, out here in the world again, she realized how tenuous her survival, and her baby's survival, was.

"There's the Children's Hospital over there!" Paul said, his voice slightly raised.

She angled the helicopter towards the building and in less than two minutes she was hovering over the rooftop.

At the moment it was empty.

"Should I set down?" she asked, unsure of what to do.

"No, wait a few minutes. I want to see what happens," he said, his eyes scanning the roof

She could see the roof was empty and the helipad was down there so she didn't understand why Paul didn't want to just set down when all of a sudden, out of the door leading into the hospital, dozens of small bodies spilled out. Most wore nothing but hospital gowns, the backs open and flapping in the wind. Most of the bodies were no more than four or five feet tall, some even smaller.

Francesca had to blink twice before she realized what she was seeing.

They were children.

Dead children were now clambering onto the roof from inside the hospital, the tiny faces staring up at the helicopter with slack-jawed expressions. A few moved too close to the edge of the roof and lost their balance, tumbling into the abyss that led straight to the ground below.

Every one of the children had some sort of mortal wound, and some were missing limbs and parts of their faces. It was a horrid sight and Francesca had to turn away, not wanting to see anymore.

"Damn it, this is what I was afraid of. There's too damn many to fight off. We need to get to a hospital that the damn zombies haven't made it to the roof yet." He pointed to the inner city.

"You might as well go, Francesca. We won't be landing there anytime soon."

"All right, I'll try for one of the others," she said and banked the helicopter away. A few small ghouls lost their footing from the backwash of the rotors, their small bodies spinning off the edge to fall to the sidewalk below. When they impacted, their small frames didn't just smack; they literally exploded, like dropped water balloons, spraying the sidewalk with blood and gore for yards in all directions. No sooner had the blood and flesh settled, then hundreds of rats appeared to feed on the gory remains.

The cycle of life continued, even in a world of the dead.

* * *

"Paul, there's Mercy Hospital," Francesca said as the helicopter dove towards the massive building. She knew this hospital had a helipad, too, because she'd flown over it with Shaun a year or so ago and she had remembered seeing it. By coincidence, a medical helicopter had been landing and she had commented to Shaun about it. Shaun had only nodded at her words, not having anything to say. He was always quiet when he was flying. It was the one place he was in total control of his world. Francesca had believed that was one of the reasons she had fallen in love with him. When she had gone up in the helicopter the first time he had asked, she had been amazed. The feeling of freedom was overwhelming, and she had transferred that feeling over to Shaun and had become his girlfriend.

She wondered if she hadn't become involved with him back then, where she might be right now. Would she still be alive? Or one of the walking dead? Or maybe nothing but a rotting carcass somewhere.

She pushed those horrible thoughts out of her mind and focused on the present. The here and now was all that mattered, and later, if they made it, the future.

She needed a future, for her baby.

As if her baby knew she was thinking about it, she felt a sharp pain in her abdomen, much more than a simple kick from the baby. She winced slightly and Paul saw her face, as he was leaning forward to gaze out the front windshield.

"You okay?" he asked casually.

She was breathing through her mouth, trying to work past the pain, when another stab went through her.

"Francesca, what's wrong? Oh, shit, is it time?" Paul asked, the worry clearly written on his face.

She shook her head no, and tried to focus on flying the helicopter. In a few seconds, her breathing slowed and she felt slightly better.

"No, Paul, I'm okay. But I think we need to land as soon as possible."

As she finished speaking, she angled the helicopter towards the roof of Mercy Hospital, the pain still fresh in her memory. She had read baby books she'd found in one of the break rooms in the office complex, some of them explaining what would happen to her when she gave birth, but she was quickly realizing experience was the only true way to get through what she knew was coming. All the books in the world couldn't prepare her for what her body was going to be doing soon.

"Well, we can't just land. What if the place is swarming with zombies, like at the Children's Hospital? Francesca, can you just wait another minute or so. We need to make sure it's safe."

She was breathing through her mouth, trying to work through the pain she was now feeling. It was a steady throbbing that felt like it was coming from her spine.

"Okay, I'll try, but I can't guarantee anything."

"Fine, fine, just get us closer to the roof and cross your fingers," he said.

She did as requested and hovered a few feet above the roof. If there was trouble, she could easily peel away none the worse for wear, but she knew she needed to get out of the pilot's seat soon.

They waited for almost a full minute and a few ghouls did appear, but not nearly as many as on the Children's Hospital's roof.

"Paul, I really need to land, the pain is getting worse," she gasped.

Paul was satisfied the roof was as safe as it could be. There were about fifteen zombies scattered around the roof below the helipad, but he was confident he could take them all out before they posed a threat.

"Fine, Francesca. Take her down, but as soon as we land you stay in the helicopter. I need to get to the rear compartment and get one of the guns we stashed there. I'm just glad Shaun listened to me when I told him to put them in there loaded. I'm not gonna have a lot of time for games."

She was barely listening, the pain growing more intense. She angled the helicopter and let up on the throttle, working the pedals as she controlled the aircraft and slowly lowered it down to the roof. When she touched down, the skids were exactly on the large **X** for the helipad. The helipad was set off from the main roof; five stairs leading up to it. The ghouls would be at least a minute, maybe less as they crossed the roof and maneuvered up the stairs to reach the helicopter.

Paul was planning on using that time wisely. Before the helicopter had fully touched down, Paul was opening the rear door and jumping onto the helipad, rolling when he landed. Coming up onto his feet, he dashed back to the helicopter, opening the small compartment behind the rear door, just in front of the tail assembly. Inside were supplies they had taken the foresight to place there. They knew there could have come a time when they may have needed to leave the complex in a hurry and they wanted to be ready. Inside the compartment were boxes of ammunition, canned food, bottled water and assorted ordnance taken from the security office inside the office complex.

Two of the latter was what Paul went for now, as he reached in and pulled out a brand new, shiny 1979 Model 88, 3.08, h26 Winchester rifle and a Single Action Army Colt .45. The small revolver was also brand new and the smell of gun oil drifted to his nose. He had less than a second to admire the polished blue finish, the checkered black, plastic eagle grip and the case hardened frame before the first zombies were climbing up the stairs and moving towards the helicopter.

Shoving the revolver in the front of his pants, he checked the Winchester to make sure it was loaded and then lined up the first ghoul's head in his gun sight.

With a casual ease, he fired the weapon, the stock bucking slightly against his shoulder. Across the helipad, the first ghoul's head exploded into a hundred bloody bone fragments mixed with brain matter. The headless body continued forward for two more steps and then pitched forward onto the helipad. The others behind it never slowed, never hesitated, but just wandered over or around the fallen corpse.

Paul could see they were all from the hospital staff, or had been before they were killed and had returned as the walking dead. Green and blue hospital scrubs adorned more than half of the zombies, the other half wearing the classic white lab coats of doctors.

But all they were now to Paul was target practice and he began firing at one after another, dropping them like ducks at a shooting game at a carnival. He was a skilled marksman and where ever he aimed, a body dropped to the helipad. When the Winchester went dry, he had no time to reload, so he set it down by his feet and pulled the Colt. Cocking the weapon, he began firing at the remaining ghouls.

Unfortunately, there were only six rounds in the revolver and there were seven more ghouls to take out. Feeling the slightest panic forming inside him, Paul continued shooting, dealing with one problem at a time. If he had to take on one of the ghouls in hand to hand combat then so be it. It wouldn't be the first time he'd done it.

It was times like this he missed Richard the most. The two men had been quite a team, and had put down more zombies than either man could have counted. But Richard was gone now, buried and forgotten for the moment while Paul was still alive and needed to deal with the here and now.

In his head, Paul was counting down the rounds, five, four, then he had two left. But with each lost round, there were more bodies littering the helipad, heads shattered, and holes leaking red and black brain matter onto the tarmac like spilled jello at a five-year-old's birthday party.

And then the Colt clicked dry, the last ghoul only a few feet away. The zombie had once been a doctor, and despite the medical garb, the dead man was a formidable specimen of male anatomy, despite the pale face, recessed eyes, and massive neck wound that had parts of his spine showing through.

Paul dropped the empty gun to the helipad, knowing there was nothing he could do with it now and prepared to grapple with the ghoul. His idea would be to punch the dead man in the face and when the head rocked to the side, he would jump up and karate kick the doctor in the chest. After that he was out of options, as he would need time to recover another weapon from the helicopter.

The dead doctor came at him and just as he planned, he punched the face and kicked the ghoul away, but instead of falling down; the doctor reached out and grabbed Paul's foot, now holding him in a very awkward position. Brown and stained teeth went down to take a bite out of his calf and Paul couldn't break the grip. The zombie doctor was nearly as big as him and was slightly more muscular.

Not wanting to admit what was happening, as he was always in control of a situation, Paul felt a small trickle of fear riding down his back. He was about to try something desperate when the doctor's head rocked to the side, the small bullet hole appearing just behind the left ear. The doctor leaned forward for a second and then pitched to the helipad, its death grip still on Paul's leg. Paul spun with the falling ghoul and came up facing Francesca, who was standing on the helipad, the door to the helicopter open, and a rifle in her hands. The same one she had used to take out the ghoul that had bitten Richard months ago.

Wiping his hands on his jumpsuit, Paul nodded quickly.

"Thanks, that was a close one," he told her as he immediately reached inside the storage compartment for more ammunition. Taking out boxes labeled with the correct rounds, he reloaded the Winchester and then the Colt as fast as he was able.

Francesca said nothing, but stood still, rifle in hand, her belly extended from pregnancy. She was the oddest looking woman anyone could have ever imagined, the picture of motherhood and the warrior spirit rolled into one. Her brown hair was blowing about her face and her lips were turned up in a wry smile.

And then her countenance changed from one of amusement to one of pain. She lowered the rifle and cried out, Paul looking up to see what was wrong, wondering if yet more zombies were coming for them. And then the front of Francesca's pants turned a dark color as if she had just peed herself. At first Paul didn't understand what had happened to her, but as Francesca's face went from one of pain to consternation, and then back to pain all in an instant, she turned wide eyes to him and nodded, as if she now knew some great truth.

"Paul, my water just broke," she said in a calm voice underlined with panic. "And I can feel the contractions. The baby's coming, right now!"

"Francesca, I..." was all Paul managed to say, and then ten more ghouls stumbled up the helipad stairs, heading straight for them.

Chapter 5

Paul looked to the ten ghouls heading their way and then back to Francesca. She was leaning against the helicopter, trying to remain standing, but from the pain in her eyes it was clear she wouldn't be able to stay that way for long.

She wasn't due yet, Paul thought, and realized the baby was coming slightly early due to Francesca's stress level. She had witnessed her temporary home, and her lover, die all in the breadth of a single day and now she was on a helipad with a crowd of ghouls coming for her.

If that wasn't a stressor than he didn't know what was.

Paul finished loading the Colt and slapped the cylinder close, then he picked up the now loaded Winchester and prepared for battle once again.

"Francesca, can you make it into the pilot's seat? It's the best place for you right now."

She shook her head no, her hair sticking to her perspiring face.

"Then, get into the back seat, and close the doors. I'll be with you in a second."

"I don't know if I have that long, Paul!" she screamed and let out a howl of pain as a contraction filled her to the core, making her teeth hurt. She tried to breathe like the books had told her to, but it seemed to do nothing. And worse, she knew she would be having a natural childbirth. No epidural for her.

She would be doing it au naturale.

Paul wasn't listening, he couldn't. He was already charging across the helipad at the first zombies. The ghouls knew nothing of warfare and so were spread out across the helipad. Paul could only hope that would be his edge. He knew from past experiences the undead were slow, their movements jerky to the point of apathy. Only their numbers were the true danger. A man against three or four ghouls could easily come out on top, all he needed to do is keep a clear head and stay moving.

And that was what Paul was doing.

He karate kicked the first zombie in the chest, causing it to fly backwards and strike two more behind it. He then spun in a half circle and the flat of his police issue combat boot slammed into the groin of another one. He could feel the testicles crushed under his boot and he couldn't help but cringe. The ghoul stumbled away with pulverized testicles, but barely flinched, the face showing no emotion of infection other than hunger.

And then Paul was through them and at the stairs leading down from the helipad.

Eight of the ghouls were turning to follow him, but two more were heading for the helicopter and Francesca.

"Come on, you two-bit chumps, I'm here, over here!" Paul yelled, attempting to get their attention. But the two ghouls ignored him, wanting the woman within the aircraft.

Paul could see Francesca's anguish covered face and he called out to her. "Stay there, Francesca! They can't get to you as long as you stay in the copter!"

He didn't know if she had heard him, the sun's glare bouncing off the glass windows. But he could only hope so.

Then the first zombie was on top of him and he spun and charged down the stairs, his eyes looking in every direction.

When he spotted what he wanted he took a chance. With the Winchester in his hand, he dashed across the roof until he was at the metal door leading deeper into the hospital. The door was wide open and he slowed as he approached the opening. With the Winchester leading the way, he poked his head into the stairwell, pleased to see it was empty. Looking behind him, the ghouls were still across the roof and he had a small amount of time before they reached him. Knowing Francesca needed him, he charged down the stairs, taking them two at a time. When he reached the top floor, he slung the rifle over his shoulder and drew the Colt. Inside the hospital, the quarters tight, the revolver would work better.

Opening the fire door, he jumped into the hallway, the time he would have preferred to take making sure the area was clear now a pipe dream. Francesca needed him now and if he was going to do her any good, he needed to find some medical supplies and get back to the roof.

At first he thought he was in luck, that the floor was empty, but then he heard the first moan of a zombie. Seconds later another wail of death joined the first and he swallowed the knot in his throat, knowing he would have to do this hard and fast.

The first ghoul shambled from a patient's room, the hospital gown draped over one shoulder, the other side slipping, exposing the aging breast of an elderly woman. The old woman had a large gash on the side of her cheek, her tongue visible when she turned her head. Paul shook his head in disgust, feeling no mercy for the old ghoul. Whatever humanity he still kept within himself was locked up tight. The things in front of him were no longer human and did not deserve to be treated as such. Lining up the revolver with the head of the old woman, he squeezed off a round. The bullet struck the old woman in the forehead; the gray head snapping back as she dropped to the floor like someone had cut the strings to a puppet. Before he could move on, he was startled when a ghoul jumped out from his right. Another room was there, the door partially closed and the zombie had opened it quietly. Paul wondered if the zombie had done it intentionally or was it just bad luck that he had been taken unawares.

The ghoul had once been a scrub nurse and he punched her in the nose, feeling cartilage crunch under his fist. Then he grabbed her by the scruff of her scrubs and tossed her across the hallway. The nurse bounced off the wall, knocking the hanging pictures of rose petals and sunsets to the floor in a crash of glass as she joined them. The crystal shards sliced the ghoul's face and arms, but she ignored it. Her left eye had been impaled by a dagger-like shard of glass, the milky eye dripping ocular fluid down her cheek like she was crying. Paul made a disgusted face and then shot her in the other eye. The back of her head exploded, brains and blood splattering over the metal chair rail. She hit the wall, bounced off it again and slumped to the floor.

But Paul wasn't watching. Instead, he was running down the hallway, and he slowed when he found the nurse's station. A zombie wearing the garb of a doctor appeared around the far corner of the hallway and Paul spun, lined up the ghoul in his sights, and sent a round straight through the doctor's open mouth.

The bullet exited out the back of the zombie's neck, severing the spine with its passage. The doctor dropped to the floor, his last rounds of the hospital finished forever.

Paul checked behind him, but for the moment he was safe, so he ran around the nurse's desk and began packing supplies into a waste basket he'd picked up off the floor. Needles, antiseptic, sheets from a cart near the desk, anything he could think of that might help to deliver the baby. He paused only long enough to empty out the spent brass from the revolver and load in new bullets.

When he had everything he could possibly carry without over-loading himself, he wrapped the trash barrel in his left arm, Colt in his right, and he headed back to the stairwell.

The Winchester bounced on his back where he had slung it over his shoulder.

Reaching the stairwell again, he was greeted by the eight ghouls coming down the stairs directly towards him. Raising the Colt, he put down six of the zombies one after another. Their bodies dropped to the stairs, sliding down like sacks of potatoes, only to remain still. But there were two more zombies left and Paul's Colt was dry. Taking a few steps back into the main hallway while the two ghouls stumbled and fell over their slaughtered brethren, Paul put down the trash barrel full of supplies and slung the Winchester off his shoulder. He then stood calmly five feet from the doorway to the stairs, rifle aimed at the opening, waiting patiently. He resembled an ebony statue carved from bronze. He barely breathed; his rifle on his shoulder, his eye lined up with the gun sight on the top of the gun barrel.

And then the first pale face emerged, stumbling into the hall-way. Paul was taken slightly off guard and the first bullet caught the ghoul in the neck. Dark maroon blood squirted from the wound to spray on the wall behind it, but it never slowed. With a growl of anger at missing, Paul recalibrated his aim, and this time put a round directly through the ghoul's nose. A three inch hole appeared in the middle of the ghoul's face, a much larger one appearing on the rear of its skull. The body was thrown back to fall to the floor, just as number eight entered the hallway.

There was no hesitation as Paul lined up the head and took the zombie down. The gunshot echoed in through the hospital, reverberating off the walls, and no sooner had the echo faded then Paul was on his feet with the trash barrel of supplies and climbing over the dead zombies in the stairwell. It was hard going with only one hand, and as he stepped on the bodies his stomach heaved slightly. Yellow pus squirted out of orifices and the miasma of death and decay filled the stairwell, causing him to hold his breath or risk vomiting.

But in less than a minute, he was stepping back onto the roof, the helicopter still on the helipad, the rotors spinning in the sun as the engine idled. Turning around, he slammed the roof door closed; making sure the doorknob was fully seated in the frame. Last time he checked, zombies didn't know how to use doorknobs. He and Francesca should be safe on the roof for a while.

He could only see the still spinning rotors from where he stood and he took off at a run, knowing Francesca needed him.

He could only hope she was still okay.

Climbing the stairs leading to the helipad, he hesitated for the fraction of a second at what he found. The two ghouls that had deviated from the group of ten were now at the helicopter. One of them, a dead woman with a large part of her torso missing, was banging on the door to the pilot's seat, while the other, a dead man, was moving around the aircraft, searching for a better way inside.

Paul shifted the trash barrel in his left hand and quickly began to run towards the helicopter. He tried yelling, wanting to distract the ghouls from Francesca, but with the noise of the rotors, the ghouls heard nothing.

Then the male ghoul wandered too close to the tail rotor. Too stupid to realize the danger the spinning blades posed, the zombie walked right into the rotor. There was a slicing sound and the ghoul's head was sliced down the middle, like his head had been divided into the left and right sides.

Blood and black ichor squirted out, the rotors spraying wet droplets behind the helicopter. The ghoul stood perfectly still for five seconds, its hands twitching by its sides. Then the two parts of the head split, each piece falling to its corresponding side. Like two cored-out melon half shells, the skull pieces rocked back and forth, only the ears stopping each peace from rolling away. Then the headless body pitched forward to land hard on the helipad. If the ghoul made a sound, the noise was lost under the thrumming of the rotors.

When Paul was only six feet from the dead woman, he set the trash barrel down and placed both hands on the Winchester. He wasn't about to risk a shot that could either hit Francesca, the baby, or the helicopter. All were precious and not worth the risk.

With a yell of anger, he charged at the ghoul, the dead woman's back to him. He raised the Winchester with the butt stock facing the back of the woman's skull, and he brought it down hard in a forceful blow that cracked her head and sent a jarring vibration up his arms and into his shoulders.

The dead woman toppled to the helipad, but she wasn't out of it yet. Paul wasn't giving her a chance to recover. Before she could attempt to gain her feet, Paul clubbed her on the side of the head, and as the skull rocked to the side, he jumped up, and came down on her face. His right boot connected hard, flattening her face and caving in her cranium like he was stomping grapes. The boot went four inches deep into gore and brains and he twisted his foot, making sure the woman was truly dead. The ghoul's arms twitched in the air, like she was raising them to God, asking: "Why me?" Then they dropped to her sides, only a few feeble flicks of dead fingers while the last of the synapses fired for a few last microseconds.

Breathing hard from the exertion, Paul looked around the helicopter. Making sure the area was clear.

There was nothing on the helipad but the two corpses, the helicopter and himself.

Satisfied they were truly safe for the time being; he turned, gathered the trash barrel of supplies, and dashed back to the helicopter.

Inside the aircraft, Francesca was lying across the rear seat. Her pants were off and her legs were spread wide. The rifle was in her hands, as she was prepared to shoot if one of the zombies had managed to open the door of the helicopter and she now dropped it to her side at the sight of Paul.

Paul was taken aback, but only for an instant.

Why he had always found Francesca attractive, he had never considered crossing that line because she had been with Shaun.

But Shaun was gone now, and though Francesca's face was covered in sweat, her features scrunched up in the pain of childbirth, he had to admit she never looked more beautiful.

"Paul," she gasped. "The baby's coming now! Oh, God, it hurts!" she screamed, her cheeks puffing up as she tried to breathe.

"What do you want me to do?" he asked, his eyes wide as he stared at the tip of the baby's head. It was crowning.

"How the hell should I know? This is my first time you know!" she screamed at him, then her face turned red as she began pushing, grunting hard.

"Oh, Jesus, Francesca, are you supposed to do that?" Paul asked in slight shock.

He was incredibly uncomfortable. Give him a building full of criminals or a bank full of robbers any day, but this? This was something far to alien for him. He was too far out of his element to even try to pretend he had control of the situation.

Francesca shook her head, as if she could deny what was happening to her.

Her hair was plastered to her forehead and her neck muscles were taut as she tried to manage the pain. Then she let out another ear-piercing scream. It was so loud even the noise of the spinning rotors could not drown it out.

"It's coming, Francesca! Oh, wow, man, I can see the head!" Paul screamed at her, excited, frightened and nervous all rolled into one taut ball of emotions.

Francesca ignored him, lost in her personal world of agony. She had never experienced a pain like this before, so blindingly bright she thought she would die. Then she felt a contraction and she pushed again, her body doing this involuntarily. She didn't believe she could stop pushing any more than she could stop breathing.

Paul was staring in shock, his eyes riveted to the juncture of her thighs. Slowly, ever so slowly, the baby's head was growing.

Francesca's eyes were so wide, it looked like they were about to pop out of her sockets.

"Well, Paul, don't just stand there! Help me, for Christ's sake!"

"What do you want me to do?" he asked in a low voice, trying to regain some of his stoic composure.

"What do I want you to do?" she screamed at him. "For God's sake, six months ago you wanted me to abort this baby? You said that I was crazy to have it. You don't know how to deliver one?"

His face went hard. "That was before, Francesca, things have changed since then, you know that," he said coldly. "And no, this is a first for me, too."

Whatever else Francesca might have wanted to say on the subject was forgotten when another bolt of pain hit her thanks to another contraction.

Breathing hard and fast, Francesca gestured with her head at the trash barrel in his hands. She could see a sheet and a few other miscellaneous items peeking out of the top.

"Forget it, just get a sheet, you need to catch the baby with it," she gasped. "And did you bring something to sterilize your knife with?"

He nodded. "Of course."

"Good, then do that fast. And you need to wash your hands." She paused to push, screaming loudly. When the pain had subsided to a dull roar in her head and lower body, she instructed him what to do.

Three minutes later, Paul was washed, the hunting knife from his hip now sterilized with alcohol and a sheet in his hands.

And just in time.

Francesca screamed again and the head appeared two more inches.

"Paul, you need to help the baby! Grab the head gently and pull. Then make sure the shoulders clear the birthing track!" she shouted, repeating what she had read. Trying to focus on what she had read helped to distract her from the pain, but not by much, and as another contraction flooded through her, she screamed again, and pushed with all she had!

Paul did as he was told, gently cupping the baby's small head in his. His large hands dwarfed the small head and he gently began to pull, working the newborn out of its mother's womb.

Francesca screamed again and at the same time Paul was gently pulling.

And then the baby came out, sliding out of the birthing track like the tiny body was coated with cooking oil.

Francesca yelled one last time and then her body went limp, the pain evaporating to be flooded with a mild numbing sensation. Her eyes fluttered and she gasped, her chest heaving again and again as if she had just run a marathon in five minutes flat.

Paul was holding the small form, and he carefully flipped the baby over and slapped it on the behind. One, two, and three! The baby howled its displeasure of being taken from the womb.

Francesca's eyes fluttered open and she gazed over to Paul.

"Paul, make sure his mouth is clear," she gasped, her energy all but exhausted.

Paul nodded, and then checked, and when he was finished, he picked his knife up from the seat, and like an intern doing his first operation, he cut the umbilical cord. Cutting a piece of the sheet into strips, he tied the cord on the baby, then wiped the viscera from the tiny face.

When he was finished, he plucked another sheet from the trash barrel and wrapped the baby in it tightly, only the small face showing.

Francesca was in slightly better condition now. She had managed to cover the lower half of herself with her jacket, and she cracked a smile as Paul handed the little package to her.

"You were right all along, Francesca. May I introduce you to your new son?"

Tears slid down her cheeks as she took her newborn child from Paul. She gazed down into the small face and she began to cry, her chest heaving with all the emotions filling her heart.

Paul said nothing, merely staring at mother and son with a wan grin.

After two minutes of silence, he broke the quiet.

"Do you have a name picked out yet?"

She nodded, wiping tears away with her free hand.

"Of course I do. It's Shaun."

"Of course it is," Paul said, not imagining the baby being called any other name.

"You need to shut off the engine, Paul. We need to save the fuel. Is it safe here?" she asked, her eyes only for the baby.

Paul nodded curtly. "For now, yes, we're safe."

Francesca pointed to a few switches and instructed Paul how to power down the helicopter. Doing what she directed him to do, the rotors soon began slowing, the whine of the engine dying in pitch.

Francesca looked down at the small form in her hands and began crying again. She couldn't stop, and all the stress of losing Shaun the night before and of the world crumbling around her seemed to slip away as she held the precious life in her hands.

Paul touched her leg, gesturing he wanted to leave her for a minute. When she nodded yes, he began to move away, Winchester in hand. He wanted to make absolutely sure they were safe on the hospital roof.

"Oh, Paul, wait," she called.

Paul turned to see what she needed.

"Yeah?"

"Uhm, well, I'm sorry about what I said earlier. I didn't mean it, you know that right?" she asked ruefully.

He nodded, his face softening. "Yeah, Francesca, I know," he said, then turned and walked away.

With the sun high in the sky, casting its golden glow on a kingdom of the dead, one new life struggled to survive.

Chapter 6

Frank, Maggie, Dale and the others waited anxiously while Don worked on the lock for the supermarket's double glass doors. The rear door of the moving van was now open and the people traveling within were now waiting to enter the building, all constantly glancing over their shoulders for signs of movements in the shadows of the alleyways nearby.

Lucy was now on the roof of the moving van, her eyes peeled for the undead. So far it had been relatively quiet. Five ghouls had been in the street as the convoy had pulled up to the front of the supermarket, wandering around in the parking lot like lost shoppers who had forgotten where they had parked. It had been simple enough to run them down, thus not firing a shot that would alert more to their presence.

She stood tall, legs wide, automatic rifle in her hands, her hair blowing out behind her. If any zombie's poked their heads out of hiding, she was ready to blow those same heads clean off.

"How we doin', Don?" Frank asked nervously. He wanted to get in there, grab everything they could and get the hell out. He knew they were taking a chance in this part of the city, not that he had a choice. His people needed to eat and drink so the only other option was to leave the city. But this was his home. He had been raised here, had gone to the Carnegie Institute of Technology and he'd be damned if he was going to leave now. Not even the dead would make him leave his home.

Others had agreed and they had bonded in adversity, making a home for themselves in the City County Building. It had five floors, a helipad and stone walls with solid metal doors. It was a fortress in its own right.

The only thing was getting in and out safely. There was a chain-link fence around the rear of the building and it was here they would park their vehicles. One of their group would get off early, before reaching the building, to then become a decoy for the others. When the undead wandered away to chase the decoy, the rest would drive through the gates, any stray zombies being quickly put down.

Once they were safely ensconced again, the decoy would run around the building, climb over the set up barricades and hurdles, the zombies not agile enough to keep up, and would then be pulled up to the second floor with a makeshift pulley system.

It had worked well so far, with the exception of one time.

A teenager, named Colin, had volunteered to be the decoy, only Colin had made a tactical error and had been surrounded by the walking dead. Frank could still remember the teen's screams as he was torn apart. When the ghouls were finished with him, there was nothing to reanimate, so at least that was a small blessing. In a world where death was everywhere, blessings were few and far between.

"You know, it's a shame the bridges are all clogged with cars and shit," Dale said. "I'd love to go see if that new office complex in the suburbs has stuff. They might even have power. If the electric lines aren't down, that is. Hell, we could move everyone over there and to hell with this city."

Don glanced at the younger man. "Dale, we already went through this before, weeks ago. The time it would take to drive around the bridges would waste more gas than we have. Plus, we don't know how bad it is over there, and once we finally got there, for all we know the place is gone, fire or something. Or worse yet, filled with so many of those things we could never get in there. No, son, it's not worth the risk, time or energy."

Frank heard none of it and was only pulled from his reverie when Don let out a triumphant bark of victory. Not too loud, though, as sound traveled further than before in the dead city of steel and stone.

"Got, it guys, there you go," Don said with a wide grin. The lock on the door was now a mangled mess of melted metal, the small torch in Don's hand sputtering before the man turned it off.

Frank turned to the faces surrounding him.

"Okay, let's get this done," he said. He turned to Don and Dale. "You two, take three people with you. We need medical supplies like band-aids and antibiotics. Go for the cough syrup and pills, too. Then work your way over to the paper department. We need toilet paper, lots of it," he said, and then turned to Maggie and another short, pudgy man named Tim. "You two take a few others and get to the canned goods aisles. I don't think I need to tell you to grab all you can find."

Tim and Maggie both nodded that they knew what was needed to be done.

"Good," Frank said and turned to the remaining faces. "The rest of you are with me, with two standing guard by the front doors in case Lucy needs any help. Okay?"

Heads nodded, and low murmurs of ascent came to his ears.

"All right, let's get this done." He turned to gaze up at Lucy who waved back the all clear, then they entered the supermarket.

Weapons were leading the way, but there was nothing to threaten them. The supermarket had been sealed tight and no ghouls greeted them. With a whooping of laughter, the survivors began collecting food, using the metal carriages to pile them high, and then bring them to the doors. Once there, they would grab another carriage and go back for more.

This went on for almost fifteen minutes, until Tim, his face awash in perspiration from the physical activity he was being forced to commit, turned at the sound of banging noises coming from the loading dock.

"Hey, Maggie, I just heard something out back," Tim told the red head as she piled canned green beans and corn into a carriage.

"You think it's anything important?" Maggie asked, creamed corn now going into the carriage.

Tim shrugged slightly. "Don't know, but did anyone go in the back? What's in there?"

Maggie rubbed her nose with the back of her hand.

"Loading docks probably, maybe some extra freezers. Don't go in there though," she warned. After six months of no power, the freezers would be a lab experiment gone mad, all the food rotting to the point of becoming deadly. The air itself would probably kill with black mold and other spores filling the air like a terrorist toxin.

"Could it be zombies?" Tim asked.

"Don't think so, they would have come at us the moment we began yelling," she said and stepped away from the carriage. "But maybe we should check it out, just to make sure."

"All right, let's go," Tim told her.

Pulling her snub-nosed revolver from her pants, she slapped him on the back and the two headed for the swinging doors leading to the loading dock. Tim let her take the lead, the small .22 rifle in his hands not much on stopping power, but it was all the team had for him so he took it happily

Maggie turned and glanced over her shoulder. In the wan light of the market, she could hear her fellow scavengers talking and working as they loaded the supplies to the front of the store. With the aisles blocking her view, she could see none of them. She gave it a moment's thought to go find Frank, then decided against it. They had too much to do to be running around on wild goose chases. Pushing through the doors that led to the loading dock, Tim could see her head framed in the brighter light coming from the docks. As he watched her, Maggie's red hair seemed to glow, and she turned and flashed him a wan smile.

And then he was suddenly shocked to see her head disappear in a glorious spray of blood and bone. His face was splattered with gore, like someone had tossed a bucket of pudding on him, and for a moment he stood with mouth agape, staring at the headless body of Maggie. Then she slumped to the floor, her neck wound shooting blood across the floor and doors, painting the linoleum red.

He was too stunned to move and so he only had the briefest glimpse of the half dozen men and women coming at him from the open loading dock doors before he felt the bullet punch through his heart, sending him flying backwards to land in a display for tampons. Blood shot from his mouth to coat his chin and he felt cold suddenly. His eyes fluttered for less than a single heartbeat and his pupils remained still, his eyes open in death, his destroyed heart squirting plasma out of the ragged hole in his torso.

The doors swung closed as Tim and Maggie fell away from them, but an instant later they were pushed open again.

Carver strode into the main floor of the supermarket, the pump action shotgun in his hands still smoking from the muzzle.

"Looks like we weren't the first ones here after all, goddamn it," he spit. "And now they know we're here after that shot, so move it!" Then he turned to his men, Lynn by his side, "I want those fuckers wiped out, all of them dead! And I want it done now!" he screamed, and with a wave of his hand, his people charged into the supermarket, prepared to take out the rival enclave once and for all. Lynn stood by his side. She wasn't another grunt; she was his partner, his lover and confident. She was the only person he trusted to guard his back.

Across from the doors, Tim stirred. His dead eyes were still open, but now they were moving again. Hands began to twitch and slowly, the head swiveled back and forth, the revived ghoul now looking around, and upon spotting Lynn and Carver, crawled to his feet and began moving towards them.

"Goddamn it," Carver spit. "That's why they have to be head shots!" he shouted as he brought up the shotgun and fired a blast directly into Tim's blank face. The slack-jawed visage disappeared in a spray of bone and blood, the top half of the skull floating in the air to drop to the floor, spinning for a few seconds before remaining still. The body pitched to the side, the open wound sputtering blood like a kinked water hose. With no more heart to pump blood, there was nothing to force the blood through Tim's dead body.

Carver barely watched the body topple to the floor. It was old news. He had killed more people than he could remember in the past six months and not all of them had been zombies.

He turned to Lynn and wrapped his strong left arm around her waist. "Come on, baby, let's go kill those bastards once and for all."

She kissed his cheek, wiped away a stray fleck of blood from his nose, and with her assault rifle in her hands, they moved off deeper into the supermarket. Already the sounds of battle could be heard, single and automatic rifle fire filling the store.

Carver grinned widely. He was looking forward to the next few minutes, and he could only hope Pearson himself was on this raid and he finally would get the chance to kill the old bastard and end this shit once and for all.

Chapter 7

$\mathbf{F}$rank Pearson looked up from the metal shopping cart he was pushing when he heard the sound of gunshots coming from the rear of the supermarket.

"Oh, shit, what the hell is that?" Frank asked as he looked to the three other men with him. The first was a middle-aged man with dark hair and bags under his eyes. His name was George and he used to be a school teacher. The second man was short and muscular, no more than five-six. He had dirty blonde hair and a hawk-like nose, giving him an aristocratic look. His name was Ken and he was just shy of twenty. The last man in their group was a heavy set man with two chins and three stomachs, so to speak. Despite the dead walking, the fat man had never lost a pound of flesh. Sometimes Frank thought the man was gaining weight. His name was Gene Hirsch and he used to be a mechanic. Frank would sometimes wonder how the man had been able to accomplish his job as he was far from agile.

Exactly how does a three hundred pound man climb under a dashboard or into the engine compartment of a Datsun?

"Could it be zombies?" George suggested, his face clearly worried. Despite learning how to use the gun in his hand, he had not adapted very well to his new life. He was a widower now, his wife dead for more than five months and he was almost always depressed.

"Probably, come on, let's check it out," Frank told him and the other two men.

Leaving the carriages full of food behind, the four men moved down the aisle, guns in hand.

Frank was the first in line, and so upon reaching the rear of the supermarket, he was the first to draw fire from Carver and his men.

Stepping to the end of the aisle, Frank was shocked when a bag of potato chips on an end cap exploded; sending chips everywhere;

a few peppering his face. Ducking low, he narrowly avoided a spray of rifle fire, the potato chips display exploding into a thousand fragments and coating the floor with crumbs.

Unfortunately, George wasn't as lucky. The man had been right behind Frank and when he stepped out from the aisle and Frank ducked instinctively, the man stood stock still, not realizing he was taking fire. Five bullets struck his body, from the groin to the neck. The first one blew away his genitals, but before he could scream in agony, the four other rounds crawled up his torso, each one spaced a few inches from the last. George danced in position, his body taking the brunt of each bullet and then he stopped moving. Behind the bullet-riddled man, Gene and Ken stared like school children at the massive holes in the wounded man's upper chest and lower back. George swayed on his feet and then pitched forward, his weapon sliding away across the floor.

Then more rounds sprayed the shelves on the end of the aisle and both Gene and Ken dove for cover, Gene catching a round in the lower leg.

The man screamed in pain and lost his balance, actually collapsing onto Ken's head. Ken had one brief glimpse of the massive body coming towards his face and then he saw no more, his neck snapping from the weight of his hefty companion.

Frank had crawled back into the aisle and was watching in horror as two of his men died in the same amount of seconds. Crawling to Gene, he tried to pull the man off of Ken, but the fat man was immobile. Finally, Frank kicked Gene in the side of the stomach like he was a beached whale, and with a groan and a cry, he managed to roll his massive bulk off of Ken.

Frank took one look at the young man and turned away disgusted. Ken's neck was turned at a ridiculously odd angle, so much so it looked like his head had been put on backwards. His mouth and eyes were still open, and half of his tongue was lying on the floor, from where he had bitten it off when Gene had crushed him.

Realizing there was nothing he could do, Frank left the man and crawled back to the end of the aisle. As soon as he saw a target, he began firing, taking shot after shot. He wasn't trying to hit any particular target; he just wanted to make the attacking force keep their heads down.

He heard a staccato of shots from his right and recognized Dale's .45, a few miscellaneous gunfire filling the void in between.

Good, his men were rallying and now putting up a fight.

He caught the lower half of Maggie as she lay sprawled on the floor and then he saw Tom. When he saw Maggie had no head, he gritted his teeth in anger.

Then he saw the man he was looking for.

Carver was standing behind stacked bags of rice, shouting orders to his men.

Frank took a chance, waiting to shoot Carver and end this feud once and for all. He was confident if Carver was dead, the rest of his people would be more than amenable to a truce. But no sooner did he try to fire at the tall, muscular man, then a cacophony of shots filled the supermarket and he had to dive back or become riddled with bullets.

But the shots hadn't stopped, and when he tried to back away, the bullets began crawling towards him on the floor as the gunner got his range. He continued to back up until he was next to Gene. Not knowing what to do, he shot a round over the fat man who was screaming about his wounded leg. No sooner did Frank get behind Gene then half a dozen rounds peppered the heaving bulk of flesh. Gene barley moved, his large body absorbing the bullets like a small blob. Frank hunkered down behind his living shield as bullets whined over his head.

Then to his right, he watched Ken and George's eyes open.

Slowly, the two once dead men moved to a sitting position and gazed around their environment. Whether the attacking force didn't know they were now zombies or didn't care; bullets entered their bodies one after another. Neither ghoul cared as pieces of their flesh were torn away.

Slowly, they regained their feet and Frank watched in horror as both men turned to face him.

"Shit, I don't friggin' believe this!" he screamed to the two men. "You're supposed to be on my side!"

Not having a choice, he raised the Glock and put a bullet into each man's head. Both bodies toppled to the floor, but no sooner did they go down then Frank felt his shield begin to shift in front of him.

Gene now had more than a dozen bullet wounds in his body, but he was still moving. And as Frank looked at the man's face, he saw the reason why. Gene had died from multiple gunshots and was now a zombie.

Heaving to his side, Gene's mouth sagged open and a guttural growl issued from cracked lips. Frank backed away, not believing what he was seeing. This man was alive a moment ago, and though he had taken down many zombies, he hadn't witnessed the rebirth, so to speak, that many times.

Gene was too heavy to try and get to his feet, the fact that one of his kneecaps was shattered only making the gesture impossible, but slowly, like a large slug, he began crawling across the floor towards Frank. More gunshots found Frank's position, but Gene was still blocking him. As the bullets plowed into the large ghoul, Gene barley flinched from the impacts. Frank didn't know what to do, but after staring at the dead eyes of the man, he pretty much had his answer.

There was only one thing to do.

Raising the Glock one more time, he lined up Gene's head and fired. The head flicked up with the shot of the round and then slumped forward, the bulk heaving one last time and then remaining immobile.

With a sigh for his newfound safety, Frank leaned over his meat barricade and fired at the opposing force to little results. Automatic fire filled the supermarket and smoke and cordite were everywhere, drifting lazily across the ceiling.

Then Dale came running down the aisle behind Frank and slid next to him like he was going for home plate.

"Oh, shit, oh, God," he said as he stared at the dead men.

"Yeah, tell me about it. Maggie and Tim are down, too," Frank growled as he fired off two more rounds. When the slide dropped back, he popped out the empty mag and slid in a fresh one, preparing to keep firing.

"Listen to me, Frank! Lucy is waiting in the van, it's clear out there for now, but she says zombies are coming right now, a lot of them! They can hear all this gunfire outside and they're coming fast!" He had to yell to be heard over the gunfire. He fired a few shots with his .45, but he too, wasn't trying to hit anything.

"Frank, we need to go, man, there's too many of them. They caught us off guard and they have automatic weapons! And Lucy's outside. She's the only one with something that might stand up to them! Frank! Are you listening to me?" he shouted, as Frank wasn't looking at him. Instead, the man was starring at Carver who was walking around at the rear of the store like a general directing his men.

Frank took a chance and fired three rounds at the man, one coming so close to Carver he had to duck. But then he ordered his men to concentrate their fire and the corpse of Gene began to jump as it was riddled with bullets once again, the blood from the wounds coating five feet of the floor and still spreading.

"Damn it, it wasn't supposed to go down like this!" Frank screamed as he ducked lower behind Gene's bulk. All around him, spent shell casings lay like marbles, some getting kicked around and threatening to trip a person who wasn't watching their step.

"Frank, we need to go before they kill us all!" Dale yelled.

That was when one of the rounds exploded out of the opposite side of Gene's body. The fat man's insides were becoming pulverized and his stopping power for slugs was diminishing. He was literally being whittled away piece by bloody piece. Then another round went through the corpse, missing Frank's head by inches.

Frank made a decision. There was nothing to do but retreat.

"All right, Dale, go tell the men to fall back, we're gettin' outta here."

"Damn right we are," Dale fired back and then crawled back down the aisle screaming at the top of his lungs for the others to retreat. Cursing under his breath, Frank fired a few more shots at Carver and his men. He saw a man go down, but another took his place.

When the man went down there was a small lull in the incoming fire and Frank took the chance and bolted back towards the front of the store. When he got there, his people were already at the doors, a few still pushing carriages of food.

"Leave that shit, it's not worth dying over," Frank snapped at them. They all nodded and took off out the doors, leaving the valuable food behind.

Don was the last one out and he stopped near Frank, firing a few shots to the rear of the store to keep Carver and his men honest, then he gave Frank a grim look and was out the doors.

Frank stood at the doors and gazed down the long aisle to the rear of the store. And it was then he saw Carver step out of hiding. The two men stood at opposite ends of the store, looking like two cowboys in the Old West at noon.

Before Frank could do or say anything, Carver raised his hands in the air and pointed to Frank.

"Kill that bastard!" he screamed and a hail of gunfire was released just as Frank fell back through the doors and into the outside light of the day. Bullets shattered the glass on the doors and flew over his head like angry bees. Don was there and he dragged Frank away from the opening, then helped the man to his feet.

"Shit, Don, it wasn't supposed to go down like this!" he yelled as he was running for the moving van.

"Well, it has, so shut the hell up and get in that truck!"

Dale and Lucy had climbed into the Camaro, and with a surge of the eight cylinder engine, he spun out, turning around and heading the way they had come only an hour ago. The others climbed into the rear of the van and closed the roll-up door, praying their attackers didn't try to shoot at the van as the thin metal would be no match for the flesh-shredding bullets of the enemy's assault rifles.

Climbing into the driver's seat, the key still in the ignition, Frank turned over the engine and placed the van into first gear. With a roar of the engine, the moving van surged forward, knocking zombies to the side as they came towards them. If they had delayed for another minute, there would have been dozen of ghouls outside the store, making their retreat very difficult.

Swinging the van around, Frank aimed the grille after the fleeing Camaro, the van bouncing as it drove over bodies, blood and gore coating the tire wells.

He barely noticed, still thinking of all the good people he had lost.

"Did we manage to get anything?" he asked Don as he steered the van around the corner and turned onto Fourth Avenue.

"Yeah, we did, it's all in the back. We got a lot, too, enough to last a couple of weeks easy."

Frank scowled heavily. "Oh, yeah? Was it worth all the people we just lost?" He thought of Maggie who should even now be driving the moving van, not him.

Don merely shrugged. After his stint in Vietnam, he was a hardened soul. Death was nothing new to him.

"Look, Frank, they knew the risks, we all did. If it wasn't Carver, it could have been a zombie. Either way, death is stalking us all; the trick is to keep dodging him until you make it to old age."

Frank chuckled despite his anger.

"That some new age shit you're spouting, there?"

"Maybe, but all I know is that death is waiting for us all, Frank. The question is whether you meet it head on or try to run like a coward. But in the end it'll getcha."

Frank glanced at his friend and Don nodded again, agreeing with his own words.

Sighing heavily, Frank turned away from Don and gazed out the front windshield, his anger still fuming inside him. For now, he needed to concentrate on getting him and the rest of his people home, after that he could deal with the loss of their numbers and break the news to the others.

He made himself a promise then. If it was the last thing he did in this lifetime or the next, Carver would pay for what he'd done today.

He swore on his future grave.

He glanced up at the clouds overhead. The sun had barely crested the sky and he already knew it was going to be a very long day.

Chapter 8

Paul gazed down at the small ball of life sleeping in Francesca's arms, his smile from ear to ear.

"He's a good lookin' kid, Francesca. Shaun would be proud."

She looked up at his grinning face and nodded.

"Yes, I know he would. I just wish he was here to see his son," she said solemnly.

"Yeah, me, too," he said in a soft voice. "Look, I'm gonna go for a walk around the roof, you'll be okay while I'm gone?"

"Sure, I'm okay." Instinctively, she reached out for her rifle, making sure it was close. There had been a time when she hadn't had a weapon and had been attacked by a zombie upon going into one of the office bathrooms. Only with an empty fire extinguisher had she managed to keep the ghoul at bay long enough for Paul, Shaun and Richard to arrive and save her. After that terrifying experience, she vowed she would never go unarmed again; and she hadn't. She was proud to say she was now a pretty good shot, too. After hours of practicing in the basement of the office complex, shooting at boxes with targets drawn on them, she could shoot the eye out of a ghoul from over a hundred feet away.

Paul touched her leg and turned and walked away, lighting a cigarette as soon as he had his back to her. Francesca was craving one, too, but she knew not to smoke around the baby; at least not in the confines of the helicopter. She was sitting in the rear seat again, the mess from the birthing now cleaned up. Thank God the seats had been vinyl and not cloth or there would have been quite a mess.

Little Shaun stirred and she thought she'd see if he would breast feed. At first he didn't want to, but soon he took the nipple in his tiny mouth and began drinking. She winced in slight pain, the feeling uncomfortable. But the baby books she had read said it would get better in time, as her milk ducts grew used to creating milk. She gazed down at the small face, the tiny hands, and the love she felt filled her to the point of overflowing.

With a weary sigh, she leaned back in the seat and enjoyed a few peaceful minutes with her newborn son.

She never noticed the zombie that had just stumbled out of a dented air duct near the stairs leading to the helipad. The zombie had once been a maintenance worker, but when the hospital had become an outbreak of the living dead, the man had panicked and had hidden in the duct work. As the days passed and the screaming below in the hospital never ceased, he stayed where he was, too terrified to leave. Eventually he passed out from hunger and later died. After reviving, the low intelligence had kept the ghoul inside the duct, but as days turned into weeks and weeks to months, eventually even the dull-witted ghoul had figured how to free itself from its small prison.

And that was why the zombie never attacked Paul earlier, but after just releasing itself, it was ready to feed. The emaciated ghoul was a withered husk of dried skin and bone, its flesh resembling dried parchment. Looking like a skeleton with a pair of overalls on, the ghoul stumbled up the stairs to the helipad, and upon seeing the gray and white helicopter with the WFDF news logo on the side, began moving towards the aircraft one plodding step at a time.

* * *

Paul strolled along the edge of the hospital roof, gazing down at the zombies below. There were dozens of them, all drawn to the hospital from the noise of the helicopter.

He stared down at the shifting, shambling ghouls, studying their pale faces. He saw many wearing the white coats of doctors and more than one had on the white or green scrubs of a nurse. More than half wore the classic gown of a patient, their bare, pale asses exposed for the world to see.

Not that there was anyone to notice.

With the exception of Paul and Francesca, there were no other humans for more than a mile. Paul couldn't help but feel alone as he stared at the remnants of humanity. An overturned ambulance was lying on the front driveway; the driver's remains hanging out the shattered window. The back doors were open, and there was a gurney half in/half out of the rear of the ambulance. No corpses could be seen, but the dark maroon stains on the gurney told the tale of what had happened.

Paul sucked in a deep lungful of smoke and let it out slowly, the wind catching the smoke and blowing it away. His eyes looked further into the distance at the tall office buildings near the edge of the city. He wondered if there was anyone left alive in there, and if there was, would they welcome Francesca, him and the baby?

They had to decide where to go next and soon, as the hospital wasn't safe. Hearing a soft pounding, he turned and began walking, wanting to check it out. Eventually, the noise brought him back to the roof access door. Standing in front of it, he could see the door actually shaking on its hinges. Touching the door, he could feel the vibration as the ghouls on the other side continued to bang on it, the soft sounds of their bare hands banging on metal.

He had no doubt that in time the door would give way, allowing the undead access to the roof once more. When that finally happened, he and Francesca would need to be gone. God only knew how many zombies were inside the hospital and they only had so much ammunition with them. And what would be the point? The hospital was too large with far too many entrances to even hope to close them all up. The only reason he and Richard were able to block the doors to the office complex was because they had access to bread trucks parked nearby in a parking lot. If it hadn't been for those trucks, the office complex would never have been secured.

Deciding it was time to go back to Francesca and decide what they were going to do; he began strolling along the edge of the roof again. In less than a minute, he was at the stairs to the helipad. Climbing up them, casually, the gray and white helicopter slowly grew in his vision.

He gasped in shock when he stepped onto the third step and was able to see the helicopter clearly, the rear doors open, and Francesca breast feeding. She was unaware of the danger only a few feet away from her.

A zombie in a pair of old overalls was making its way towards her, and Paul jumped up the remaining steps and dashed across the helipad, calling out to Francesca to look out.

But she was slow to react, now having to worry about the baby, and he knew she wouldn't be able to fire the rifle next to her without having to take the time to put the baby down first.

That was time she desperately needed.

As Paul charged across the helipad, the ghoul reached the helicopter, its rotten hands touching the rear fuselage as it moved along the aircraft towards the open doors.

Paul knew he couldn't use one of his firearms for risk of hitting Francesca or the helicopter. If the aircraft was damaged, any hope of them surviving would be lost with it.

So he powered down and ran for all he was worth, his long legs thrusting him forward.

Just as the ghoul arrived at the open doors and Francesca was staring in shock and surprise, Paul reached the ghoul. He plowed into it, his body low like a football player tackling an opponent. The ghoul bounced off the side of the aircraft, then fell to the helipad. Paul never slowed his momentum. With a foot on the lower struts of the landing skids, he spun around and kicked the ghoul in the head, rocking the skull to the side. The zombie let out a moan and hands reached up to grab Paul, but the tall man wasn't there. Instead, he had jumped over the prone ghoul and had grabbed it by the scruff of its overalls. He then began dragging the zombie across the helipad, his destination the edge of the roof. The ghoul fought to reach his hand, but the odd angle prevented it.

When Paul was at the edge, he dropped the ghoul and took a step back.

From the safety of the helicopter, Francesca watched perplexed when Paul took a step away to let the zombie regain its feet. She didn't understand what he was doing. But then it all came clear as the ghoul stood up, and before it could take one step forward, Paul ran at the corpse and karate kicked the zombie directly in the middle of its sunken chest. The ghoul went flying backwards, but instead of landing on the roof, it went out into empty air. Arms waved around the zombie, as if the ghoul thought he could fly if he only flapped hard enough. And then gravity did its job and the body dropped to the hard ground below.

By coincidence there was a Mustang parked below and the body fell onto the roof of the car, all the windows shattering with the concussion. The bones in the ghoul were pulverized from the impact, only the leathery skin preventing the soupy insides from spilling forth onto the caved-in roof.

Paul stared down at the ghoul, his jaw taut.

"No good sucker," he said under his breath and then turned to see how Francesca was doing. Jogging across the helipad, he was soon at the helicopter.

"Thank you, Paul, I didn't...I mean, I almost..." She became choked up and he reached inside and took her hand.

"It's all right. Nothing happened. It's gone now. How's the baby?"

Francesca gazed down at the face of little Shaun, the baby sleeping through the entire event, his belly full of breast milk putting him right out.

"He's fine."

"Look, Francesca, we need to talk about what we're gonna do next."

She nodded, not replying, the gesture enough.

"I was thinking, maybe we should try one of these high-rise buildings to the north."

"Can't we stay here for a while, Paul? God I'm, tired. We haven't even had a chance to mourn Shaun. Christ, he just died a few hours ago!" She was emotional, her hormones all out of whack. She didn't want to cry, not finding it becoming in a woman. Just as she never screamed. No matter how frightened she might be, a scream would not escape her lips.

Paul slammed his fist against the side of the helicopter, his white teeth flashing in the sun.

"Don't you think I know that? Damn it, Francesca. He was with me in that complex. And I let him down. I was the one who left him even though I heard his gun. He could have been alive in that stairwell. Damn it, I thought it was the right decision at the time, but..." He trailed off, his eyes burning.

He turned away from her, his gaze going out to the horizon. The sun was high in the sky, the air brisk. He was tired, too. It had been a long night and he needed rest, but not yet. Not until they were safe.

"Paul," she said softly. "It's not your fault. What happen to Shaun…" She trailed off, not wanting to think about it any longer. But she knew she would. She would always have that last picture of her lover in her mind as he stepped into their haven and Paul shot him in the head with his shotgun. The way he had leaned against the wall and had then slouched to the left; the other zombies stumbling into the room after him.

It wasn't fair. No woman should have to remember her man like that. But she had seen it and she couldn't wipe it away.

"Paul," she said again. "What the hell are we going to do now? Where will we really be able to go that's safe? We're low on fuel and there's only so much ammunition and there's only enough food for a few days. Shaun said we couldn't overload the helicopter with more because of fuel consumption." She sighed heavily and shifted in her seat. "And now I have him to worry about?" She referred to the baby, still sleeping softly despite the loud voices of the two adults.

Paul pulled his gaze from the horizon and turned to face Francesca. Now his eyes were hard, his jaw set, his mind made up.

"It's simple, Francesca, we go where we can until the damn copter runs out of gas. It's all we can do." He considered something, biting his lip in thought. "How are you feeling, really? Will you be okay to fly soon?"

"Yeah, I'm okay. Just give me a few more hours and I'm sure I'll be fine. You know, in other countries, women have babies and go right back into the rice fields again hours after giving birth. I think I can handle flying this helicopter." She grinned, thinking about something far away. "Shaun was a good teacher."

"So we'll stay here for the time being," Paul stated.

She sat silently weighing his words, deciding if she was going to agree with him. Then she nodded.

"Fine, yes, we can do that, Paul. Let's rest a while, maybe get some sleep, then we'll leave."

Paul slid down to the helipad to a sitting position, his back against the landing strut. He pulled out another cigarette and lit it, cupping his hand to protect the small flame from the wind. The lighter he was holding had been Richard's and a pang of loss filled him. But he pushed it aside. Even after six months he still missed the little guy. The two had become brothers in arms in a very short time and Paul wished like hell that Richard could be with him now.

But he was dead and gone, like thousands, millions of others.

"That's cool, Francesca. We'll stay here for now and leave when it starts to get dark. That way, if there's any lights in the city, we'll be able to spot them from the air."

"Sounds good, Paul," she said softly and then leaned back and closed her eyes, finally resting while Paul stood watch over her and the baby.

His Winchester was across his lap and the Colt was by his side. If anything tried to get near them, it would find out what a hollow point to the head felt like.

With the baby sleeping softly, Francesca soon followed, while Paul smoked cigarette after cigarette, remembering times long lost and wondering what the future would hold for the three of them.

Chapter 9

The moving van slowed to a stop one street over from the City County Building. Placing the van in park, Frank jumped out the cab and walked around to the front of the vehicle, the radiator ticking softly in the sun. The Camaro had slowed to a stop, as well, and Dale and Lucy now jumped out of the car, their faces a mask of angst from what had happened only minutes ago.

Frank punched the air, his anger a palatable thing. His talk with Don had not quelled his rage at the loss of the others.

"Damn it, guys, what the hell just happened back there?" he yelled at Dale, Lucy and Don, who were climbing out of the cab while Frank talked. He had talked to Don for most of the trip back, but his anger had only grown worse, especially because the men he'd lost were his responsibility.

No one spoke, as there wasn't anything to say.

"Goddamn it, we were supposed to be the only ones there! We shouldn't have been first only to be caught off guard like that. Goddamn it!" he screamed.

Dale and Lucy were looking around the area, knowing the yelling and noise from the engines would alert the dead they were there.

"Frank, I thought we went through this inside the truck, man, it wasn't your fault. Shit happens and we lost good people in the process," Don said in a reasoning tone.

Frank spun on his friend, a finger jammed at his face accusingly.

"Well, I can't accept that. Maybe you can, but not me! We should have been ready for anything, not just the damn zombies."

"Uh, guys, we got company," Lucy said from behind Frank and Don. She didn't receive an answer and so waited a half-second, then spoke up again. "Frank, you really need to hear this."

"Damn it, Lucy, what now?" Frank snapped at her as he spun around, prepared to vent his frustration on someone else. But no sooner did he turn around, then he held his tongue, seeing the street ahead of them.

More than thirty ghouls were appearing from hidden alleyways and from behind cars, some climbing out of the old derelicts. Already the moaning could be heard and if Frank hadn't been so pissed off, he would have heard it, too, almost immediately.

"Shit, goddamn bastards. Why don't you leave us the fuck alone!" Frank yelled, finally having something tangible to let out his anger and emotions on. Pulling his Glock, he moved past the others, already firing at the first zombies in the undead line. The first round took a ghoul in the head, the back of its skull literally lifting up like a hatch, the brains popping out. Then the flap dropped back down and the corpse dropped to the pavement, now missing more than half its brain. Next came an old man ghoul, still wearing his hat. How the geriatric zombie had managed that for months was a mystery, but Frank lined up the zombie in his sights, and fired directly at the hat.

The head snapped back and the hat flew off the head, half the scalp going with it. Blackened brains glistened in the sun, but the old man still continued forward.

"Bastards, why don't you die?" Frank yelled, not paying attention to his surroundings. Before he realized it, he had three ghouls coming at him, one from his left and two on his right. He was fast becoming trapped and his carelessness was about to get him killed.

His head snapping left to right, he tried to decide which danger was more predominant, when automatic rifle fire came from behind him. The ghouls to his right were chewed by a dozen rounds peppering their bodies. The zombies danced a jig of death as the bullets found arms, legs and kneecaps. They dropped to the street, writhing, one or two without arms and legs, the torsos still trying to roll towards Frank.

He took the opportunity, and with a wave to Lucy in thanks, he turned to his left and dropped the other zombie before it could reach him.

With his life on the line, he regained his faculties and felt very foolish for what he had just done.

Retreating back to the others, he bashfully nodded to Don, who stoically returned the gesture. He had seen more death than all of them combined and Don knew how Frank felt. He also knew Frank would have to deal with his responsibilities as their leader on his own, and there was only so much advice that the veteran could give him.

"All right guys, I got whatever it was out of my system, thanks again, Lucy."

"Happy to oblige," she grinned.

"Okay, now that we're all friends again, can we get the hell out of here?" Dale asked as he eyed the closing zombies. They had half a minute, if that, to try and escape the approaching undead horde.

"Okay, let's go, let me take lead, Dale, I'll clear a path for you. Whose gonna be decoy today?"

"I got it, Frank," Lucy said. "I needed a good run anyway."

"Good, sounds real good, Lucy, you just watch your ass," Frank warned.

"No shit. That ass is mine and no one gets to chew on it but me," Dale quipped as he slapped her on the behind. She squeaked like a little girl and the couple climbed back into the Camaro.

Frank and Don were doing the same, climbing inside the moving van, and once back in the driver's seat, he put the vehicle in drive and shot forward, going wide around the Camaro. The line of zombies was right in front of him, so he put the van in low gear and floored the gas pedal, the front grille impacting with the first ghouls in the line. Bodies rebounded off the grille like soccer balls, arms and legs dislocating or just plain falling off. One ghoul was struck so hard its head spun around on a broken neck, the eyes still looking around as it was forced to the street before the tires of the moving van rolled over it, crushing its chest and flattening its ribcage.

Then they were through the crowd and on the move again. He glanced in his side mirror and was pleased to see Dale right behind him. The wind blew inside the cab chilling him, but with the glass shattered it couldn't be helped.

Putting the transmission into second, Frank continued driving to their haven in the middle of the Hell once named Pittsburgh.

* * *

Carver slowed the pickup truck full of supplies as he rounded a bend in the road leading to the City Courts Building, his eyes scanning the distance for possible threats.

Though the city was infested with ghouls, most were spread out, and if any gathered in too great a number near his building, he and his men would usually take them out, thus keeping the dead population down.

He could see there were a few too many there now, most at the rear of the building where the loading bays were. A tall wall of chain-link fence surrounded the parking lot, razor wire adorning the top.

Three men stood guard at the only gate in or out of the parking lot and it was only because they stood on small podiums that Carver could see them at all. This gave the guards a grand view of the area, so they could keep track of how many zombies had arrived. Sometimes, if the numbers were too great, a few men would go out to the fence with sharpened broomsticks and jab the ghouls in the eyes. While this didn't kill them, by blinding them the zombies became all but helpless. Then later they were easy to dispose of.

Carver could see more than a dozen ghouls shambling about, their eye sockets nothing but weeping, open wounds, an aqueous fluid dripping down their cheeks from the violent loss of the eyes. Near their eyes, or where they once were, numerous circular wounds could be seen. This was the result of the jabber missing and instead of puncturing an eye, the point of the spear had penetrated flesh. Not that the ghouls minded.

A BMW M1 pulled up next to Carver, the back seat and trunk overflowing with food and other miscellaneous items, including an eight track tape player with some of the most popular tapes at the moment.

Donna Summer, The Eagles, The Doobie Brothers, The Knack and a half dozen more were piled high against the rear window.

David O' Hara rolled down his driver's window and turned to look at Carver.

"We goin' or what?" O'Hara asked bluntly. Fred Sherman was sitting next to him in the passenger seat and he tossed his hair off his shoulder as he nodded in agreement.

"We're goin', Dave, relax a minute, you'll live longer," Lynn said askance of Carver. He grinned at her statement,

"Yeah, Dave, relax. Listen to my lady," Carver said, backing up his woman.

O'Hara frowned, but he said no more.

Behind them the last vehicle pulled up, waiting for the others to move.

"So how we gonna do this?" Lynn asked Carver as she eyed the ghouls around the fence.

"Same way we always do it. Slow down, let them come to us, and when they do, we drive over, around, or through them, and get to the gate. It's worked so far and today'll be no different."

Lynn stared at the zombies in the lot and frowned, but knew he was correct. They had done this hundreds of times and today would be no different.

David revved the car's engine and Carver glanced his way.

"All right, let's move out," he called through the window.

"Finally," the old biker said as he pulled forward, taking the lead.

The beat up Pontiac rolled forward and Carver pulled up behind it. The last car in line, a new Saab 900 GLS, soon followed. The driver name was Wes Towers, and he had liberated the vehicle from a car dealership a month ago. Seems that all the salesmen were zombies at the time, he didn't think anyone would mind.

He was a tall man with lanky arms and a thin face. He had been a security guard before the world had collapsed in on itself and had been very lucky to have found Carver and his men. He was the weak link in the chain of cars heading towards the chain-link gate, the man not strong enough to handle his new world. He tried his best, but panic was always there, hidden just below the surface. He knew better than to let Carver or any of the others see it, though. He kept on a strong face and did his best to survive. Even at the supermarket, when all hell had broken loose, he had stayed in the shadows, only firing when he knew it was absolutely safe to do so.

He knew he wasn't cut out for this crazy life, but what choice did he have? He didn't want to die and he definitely didn't want to become a zombie.

So he kept up a false front of confidence, while inside himself he wanted to curl up into a ball and cry.

The BMW had just reached the edge of the parking lot and already the ghouls were turning at the sound of the engines. Carver pulled to the side of the car and together they began hitting their horn. The cacophony filled the area, alerting every zombie there was new meat only a few hundred yards away.

Soon, all the undead were leaving the fence, shambling and stumbling towards the vehicles. The men at the gate quickly took out the few that remained behind. There were always at least a dozen that refused to leave, wanting to reach the guards inside the fence with a determination that went beyond their dead brains.

With the sounds of gunshots filling the parking lot, Carver grinned as he glanced to Lynn.

"I love this shit, did I ever tell you that?"

"All the time, baby," she replied.

Carver glanced in his rearview mirror to see the Saab behind him. Wes was biting his nails in anticipation of what was to come. Carver frowned as he watched the man in the small mirror. He was beginning to worry about the guy, wondering if he could truly rely on the man to watch his back. Carver had gotten rid of others who he'd decided couldn't, or wouldn't, pull their weight.

"All right, it's time, let's go, baby!" Carver yelled and floored the gas pedal, the old pickup truck shooting forward. No sooner did Carver take off then the BMW followed, both vehicles plowing into the first ghouls in the parade of the dead. The SAAB took up the rear, swerving in and around the zombies. Carver plowed head long into the melee, the front grille of the truck whacking the ghouls down like ten pins. One was struck so hard its head snapped off, the dried skin already weakened from decay. The head bounced on the hood and then struck the windshield, the dead face staring at the driver and passenger. Then the head rolled to the side and fell to the pavement, where the BMW promptly drove over the skull like the tires had run over a small cantaloupe. Brains and viscous fluid shot out of the neck cavity, spraying the tire wells with gore. Then the car was moving on, the tires crunching over the pickup's leavings.

Wes gritted his teeth as he fought the car between the zombies, weaving back and forth like a drunkard driving after last call and had managed to keep his car keys.

As he sped through the parking lot, he overcompensated, and before he realized it, he was heading straight for a light post fixed in the middle of the lot. The posts were placed at ten foot intervals, so the parking lot would have been well lit at one time, but now the thick metal posts resembling telephone poles were nothing but obstacles to avoid, and Wes had done a terrible job of it. Before he could swerve away from the oncoming steel post, the SAAB struck it with bone-crushing force. The SAAB was a marvel of engineering, built to take the abusive impact, but not so for the human being of flesh and blood inside the steel body.

Wes was thrown forward, and before he knew what was happening, he was catapulting through the shattered windshield, the safely glass peppering his face with small slices and cuts, his neck all but snapping upon striking the glass as he flew over the hood and into the parking lot, where he rolled for a few feet and came up lying on his back.

He lay still, staring up at the clear blue sky, wondering what he was doing on the ground. Wasn't he driving a second ago?

Then he heard the first moans of the dead and he was able to turn his head slightly to the right. He saw legs, a lot of them, and when he glanced higher up, he saw the legs were connected to dead things.

Rotting, putrefying, and desiccated dead things.

His mind told his body he needed to move, that he needed to get up and run away, but as he tried to get to his feet, he realized his legs wouldn't respond.

It was then he realized he couldn't feel his legs!

Something had happened in the fall to the ground and now he was numb from the waist down!

Screaming in fear, he rolled to his side and began crawling away, his legs dragging behind him like two dry stalks of corn.

He didn't get far.

Before he had managed to cover four feet, his elbows and lower arms already cut and bruised from the accident now more so from scraping the pavement, the ghouls were on him.

One of the first ghouls in line held a sharp piece of metal, something shiny the zombie had found and had never put down. As the zombie bent over Wes to get at his body, the metal sunk into his upper torso, slicing deep into his chest right through his shirt. The ghoul drew back its arm like it was pawing at the body, and the metal slid down the torso, all the way to the screaming man's groin. Wes was shrieking in pain, blood seeping from the jagged tear in his body as he tried to escape the onslaught of the dead.

But he was totally, utterly lost.

With the jagged tear in his chest, the other ghouls had easier access to the organs within and a dozen hands dove in to plunge rotting fingers into the open wound. Then there was a loud tearing sound, like a sheet was being ripped, and Wes screamed as his chest cavity was peeled open on the left and right sides, exposing the rib cage beneath. His ribs glistened in the warm sun, reflecting the light in small sparkles as the blood seeped out the sides to coat the ground beneath him. Dead hands reached through the ribcage, and with a strength inherited in death, pulled on the bones.

Wes' body was lifted off the ground a few inches as the ghouls yanked on his ribs, but then the ribcage snapped apart, and the ghouls spread them wide, wanting access to the juicy organs within.

In the glare of the sun, Wes' heart pulsed amid muscle and tendons, fibers flexing as he screamed louder, his lungs still processing oxygen. Blood was everywhere, pooling under Wes like he had sprung a leak, which he had in many places all over his body.

A set of pale hands dove into the exposed cavity of organs and one hand wrapped hooked fingers around the beating heart and as Wes screamed one last time in unbelievable agony, the ghoul pulled backward, yanking the heart from the chest. With the heart still beating its last pulse, the ghoul sunk rotting, brown teeth into the muscle, blood squirting out of the sides to cover its chin and drip down to the pavement in red rivulets. Other hands were inside the corpse of Wes, as well, ripping out organs and muscles like he was a piñata at a child's birthday party. Wes' eyes glazed over and his mouth opened and remained that way. Soon, teeth sank into his neck and half his face was eaten, the exposed white of skull peering through the mottled flesh.

The feeding frenzy continued for more than three minutes before Wes' eyes seemed to move again, the orbs shifting back and forth in their sockets.

While the ghouls fed, the man named Wes sat up, his dead eyes staring at the other zombies.

Suddenly, there was a loud crack and Wes' head grew a blossoming hole in his forehead. No sooner had the body sat up then it dropped down to the ground again. The ghouls continued feeding, barely noticing what had occurred.

Across the parking lot, at the entrance to the open gate, Carver stood stock still, a sniper rifle in his hand. Lowering the weapon, he handed it back to the guard he'd borrowed it from.

"Nice shot, Carver," O'Hara said from his side.

"Yeah, wasn't bad, was it. Poor, bastard. No one deserves to go like that and then have to walk around like one of those things," Carver said, showing unaccustomed emotion.

While he talked, his men were firing at the few ghouls who had wandered too close to the gate. Carver turned and walked inside, the gate closing after him as a guard secured it with a heavy padlock.

Lynn was waiting inside with her arms folded, her hip cocked to the side seductively.

"What about all the shit he had in the car?" she asked, gesturing to the wrecked SAAB.

"We can get it later, it's not like the stuff's going anywhere, right?"

She nodded. "Guess so."

Carver turned to O'Hara and pointed to the BMW and the pickup truck. "David, get the men to unload that shit and then have everyone who came with us get some downtime, they've earned it."

O'Hara nodded, and moved off, yelling at the others to begin unloading the supplies.

Carver grinned at Lynn.

"Come on, baby, I'm so horny I can't stand it."

She smiled sexily, and with her arm in his, they left the parking lot behind and entered the stone building, prepared to have some fun.

He had always found that after a raid, the sex was more intense, more electrifying as the adrenaline from the adventure still flooded through his veins, making him fly like a bird in the sky.

And when he added a little acid to the mix, he felt like he was touching God Himself.

No, wait, scratch that. He felt like he *was* God, and beware anyone who angered him.

Chapter 10

Carver entered the building with Lynn by his side.

Bullet marks and blood stains could be seen etched into the stone walls. Someone had tried to repair some of the holes and had tried to clean up the blood, but the stone was porous and had absorbed the blood like a sponge, a constant reminder of the world they all now lived in.

Carver and Lynn strolled through the long hallway until reaching a vast, grand lobby. From here, there were wide stairs, one on each side of the room. Both stairs led up to the second floor, where banks of elevators sat useless. Also on the second floor was one of the courtrooms, once used to practice law and hand out vengeance under the guise of law and order, but now nothing but sleeping quarters for some of his people.

As he entered the wide lobby, he could hear the distinct sound of music. Rod Stewart was asking if people thought he was sexy, the generator powered electricity allowing the building a small amount of lighting and other necessities. He allowed the generator to be run for three hours a day, and in that time he expected anything needed that was electrical to be done and finished in that time. That was when a blender would be used for preparing food, coffee would be made for the rest of the day, and of course, letting his people enjoy some of the newest, and probably last music hits of this year and perhaps all years to come.

Walking up the wide stairs, Lynn at his side, people moved about on the second floor, some cooking by the many windows. Makeshift ducts had been constructed to allow the smoke to vent out of the building, thus allowing an open fire to be used for cooking and boiling water which was retrieved from the nearby river. It was a chore, but they had no choice.

Carver nodded to the people he passed, Lynn being more polite, she was the queen everyone loved and he was the hard king, ruling with an iron fist.

The two reached the end of the balcony overlooking the lobby and entered the courtroom where the music was coming from.

Hard-faced men and a few women glanced up at his approach, but no one moved or did anything other than nod in their direction.

Carver and Lynn stomped through the courtroom and stopped at an ornately carved door. The room had once been the judge's chambers, but now Carver had made it his own. Stepping inside, he saw it was how he had left it. The desk had been pushed to the side of the room and there was a king size mattress on the floor. Trash and debris littered the floor around the bed, the result of past meals and snacks. One small lamp was in the corner, the only illumination in the room. If the generator hadn't been on he would have settled for candles.

Sliding out of his weapons and dropping them onto the desk in the corner, he turned to Lynn and held out his hand. She had done the same, now devoid of weapons and she moved swiftly into his arms. The two kissed, softly at first, but with each passing second the embrace became more passionate. Tongues explored mouths and breathing grew excited. Soon clothing was removed and Lynn took a step back, allowing Carver to gaze at her. Her skin was milky smooth, what was called alabaster by some, and her blonde hair flowed down her back, stopping above the small arc. Her firm breasts defied gravity and her nipples were hard from the heavy petting the two had just shared. Carver quickly slipped out of his pants and shirt and moved closer to her, his manhood already at attention.

Crushing her to him, the two lovers kissed again, slowly and then faster as he gently laid her down on the bed. There was no foreplay, not this time; he was too revved up from the raid. So with a gentle positioning of himself, he slid into her warmness and she gasped in happiness.

At first he was gentle, slowing moving his hips in rhythm with her gasps of pleasure, but soon his excitement and selfishness got the better of him and he began to pump harder, slamming himself into her. Her eyes were closed, only the slightest flutter of her eyelids as she writhed in ecstasy under him. He could feel himself growing close and he nuzzled her neck, biting down ever so lightly with his teeth. She gasped once again, but this time a soft squeak was added to the mix and she began to quiver beneath him, her muscles gripping his erection like a clamp. When he could take no more, he found the sweet release of passion, and he filled her with himself for the last time, grunting in pleasure into the nape of her neck. She moaned loudly, arched her back, and then collapsed beneath him, her arms and legs going limp. He too, was spent and he collapsed on top of her, breathing heavily as he basked in the latent glow of their love.

"Wow, baby, that was great," he whispered into her ear, nipping at the tip of her earlobe.

She nodded, her cheek brushing his as she moved beneath him. Neither wanted to move, but knew in a moment they would have to.

The light in the room flicked out, and both were bathed in darkness. Neither moved, barely registering the lost lighting, too exhausted from their bout of lovemaking

Before he could get up, the door to the room shook on its hinge's, someone pounding on like it was the end of the world. Which didn't make sense, because it seemed that had already happened.

"What the fuck? Who the hell is that?" Carver snarled while rolling off Lynn, who only stretched and covered herself partially with a dirty sheet, her eyes still closed.

Still naked, Carver stood up and went to the door, not worried about his state of undress. Opening the door, David O'Hara stood there, his right hand held in the air for another round of knocking on the door. He got one look at Carver's nakedness and he lowered his hand, his eyes looking in every direction but forward. Suddenly a small scratch on the floor looked very interesting.

"Oh, shit, Carver, I'm sorry to bother you, but we got a problem with the generator," David said as he kept studying that scratch. It looked like a fish if he turned his head the right way.

Carver turned back to Lynn and realized the light was out, as was the music he'd heard only minutes before.

"Shit, stay there, let me get dressed," he snapped as he walked away from the open doorway. David waited at the door and the light from the main room cascaded into the judge's room, illuminating Lynn's prone body. One shapely leg and one breast were exposed to the air and David found his eyes wandering to her smooth, firm body. Carver had finished dressing and as he turned to leave the room, David immediately made his eyes look somewhere else, not wanting to piss off Carver. All the people who lived at the courthouse knew Lynn was off limits.

"Okay, let's go," Carver told him as he grabbed his shotgun. "I'll be back, baby, you get some rest," he told Lynn. She merely nodded, already half asleep.

As he entered the main courtroom, voices asked him questions, all wanting to know what had happened to the genny. They had another hour before the designated time to turn it off for the day. Carver told them he was looking into it and to relax, his voice hard. That tone was enough to shut them up. Carver had kept them safe, but he was also not one to disagree with.

David led Carver to the lower level of the courthouse, though Carver knew the way by heart. The generator, or genny to the people, relied on it heavily. The genny was one of the only things saving them from falling into the dark ages and having to play music on guitars and cooking over open flames forever. The generator was a tie to the past, what the world once was, before the dead rose and squelched any hope that mankind would continue to prosper.

Fred Sherman appeared from a side corner, joining Carver and O'Hara with a flashlight in his hand and the three men made their way to the generator room. Before reaching it, Carver slowed at a small side door. The small room had once been used as a utility closet, but now it was the armory for the enclave. A small battery operated lamp was hanging on the wall so there was light. Carver stopped and glared at the man standing in front of a waist-high table. The man was short in stature and wore a beat up fedora on his head. A pair of wire rimmed glasses adorned his face and his small eyes peeked through like a field mouse out of a hole in a log. In his hand, he had a small stick, red, like a candle, in his hands, and he glanced up at the sight of Carver and the other men behind him.

"Hey, Boss man, what's up?" The amorer asked.

"You tell me, Dax," Carver told the man.

Dax shrugged and gestured with the hand holding the stick. "Just inspecting the dynamite that got brought in the other day. So far it looks good. No sweating. And best of all we got a bunch of detonators, too. You got any plans for this shit?"

Carver nodded, pleased, his eyes playing over the weapons adorning the walls. M-16s, rifles, shotguns, a few Winchesters, and half a dozen handguns were hanging on hooks. While most of the enclave was always armed, the extra weapons were stored down here. Dax had worked in a gun store and was an expert craftsman when it came to ordnance. He could take apart and reassemble almost any firearm in minutes, so it had been a simple task to assign him the armory for his responsibilities in the enclave.

"No, Dax, not at the moment, but it's good to know it's here. Better to need it and not want it than to want it... well, you get the fucking point, right?"

"Sure, Boss man," Dax nodded, setting the dynamite down and picking up another stick. "I get it."

"Good, carry on, I'll see you later." He gestured to his shotgun on his shoulder. "My baby here is gonna need a good cleaning soon. She got a work out today."

"No problem, Boss, just have someone drop it off when you're ready. I'll get to it immediately."

Carver grunted, pleased. Dax was a good man and they were lucky to have him. Turning away, he continued to the generator room, Fred and David right behind him, Fred keeping the beam of the flashlight in front of him so all three men could see where they were going.

Upon reaching the room, the first thing he detected just before entering the room itself was the odor of burnt meat, sickly sweet and cloying, like cloves. As he entered the room, he saw the generator on his left and behind that, on the far wall were ten barrels of gas, all lined up neatly two levels high. But the most disturbing thing in the room was the fried, blackened and charred corpse lying on the cement floor next to the generator.

As Carver stared at the dead mechanic, he realized fried wasn't the appropriate word description to use for the husk of death on the floor. The man had been burned beyond recognition, his true semblance roasted off like a Christmas turkey after spending all day in a 400 degree oven.

"Jesus Christ, what the fuck happened here?" Carver snapped as he stood a few feet from the blackened corpse. The redolence of cooked human flesh permeated the room and made them all cover their noses and try to breath through their mouths.

"I found him this way, Carver," O'Hara said. "I came down to check on him and he was like this. Looks like he touched the wrong wires."

"Ya think?" Carver spit. "Stupid bastard. Look, that's where he must have done it." Carver pointed to the end of the generator where the thick electrical wires led from the machine to the circuit box of the courthouse. The black coloring on the wall stated to where the sparks and flames had shot out, cooking the man with enough burn to cook him from the inside out.

And then something happened that all three men should have expected, but given the condition of the dead man on the ground, none of them had given it much thought.

The charred man moved.

At first only his hands twitched, the brittle fingers cracking in the quiet room, but then the head shifted and soon the torso was rising to a sitting position.

"Oh, shit, I don't fucking believe it," Carver gasped, even his hard exterior cracking for a moment. David and Fred merely stood transfixed, both in a mild case of shock. Then David pulled his sidearm, preparing to send the newly risen zombie back to whence it came. Carver saw what the man was doing and he slapped his hand down hard enough to cause David to cry out.

"What the hell did you do that for?" the old biker snapped.

"What are you, an idiot? Look at all that gas stored back there. One shot you either miss or it goes through the body and, boom, we all go up in a blazing fireball." He shook his head. "No, man, this one needs to be taken down close and personal." He handed his shotgun to Fred and picked up a piece of rebar lying to his right, amongst some other miscellaneous debris. Fred kept the beam of the flashlight on the zombie so Carver could see clearly.

Whacking the rebar into the palm of his other hand, he stepped forward to take down the dead mechanic.

Chapter 11

The sun was high in the sky, a little past one o' clock by Paul's watch.

He had owned a thousand dollar time piece only a day ago, but when the rogue military faction had attacked the office complex, he'd tossed the watch and the frivolous gold rings on his fingers to the floor, once again donning his old watch for battle.

The timepiece was impact resistant and water proof, and though it was relatively inexpensive, when he was out on the road, it was the better watch to have.

He thought back to all the glittering items he and Francesca had possessed when the office complex had been taken from the undead, the floors filled with storage rooms for the import/export businesses. Furs, gold, silver, diamonds, all of it useless in the world he now lived in. You couldn't eat diamonds and drink gold, so what was the point?

In his opinion, a full load in his Winchester was worth a thousand tons of pure gold or a mountain of cash. He stood up from the helipad, the spent cigarette butts near his feet blowing in the wind as he moved away. He had gone through more than a pack, smoking being the only thing to do as he stood watch over the empty roof.

Francesca was sleeping soundly in the rear seat of the helicopter, the baby curled up in her arms. He gazed down at them both for a minute and then decided he needed to relieve himself.

Walking to an air conditioning unit, he quickly undid his fly and emptied his bladder.

All the while, he could hear the sounds of pounding, the roof door still being pummeled by undead fists. When he was finished, he zipped up and decided to check out the door, not wanting any surprises at an unfortunate time.

Crossing the helipad, he moved down the stairs leading to the main roof, his eyes scanning everything. He had been disappointed not to find a refueling station on the roof, just the helipad, but at least he had found the medical supplies he needed to help with the birth of the baby. But they still needed fuel, and if they didn't find some soon, they were in for more trouble than he wanted to think about.

He strode across the roof, the sun warm on his face, and as he approached the roof door, he could already see the situation wasn't good. The hinges were on the outside of the door, and when he studied them more closely, he could see the paint around the frame was flaking off, the pounding affecting the metal. And now that he was standing in front of the door, the noise was almost deafening. Thumps of dead flesh continually slapped the door and every now and then he heard the distinctive sound of scraping. Could that be hands that had been destroyed, now exposing the bones beneath?

He was deciding what he should do, figuring he and Francesca should consider leaving earlier than their planned departure when the door rocked in its frame. Paul took a step backward, his eyes on the door like it was about to become animated when the door jumped again.

"Shit," he muttered, knowing what was about to happen. As if he had seen the future, the door rocked yet again, and this time the hinges separated from the door.

The door fell straight down, landing heavily onto the roof, the three ghouls pressed against it now horizontal. But these three weren't the real problem.

It was the three dozen behind them, now desperately trying to force their way through the exposed doorway that was the real threat.

"Damn it, you've got to be kidding me," Paul said under his breath as he swung the Winchester off his shoulder and aimed it at the first zombies to step out onto the roof.

The rifle barked and a head imploded, splattering the other ghouls with blood and gore. None of them slowed an instant, but pushed onward onto the roof. One of the ghouls that had been lying on the door was crawling across the roof and when it was closer to Paul, the large man stepped up and kicked the pale face hard, dislocating the ghoul's jaw and sending the body rolling to the side. The ghoul rolled and then looked up, its jaw now off center, the tongue lolling out of the open mouth like a piece of liver.

Paul fired repeatedly at the bodies. Some were headshots, but in his haste, many bullets found torsos and limbs only. He was still backing away from the undead army, and when he reached the stairway leading up to the helipad, he was able to get a better view of the roof around him.

There had to be at least a score of zombies shambling towards him, most wearing hospital garb in one way or another. A few wore security guard uniforms, and others wore janitorial outfits. But it didn't matter anymore. Doctor, nurse, janitor, all classism was past. Now they were one team, and they were playing for the side of death. Turning, Paul charged up the stairs, already yelling out to Francesca.

When he was halfway across the helipad, Francesca was awake, her eyes wide as she gazed around her. At first she didn't understand what was going on, but then, as Paul dashed across the helipad, she looked behind him and saw the first zombies appear as they stumbled up the stairs from the roof.

"Oh my God," she whispered as she immediately gathered baby Shaun in her arms and moved to the pilot's seat in the helicopter.

She began flicking switches, the baby already stirring in her arms, unhappy about being disturbed. She ignored him now, knowing getting the helicopter running was the priority.

The engine sputtered and she sent fuel through the lines just as Shaun had taught her, and in another second the engine came to life, the main rotor beginning to spin.

But as she glanced at the zombies following Paul and then up at the slowly moving rotor blades, she knew there wasn't going to be enough time for their escape.

Paul had reached the helicopter and he literally ran into it, his body banging off the rear door in his haste. He opened the door and hopped inside, his face covered in sweat.

"Go, Francesca, now, before they get here!"

"Paul, I can't! Not yet. The rotors need time to cycle!" she yelled back. The baby had begun crying, sensing his mother's angst and Francesca tried to soothe him.

"Damn it all to hell," Paul snarled. "Fine, you get the copter ready and let me know when we can leave. I'll keep those things off us."

He opened the door, stepped out, closed it, making sure it was secured, and then turned to the oncoming horde of zombies.

They had fanned out now, some drifting to the sides as they moved towards the helicopter. Their moans filled the roof and caused Paul to feel a chill down his spine, their wails overriding the cycling engine. He glanced above his head to see the rotors moving faster, knowing in less than a minute the helicopter would be ready to go.

But the first ghoul would be on them in thirty seconds, so again, he raised the Winchester and fired, taking out the first ghoul in line. The head snapped back and the body dropped to the helipad, the ones behind it stumbling as they stepped over the prone corpse. But still they came onward. They knew no fear, no hesitation. All they knew was hunger.

Paul fired again, and again, putting the zombies down like he was target shooting at a carnival. But there were still too many.

When the Winchester went dry, he slung it over his shoulder and pulled the Colt, firing with smooth shots, not wanting to waste a single round. He took three ghouls down before the first one got too close for him to shoot.

The head dove into his outstretched arm and he pulled away, cracking the ghoul over the head with the butt of the revolver. The ghoul dropped to the helipad, but there were more right behind it. Paul spun around, trying to stay out of reach of the grasping hands, a few getting past him to the helicopter. They began pounding on the glass and doors, shaking the aircraft on its landing skids, and Francesca bit her lip in fear. She would not scream, that was a given.

The gauges told her the rpm was high enough for lift off and she called to Paul through the glass, a ghoul pounding on her door inches from her face.

Paul couldn't hear her, the man fighting for his life, trying to keep the ghouls from swarming over the helicopter. If too many got their hands on it, the weight would be too much and the machine would never fly.

He was punching and kicking at each zombie that got near the helicopter, knocking them to the helipad. He wasn't worried about killing them all, only slowing them down.

Francesca decided she had no choice and began lifting the helicopter off the helipad, hoping Paul would see what was happening and know what to do.

Paul did.

As he felt the wash of the rotor blades blow across his face and body, he knew she was taking off. He punched a zombie in the face and then turned and jumped for the left landing skid, wrapping his arms around it, his lower body hanging like an acrobat.

The helicopter ascended, and just before Paul's legs were higher than five feet from the helipad, a spry zombie reached up and wrapped dead hands around his shins.

Paul felt the tug of weight and held on for dear life as the helicopter swayed back and forth like a small row boat on choppy waters. As he held on, gritting his teeth from the added weight, he glanced across to the other landing skid to see two more zombies had done the same as him.

The ghouls were holding on to the skid with their hands in a death grip and when one of the pale faces turned to see him, the ghoul got the idea that all it had to do was let go and walk over to him.

Unfortunately for the walking corpse, Francesca had taken the helicopter up and out over the city, and when the ghoul let go, reaching for Paul, it dropped away to plummet to the city and the hard ground waiting below.

The helicopter rocked again and Francesca struggled to keep it under her control. She was inexperienced and could barely keep the aircraft level, and she winced every time the weight under the helicopter shifted as the bodies swayed back and forth like flags in the wind.

"Keep the damn thing steady!" Paul called out over the wash of wind blowing across him. He didn't know if she had heard him, but he had to try.

"I'm trying!" she yelled back, but it was doubtful Paul could hear her.

Paul felt his grip slipping and he set his jaw tight and pulled himself back up. The ghoul holding onto his ankles was now crawling up his legs, and it would be seconds when the teeth of the pale face would sink into his thigh. He tried kicking the body off him, but the corpse was on tight. He decided there was only one way to get rid of his uninvited passenger.

With a yell of exertion, he pulled his body higher, then wrapped his right arm around the landing skid so his armpit was now holding him up. He then pulled the Colt from his holster, and with his arm and hand swaying in the wind while he tried to line up the shot, he tried to shoot the ghoul below him. The vantage was awkward and he knew he had as much chance of shooting his leg as he was of shooting the zombie, but he had no choice. Already his limbs were tiring and he needed to get rid of the excess weight.

The ghoul on the other landing skid was smarter than its brethren and it held on tightly, not letting go, though its dead eyes stared at Paul. Every time the zombie shifted, the helicopter rocked, Francesca trying to keep it steady.

Paul aimed straight down, knowing he had three bullets remaining in the revolver. When he was sure he had a shot, he fired, the echo of the gunshot lost in the swirling maelstrom that was now enveloping his ears thanks to the helicopter's altitude.

The bullet missed, disappearing into empty air and Paul cursed, knowing his chances were sliding with his loosening grip. He lined up the head of the ghoul again, and when he was as sure as he could get, he fired just as the pale face had reached his thigh and was about to sink its fetid teeth into his flesh.

The bullet caught the zombie in its open mouth, shattering its jaw and causing more than twenty of its teeth to fly off, falling away into the air. But better yet, the impact of the round caused the zombie to loosen its grip and fall away from Paul, tumbling head over heels as a thin spray of blood spread out from its body to disperse on the wind.

Paul immediately felt better when the excess weight was lifted from his arms and he swung up with his other one, letting out a loud grunt. Now he had to deal with the other ghoul on the opposite landing skid, so he turned and leveled the Colt at the swaying body. The ghoul snarled at him, almost as if it could sense what was about to happen.

Paul took his time, knowing this was his last round, and when he was confident of a hit, he fired, the bullet crossing the few feet separating him from the ghoul in less than a second. The zombies head snapped backwards and its hands let go as it tumbled backward into space.

Paul watched it fall for a second, realizing that could just as easily been him, then he holstered the empty gun, and with both hands on the landing skid, grabbed another part of the strut and pulled himself up.

It was hard work, his arms protesting the entire time, and for a few moments he almost didn't think he had it in him. But his will was strong and he wasn't about to give up now.

With one last push, he reached up to the rear door and managed to open the latch, then he pulled himself inside. He was on the floor and he had to dig deep one last time and pull himself in the remaining inches, then crawl onto the seat. The door slammed closed from the wind and he leaned back against the seat, his chest heaving like he'd run a mile in less than two minutes.

Francesca glanced over her shoulder at him and smiled, relieved he'd made it.

"Are you okay?" was all she could think to ask.

He merely nodded, too winded to speak, and he gestured with his right hand that she should go.

"But where do I go?"

"Anywhere," he gasped, closing his eyes and sucking in large lungfuls of air. The Winchester was poking his back so he shrugged out of the strap with a grunt and a moan. Baby Shaun was crying and she tried to soothe him again, but she needed her other arm on the control stick. She banked the helicopter deeper into the city while Paul watched her fly the aircraft.

"He all right?" he asked brusquely, referring to the baby.

She nodded. "Yes, he's fine. Thanks to you. We almost didn't get out of there alive."

Paul brushed her comment off.

"Just look for another helipad on a tall building, and when you find one, set down there. We still need to figure out what we're gonna do before we just start flying around."

She said okay and Paul sighed heavily. He leaned back, his head touching the smooth metal behind him, the vibration of the engine going right into his skull. He closed his eyes and let the vibration fill him, his heartbeat slowing down with each passing breath. His arm's tingled from the exertion he had just forced on them, and while he rested, the adrenalin fueling his body slowly drained away, leaving him more exhausted than he could remember being in a long time.

Chapter 12

Carver took one step forward, ready to take down the charred ghoul in front of him. As he moved, his eyes took in the unbelievable condition of the dead mechanic.

The man's face was charred a deep black, the hair all but cooked away in the flames. His clothes were burned on over half his body, the material flopping on him like old rags.

His eyes were missing, nothing but dark holes where the white orbs once resided after being cooked away, bubbling like hard-boiled eggs. A small amount of viscous ooze still seeped out of the tiny caverns to drip onto the burnt cheeks.

The mechanic didn't seem to mind and never missed a step as he began moving towards Carver, his ears telling him where the three humans were standing, though his outer ears were nothing but melted flesh resembling candle wax.

Pieces of charred skin flaked off to drift to the floor, and when the mechanic opened his mouth as if he was trying to speak, only a hollow rasping could be heard, the dead man's vocal cords burned to a crisp in the searing heat. Carver noticed inside the man's mouth the tongue was shriveled and black, like an onion that had sat on a barbeque grill for far too long.

The mechanic reached out with his right hand and leaned on the generator for support, and when he removed his hand, pieces of blackened flesh stuck to the metal of the generator. The dead man's palm glistened red in the light beam of Fred's flashlight, the raw meat underneath the charred skin now exposed. In a few places, the white of bone peeked through.

Flies were already circling around the body of the ghoul, resting to feed and then taking flight again. Carver marveled at how the insects had found the corpse so fast.

The zombie stumbled forward, arms out like he wanted to embrace Carver in a loving hug, but Carver had other ideas.

Bringing the rebar high over his head, he sidestepped the out-stretched arms and cracked the dead mechanic over the head.

Blood shot from the wound and mixed with the blackened skin and Carver was reminded of barbeque ribs, as sickening as that seemed. The zombie was knocked to the side, but recovered in an instant and turned towards Carver, as if the mechanic could now sense where he was. Before Carver realized it, the mechanic was lunging for him. Carver sidestepped the clumsy move and brought the rebar down flat onto the top of the skull. There was a meaty thwap that filled the room and the ghoul dropped to the cold floor. Not wanting to take chances, Carver raised the rebar over his head like a spear and plunged in down through the zombie's spine, severing the connection from head and body and the arms dropped to the floor like limp spaghetti. The corpse slumped to the floor and rolled onto its back and Carver could see the mouth still moving, the charred tongue flicking around like a burnt twig.

"Son of a bitch just won't die!" he snarled and brought the sole of his left boot down onto the ghoul's face, crushing it flat as brains and gore spread out like a spilled bag of chicken livers fresh from the supermarket.

The body was still after that, and Carver stepped away, his face a mask of revulsion as he stared at his boot. Stepping back to the door, Fred aimed the flashlight at him, wanting to see him better.

Carver took off his boot and dropped it onto the floor, then pointed to the charred corpse while taking his shotgun back from Fred.

"Clean this shit up and my boot, too," he said, and without an-other word, turned and walked back down the darkened hallway, now with a subtle limp as he strode away with one boot missing.

David and Fred looked to one another, and then glanced at the corpse. They were so high up in the hierarchy of the enclave they knew they didn't have to clean up dead bodies, so with a quick smile to one another, Fred spoke first.

"Get one of the shitheads to do it, right?"

"Hell, yeah. I ain't doin' it," David replied.

Both men turned and moved back down the hallway. There were plenty of lower men and even some women on the ranking system of the enclave and Fred and David knew just who to get.

* * *

Carver moved through the dark hallway until he was at the stairwell leading to the first floor. The instant he opened the door, a wan light filled the hallway. Small circular windows were on one side of the stairwell allowing natural light to filter in. Glad to be out of the darkness of the lower level, he moved up the stairs, careful not to step in anything sticky on the steps with his bare foot. The stairwell was a popular place for couples to screw when they wanted a few minutes alone. Most shared their sleeping quarters with five or six others, and only Carver and a few others were high enough in the chain-of-command to have sleeping quarters all their own.

Crossing the large lobby, he climbed the stairs and was about to return to Lynn, already thinking about her soft, shapely body, and what he would do to it in a few minutes, when he paused as he approached a small courtroom at the opposite end of the floor from where he wanted to go.

He could hear someone crying as he crossed the polished marble tiles, and when he stepped inside the courtroom, he spotted an old woman sobbing on her knees near the front of the room, a supine old man in front of her, his arms folded across his chest.

He recognized her at once. Her name was Margaret and her husband was Wilbur. They were a few of the refugees he had taken in, although most were healthy and had integrated into his enclave. But Margaret and Wilbur were old and so weren't up to the task. Carver had always wondered how they had managed to survive for more than three months in the city before he had found them. Usually the old and weak were the first to become food for the undead, but somehow they had survived, hiding in a delicatessen on Grant Street.

"What's wrong with Wilbur, Margaret?" Carver asked while he approached the kneeling woman. Though a hard man, Margaret had reminded him of his mother and even the toughest bastards around still loved their mothers.

She looked up at him with tear-filled eyes.

"He's dead, Ben. I think it was his heart. He said he was having pains and that his arm hurt and then...and then, he just collapsed to the floor."

With a deep frown, Ben Carver leaned over and touched the side of Wilbur's neck, trying to see if there was a pulse. He waited for more than a minute, slowly moving his two fingers as he searched, but after the full minute was finished, he shook his head and stood up.

"I'm sorry, Margaret, you're right. He's dead. And you know what we have to do now, right?

He was already unslinging his shotgun from over his shoulder, his jaw taut with determination. He glanced around the room, but there was no one else in sight. Footsteps could be heard coming from the outside lobby, but inside the room it was just two living beings and one dead one.

Margaret threw her body over her husband, as if she could protect his form with her own, as if her frail body could stop the penetration of a shotgun blast.

"No! You can't! He's my husband, Ben!"

Carver sighed wearily. He'd seen this hundreds of times. Some people just couldn't accept that when a person was dead they were gone, and worse, were now the enemy.

"Damn it, Margaret, move away from him before he comes back!" he snapped through gritted teeth.

"No! You can go to Hell, Ben. I love him, you can't!"

But the decision was taken from her when Wilbur's eyes snapped open and before she could so much as gasp in surprise, he raised his head, craning his neck to do so, and sank his dentures into her left arm, the teeth going in so deep they only stopped when they hit bone. Margaret screamed and pulled away instinctively, leaving a large chunk of her arm in her husband's mouth. White bone from her ulna peeked through the blood and tattered skin as she screamed to the heavens in pain.

Cursing a blue streak, Carver pumped the shotgun and then kicked the old woman aside so he had a clear shot at Wilbur.

The old man was already sitting up and as he leaned forward to try and stand, chewing happily on his wife's flesh, he suddenly had even more of a mouthful to chew on when the muzzle of the shot-gun was jammed between his fake teeth.

"Eat this, you dead bastard," Carver growled as he fired from the hip.

The blast took off Wilbur's head from the lower lip, severing the cranium like a dull edged blade had swiped it away. The tongue was still there, however, having been pinned down by the barrel of the shotgun, and as Carver pulled the muzzle out of the half-mouth, the tongue flopped upward like a landed fish. With less than half a brain, Wilbur wobbled on his butt, and then collapsed to the floor, the lower half of his remaining brain matter spilling onto the floor like spilled beef stew.

Margaret was screaming uncontrollably as she watched her husband lose the top half of his head in the blink of an eye. She was on her butt, legs kicking at the air, her one hand covering the large gash in her arm. With a sad look on his face, Carver pumped the shotgun, expelled the spent shell and racked another into the chamber. He turned and walked to Margaret, towering over her like a giant. She stopped screaming when he gazed into her eyes and as she stared into those cold orbs, she realized she was looking at her executioner.

"No, Ben, don't!" she screamed, tears running rivers down her wrinkled cheeks.

Carver never slowed, never wavered, and despite his cold heart thawing slightly at what was about to happen, he knew there was no choice in the matter.

"I'm sorry, Margaret, but it has to be this way. You've been bit. And we all know what happens then."

She raised her hands into the air, her arm wound now squirting blood into the air. Wilbur had nicked a vein with his dentures. She now had her palms out in front of her face, her eyes closed as she screamed for Carver to stop, to not do what he intended. Carver didn't hesitate. Raising the shotgun, his fingers white on the shotgun, he fired point-blank at her.

The blast sheared her fingers from her hands and then contin-ued into her face, destroying her visage in an instant.

With no more face and very little upper skull, Margaret's neck geysered blood into the air and the body fell back to the floor, the plasma now shooting horizontal as the heart beat its last. Her arms and legs kicked a staccato beat onto the floor and Carver stepped back, waiting in case he needed to fire again.

No sooner did he fire, then three men charged into the courtroom, guns in their hands.

"You okay?" one of them asked.

From where he stood, the two bodies were behind the wooden benches for seated spectators in the courtroom.

Carver stared at the corpse of the old woman for three more seconds, and when he was satisfied she was down for good, he nodded.

"Yeah, I'm fine. Come over here, will ya?"

The man did as he was told and his breath caught in his throat when he saw the two bodies, heads all but destroyed.

"Take care of this for me."

"Uh, okay, but what do I do with them?" the man asked as the other two men filed inside to see what was going on. Both men gasped in surprise.

"I don't fucking care, you dumbshit! Just get rid of them! Jesus Christ, do I have to think of everything? They're fucking dead! Toss them off the damn roof for all I care!" He spun around and walked out of the room, and when he knew the men couldn't see him, his face softened slightly.

He regretted what he'd just done, and though he knew he had no choice, he still felt a slight pang of guilt.

It was like he had just killed his mother.

Pushing the unpleasant thoughts down deep inside himself, knowing he needed to purge the distasteful feelings, he headed off to see Lynn. Only now he wasn't as horny as before, in fact, he was hoping she would just hold him, even if it was just for a little while before he would then have to put on his facade of hardness once more.

Chapter 13

"**P**aul, look down there! Is that a place to land?" Francesca asked as she gazed out the front windshield of the helicopter. There were streak marks and handprints from where the zombies had slapped the glass. She tried to ignore them, the reminder too painful to contemplate.

It was still odd sitting in the pilot's seat, she thought. She felt like she was in the wrong seat. Shaun should be here, flying his helicopter like he had done every morning for the traffic report. But he was gone, and she needed to accept that.

Paul craned his neck to see where she was pointing and nodded curtly.

"Okay, that'll work, can you make it down there okay?"

"We'll just have to wait and see," she told him as she pressed the pedals under her feet and pitched the rotors so the helicopter would begin descending.

Paul felt his stomach drop and the helicopter dove downward slightly faster than Francesca had planned.

"Sorry," she said while leveling the aircraft out. "I still haven't entirely gotten the hang of it."

"You're doin' fine, Francesca. How's the baby?"

"Sleeping. One of the books I read told me newborns sleep a lot in the first few weeks. So hopefully he won't be much trouble. Though I think we may be in trouble in a little while."

"How so?" Paul inquired from the rear seat. The building was growing closer and he could now make out images on the roof.

"We're gonna need diapers for him, Paul. If not, we're going to be in big trouble."

Paul frowned, realizing she was correct. He reached down and picked up a white sheet, one of a half dozen he had ransacked from the hospital.

"How 'bout using this till somethin' better comes along?" he suggested. "I can cut these into cloths for you."

"Hey, yeah, that just might work. For a little while at least."

"One thing at a time Francesca, okay?"

She nodded, her dark brown hair falling over her aquiline face, showing her European heritage. If she had a free hand she would have brushed it off, but one was holding the baby and the other was on the control stick for the helicopter.

Paul gazed out the side window once more, studying the rooftop of Francesca's destination. The roof had a small helipad near the north corner and he saw what looked like a small fuel refilling station. A small tower stood on the center of the roof, the once blinking light at the top now dead.

"Hey, it looks like there's a refueling station there, too. If we're in luck, there might be somthin' left in that tank."

She followed his pointing finger and nodded, concentrating on flying the helicopter. All the things Shaun had taught her were flooding back and she bit her lip as she tried to maneuver around the tall metal tower and towards the helipad.

Paul eyed the rooftop warily, wondering if any zombies were going to pop up. At the moment, the roof was clear, but that could change at any moment.

He fingered the Winchester next to him, the Colt still in its holster on his hip. Both weapons had been reloaded and he felt good knowing he was at least prepared for whatever would happen next.

Francesca eased up on the stick, the rotors changing pitch as she angled downward. Paul gripped the seat under his legs tightly, his face awash with his concern. The landing was shaky, Francesca juggling the sleeping baby and setting down the helicopter. She touched down once, but the landing skids bounced up a foot in the air and she growled in her throat and then tried again, this time with a more gentle touch. The landing skids floated over the rooftop, three inches high, then two, and then she was down. Letting go of the stick, she glanced over her shoulder at Paul, her smile a mile long.

"Great job, Francesca, you're doin' great. Now stay here and keep the engine on, like when we set down at that abandoned gas station with Shaun and Richard. You remember?"

"How could I forget," she replied, thinking back to the harrowing adventure at the dilapidated small-town gas station. That had been the first time she had seen a real and true zombie, and though she had been scared out of her wits, she had maintained her composure. Shaun had been the gallant hero and had saved her, cracking the ghoul over the head with a crowbar he'd found.

Then later, Richard had taken out the others with his shotgun and knife.

So many memories and all so painful. How could all this happen? What did humanity do to deserve this?

She was pulled from her reverie and Paul opened his door, stepping onto the helipad. Where the last one was clean and pristine, this one was covered in debris. Stray candy wrappers, newspapers, old and dented soda cans, Coke being the predominate one, littered the helipad and roof top.

With his Winchester leading the way, Paul moved off from the helicopter, staying low because of the spinning rotors, he doubted he was in any danger, but he wasn't taking any chances.

No sooner did he move away from the helicopter then a zombie popped up. It was ghastly in appearance; its teeth falling out from rot, its flesh peeling on its face to the point white bone peeked through, like a wood floor from under a frayed carpet. It was wearing a business suit, gray, if Paul was correct, right down to the vest. The once white shirt was almost black; crusting pus, blood and gore now the attire for the best dressed zombie.

And this one was decked out to the max.

Paul would have shot it there and then, but he realized the refueling tank for the helicopter was right behind it. And he couldn't risk what might be in that tank.

The ghoul was already moving forward, the once shined shoes now covered in muck. Its mouth opened and a sort of wail/moan emerged, sounding like a one year old who couldn't talk but wanted its bubba. Paul glanced over his shoulder, the helicopter still there of course, and he got an idea.

Slowly, he backed up until he was almost to the helicopter. Above his head, the rotors cycled round and round, the downdraft blowing all the refuse away from the area. The ghoul was still moving forward, arms out in a stiff reach, hands clasping empty air as it wailed for Paul.

"Come on, sucker, just a little more," Paul grinned as he waited with his Winchester now over his shoulder again.

Francesca watched from inside the helicopter and she was growing concerned. Why hadn't Paul shot the zombie? What was he trying to do?

When the ghoul was no more than three feet away from Paul, the tall man went into action. Compared to the slow moving ghoul, he was like lightning.

He darted to his left, spun around like a football player dodging a foe and came up behind the ghoul. Before the ghoul could turn around, Paul grabbed it by its shirt collar and belt and heaved upward as high as he could.

The ghoul wasn't heavy, desiccation helping to take away its body weight and the corpse shot straight up into the spinning rotor blades.

The top of its head was sliced off like a hot blade through butter, and the upper half of the skull and blood rode the rotor blades as it flew into the air to fall to the streets below.

The ghoul was twitching in Paul's arms and the man tossed the body to the side, making sure to stay low to avoid the blades himself. The corpse rolled onto its side and remained still; the brains in its cranium seeping onto the rooftop like someone had dropped an open can of cherry pie filling onto the ground.

Wiping his hands on his pants, Paul waved to Francesca who was staring at him, dumbfounded. He nodded he was all right and then pointed to the roof behind him, signaling her that he was going to keep exploring. She nodded, her mouth slightly agape, the visceral scene of the ghoul's head flopping off to fall away over the roof still in her mind.

Taking his Winchester off his shoulder, Paul moved off again, now more leery of what might await him on the rooftop. He moved slowly, the sun overhead warming his back and the top of his head.

Circling around some old vents and ductwork, he came upon a small shack with dead pigeons lying around the outside. As he moved closer, he could see the pigeons had been drained of blood, their small carcasses nothing but empty, feathered shells.

He debated if he should check inside the shack and in the end decided to leave it for last. So on the move again, he wandered around the roof. He was almost finished when he came upon a prone corpse, a woman's body by the dress and feminine wrist-watch. That was all he had to go by because the body was missing its head. He moved closer, waving away the flies gathering on the corpse and as he studied the neck wound, he could see something jagged had severed the head from its shoulders. Any blood that had spilled onto the rooftop was long dried and Paul stepped back and moved away.

Then he did a half step forward and decided he wasn't going to let this body remain where it was, not with Francesca and the baby on the roof, too. So as the corpse was close to the edge of the roof, he reached down, grabbed a piece of the dress and pulled the body across the rooftop, the flies buzzing about, angry their meal was being disturbed. When he had reached the edge, he moved to the torso itself and with his right foot, shoved the body off the edge.

Taking a glance over the edge, he watched it tumble away to fall between a pair of parked cars. Like a water balloon, the corpse exploded, splattering the front and rear of the parked cars with black ichor and dried bones and cartilage.

Turning away disgusted, he spun around and was caught entirely off guard.

There was a man charging at him, waving his arms in the air like a crazy person, and as the man came at Paul, the tall man realized his attacker was going to plow into him and take them both over the edge of the roof.

In an instant before the man struck him and he felt himself going over the edge, Paul realized he was about to join the corpse already splattered on the street below, and he figured his body was going to look about the same in about four seconds.

Chapter 14

Frank glanced over to Don as he drove down the road. The City County Building was almost in sight and he knew the men on guard needed to go into action if they were going to make it inside the building safely.

"Better let them know we're almost there so they can get started," he told Don as he struck a zombie walking in the middle of the road with the front bumper of the van.

The body was catapulted across the road, where it then bounced off the hood of a parked car. The ghoul was still alive, but all its limbs were shattered; bones sticking out at odd angles. Half a dozen bloody ribs poked through its torso, making the zombie look like a pathetic porcupine.

Don reached into the glove box and pulled out a two-way radio. It was only used when they were approaching the County Building for the simple reason they were low on the batteries for the radios. They weren't as fortunate to have a generator.

The building had been tied into the main power grid, and when it had failed months ago, so too, did their power disappear.

"Hey, guys, this is Don, we're almost back, send down the decoy, over."

There was a crackle of static and a man's voice could be heard.

"Ten four, Don. Sharon's got her turn in the swing. You want us to send her down right now?"

"Hell, yes, right now! Jesus Christ, I wouldn't have called if I hadn't wanted ya to, over."

If the man on the opposite end of the radio was offended by Don's unctuous reply he gave no sign of it.

"Okay, Don, we'll send her down in two minutes, over."

"That's fine, two minutes, got it, over and out." Don turned off the radio and set it back in the glove box.

"There you have it, Frank. Sharon's going down today."

Frank nodded curtly.

"Yeah, Sharon's good people," Frank said. "Her husband, too. I still remember when we found them both holed up in the small apartment building. If they hadn't heard us driving by and shooting all those zombies I don't think they would have lasted another week."

Don said nothing. He remembered the incident like it was yesterday. The convoy had been on the west side of town foraging for food, and had stopped by a small convenience store. While they were ransacking it, more than two dozen ghouls had arrived and it had been a damn close call when they all made it back to the vehicles and drove away. Not one casualty that day. Yes, sir, it had been a good day.

It was while they were driving away that they heard shouts for help. It was a woman and then a man's voice. Don had been driving one of the other vehicles from the garage and he had spotted them hanging out a second story window. He had taken a chance that day, and with Dale in the passenger seat, they had managed to get under the window, where the couple had dropped out using a makeshift rope made of bed sheets. They had dropped onto the hood of his car and he had ushered them inside. Then they had gotten the hell out of there while the zombies chased them down the street.

Later, back at the County Building, Sharon, and her husband, Bob, had filled the enclave in on their story of survival.

When the outbreak had first began, they had stayed in their apartment building like the news stations on the television had told them to do, and later when the same news stations had told people to leave their homes and go to rescue stations, Bob had decided against it. He had always been somewhat of a conspiracy nut, ever since Nixon had been in office.

So they had stayed, and when things went from bad to worse, they had tossed all the extra furniture from their apartment onto the stairwell, thereby blocking it off. Later, when the undead tried to reach them, they were blocked from gaining entry. Unfortunately, so too, were they trapped in their apartment, and when the water stopped running from the taps, the power went out, and the phone lines went dead, they realized they might not have made the right choice in staying. Sharon had been more concerned for her mother in Johnstown than for her own life and only Bob had kept her focused on the here and now.

They were dangerously low on the water they had saved with buckets and empty containers, as well as food, when the convoy had arrived on the street outside and saved them.

"We're here," Frank stated, pulling Don from his reverie.

The war veteran looked up and out the front windshield of the moving van, seeing the County Building standing alone in a large parking lot. All around the building, the undead wandered, some banging on the lower level, trying to gain access.

They knew there were living people inside and they wanted in.

But the windows and doors on the first floor had been secured months ago with heavy wood and metal. Nothing short of a tank would be getting through them any time soon.

Next to the moving van, the Camaro idled, waiting for Frank to head out again. Dale didn't have a radio, but he had been through the operation enough to know what was happening. Don waved to Dale from the window and the man waved back. Lucy was sitting next to Dale and her hand was hidden from view. As Don looked closer, he could see her hand was actually inside the front of Dale's pants. Don chuckled to himself, slightly jealous of the young man.

He may be getting older, but he still had needs and he considered hitting some of the more mature women in the enclave when he returned. He knew there were at least three that had an eye on him and all three weren't bad lookers, either.

The sound of a woman screaming could be heard now, floating across the parking lot to the waiting convoy.

Almost immediately, the ghouls turned and began moving around the building as they all headed in the direction of the shrieking woman.

None of the occupants of the small convoy made a sound. They had been through this dozens of time and knew there was no one in danger.

If someone had been fearless enough to brave the undead, they could have walked around to the opposite side of the building to see where the zombies were going. If they did this, they would have seen a woman, sitting on what could only be called a swing, like on a swing set. She was holding on with both hands to the ropes, while she gently swung back and forth while she was lowered to only a few feet above the grasping, reaching hands of the undead.

She was screaming, shrieking, and pretending she was crying as loud as her vocal cords would allow, her mock song of pain and anguish riding the air currents, calling the ghouls to dinner.

And that was what she was doing.

She was the human decoy.

As she screamed, the ghouls all herded towards her like she was a steak sandwich to a starving man. Almost every ghoul in the parking lot was now in a massive crowd under the screaming woman.

Her face was filled with concern as she eyed the undead warily, and her knuckles were bone white as she gripped the ropes holding the swing above the heads of the ghouls.

"Okay, that's good enough," Frank said as he put the moving van in drive and began rolling across the parking lot.

His destination was the loading dock at the rear of the building. It was a two bay dock with rolling metal doors. This was where all the delivery trucks would come to deliver paper, food, and other miscellaneous items to the building once upon a time.

As the two vehicles rolled across the pavement, a few ghouls had stayed behind and now turned to face the oncoming moving van and car.

Frank never slowed, never so much as shifted an inch with the steering wheel. As the van shot across the parking lot, the first ghoul found out its face was no match for the radiator grille of the moving van.

The skull was smashed into the metal grille, the face sliced to ribbons. The skull bounced off the grille and the body followed, flying ahead of the van to roll on the asphalt. But the van was still moving and no sooner did the body land on the ground then the van's large tires were driving over the corpse, crushing the chest to mush, bifurcating the body like a large knife.

As the two vehicles shot past, the zombie reached out with shattered hands and began pulling its upper part across the pavement in the direction of the moving van, only the rumbling engine giving the vehicle's direction away. The ghoul's face was a mask of red ribbons of flesh and both eyes had been punctured, a milky white viscous fluid seeping out the gaping eye sockets.

With the severed legs forgotten, the ghoul crawled one painstaking inch at a time, as determined as the ant and the rubber tree plant.

Meanwhile, the woman continued screaming, keeping the undead's attention.

The bay doors of the loading dock were opened and the van and the Camaro pulled inside. There were two other vehicles inside and the two returning ones parked behind them. There was just enough room for Frank to drive the front of the van to the side, tucking it up tight against the platform. As the loading doors closed, the van's rear bumper missed the metal doors by a mere inch and a half.

An instant later, Frank tapped on the wall of the van and the rear door rolled up, the rest of his group climbing out of the back of the moving van, having to slide by the closed bay doors. All were happy to get out of the small box, the air inside growing stuffy, not to mention no one had known what was going on.

A few ghouls had managed to get inside the loading dock and the guard on the platform took each one out in succession, the echo of gunfire bouncing off the stone walls of the bays.

"All clear," a man called out as he lowered his rifle, satisfied at his marksmanship. His name was Jeff Durham and he was the man who was usually sent to the loading dock upon the arrival of a returning scavenging team.

He was medium height and medium build. He had short brown hair and a half-moon face. His big blue eyes were always twinkling, as if he knew something you didn't and wasn't going to share. He had once been the owner of a record store, but after the dead began to walk, his business was worthless. He was single and all his relatives were either dead or lived in other states, so even before the dead rose he was relatively alone in the city.

Frank hopped out of the cab and climbed the four stairs to the upper platform, Don right behind him.

"Good shooting, Jeff, as always. Will you supervise the offloading of the truck, please?"

He nodded, his eyes looking over Frank's shoulder. He was searching for someone. More than one actually, and Frank had a feeling he knew who.

"You're looking for Maggie, right?"

Jeff nodded. "Yeah, where the hell is she? I don't see her." Then his face went ashen as he stared into Frank's eyes.

"Oh, shit, Frank, don't tell me..." he said in a whisper.

"Yeah, Jeff; I'm so sorry, but yeah, she's not with us anymore."

Jeff's face went slack and his rifle slumped to hang from his hand, like the weapon was too heavy to hold onto.

"We lost some others, too," Don added. "George, Gene and Ken to name a few."

"Oh my God, they killed Kenny!" Jeff asked, incredulous, his face full of pain. He turned to the prone corpses lying inanimate on the loading dock floor. "You bastards!" he screamed, glancing at the destroyed zombies on the cold floor. "You no good bastards."

Don moved next to Jeff and grabbed the man's shoulder with one hairy-knuckled hand.

"Sorry, partner, it sucks, but it happened, look, there'll be time for mourning later, but right now we need to get this stuff into the building ASAP. Especially what we could get for medical supplies."

Jeff raised his head and nodded, a tear rolling down his cheek. Maggie and he had been close and Ken had become like a brother to the man.

Frank moved closer, too. "Go ahead, Jeff, get to work, when you're through, take some time off, let anyone who says anything come talk to me."

Jeff grinned wanly. "Yeah, okay, Frank, thanks, thanks a lot." He moved away, knowing he needed to help the others as they unloaded the rear of the moving van.

"Oh, and Jeff?" Frank called.

"Yeah?"

"When you're done, make sure someone takes care of those stiffs. We don't want them stinkin' up the place," Frank added as he gestured to the ghouls littering the dock.

Jeff nodded and moved away just as Dale and Lucy walked up, waiting for the conversation to wan.

"Took it hard, huh?" Dale asked as he watched Jeff climb down off the platform and begin organizing the offloading of the moving van.

"Wouldn't you?" Don asked.

Dale shrugged. "Suppose so. I heard him and Maggie were, you know, bumpin' boots."

Frank's eyebrows went up a notch. "No shit?"

"No shit," Dale replied.

"What's wrong, Frank?" Lucy asked. "Can't an older woman get a little young love once in a while? Why does it always have to be the man who's older?"

Suddenly there was the sound of heavy footsteps coming from the hallway leading into the building, and a second later a man with a long beard and a bandana came charging into the loading dock.

His face was filled with worry and he ran directly towards Frank.

"Frank! We got a problem, man."

Don was the one to speak first. "Well, out with it, Duane, what the hell is it?"

"It's Sharon, the goddamn rope snapped and she's hanging on for her life! We can't pull her up because she's caught on the side of the building and she says she's in pain and can't hold on for much longer!"

"Shit, you've got to be kidding me," Frank spit as he turned and followed the bearded man out of the loading dock with Dale and Lucy on his heels. Don was a little slower, so he brought up the rear, taking the last place in line like a tired, fat kid running a marathon.

Chapter 15

Paul felt the man impact his chest and send them both flying off the edge of the roof. If it wasn't for the simple fact that Paul was over six inches taller than the man, he had no doubt in his mind he would have been watching his own death happen.

But that difference in size was the deciding factor, and as both men flew off the roof, Paul reached out and just managed to grab onto the edge, the sheet metal curved around the corner of the roof cutting into his palm and causing him to cry out in pain. Then he felt his body falling and he braced himself for the inevitable jolt.

The force of his body slamming against the side of the building was confounded by the fact that the man was still holding onto him. Paul was only holding on with his left hand, his right dangling out in the air, and he knew if he wasn't able to regain a grip with his other hand fast, in seconds he would be falling to the earth to splatter on the ground like a plate of spaghetti and meatballs.

Vertigo filled him as he gazed down twenty stories below. The wind blew at his face, drying the sweat as fast as it appeared.

"Please, wait! Don't drop me, I'm sorry!" the man screamed as he clung to his waist.

"You stupid bastard! Why the hell did you do that?" Paul yelled and gasped at the same time. His fingers were already growing numb and he could feel them beginning to slip.

"I'm, really sorry, I saw you push my wife off the roof and I just went crazy. I didn't realize what I was doing until it was too late to stop myself. Please, I don't want to die!"

"No shit, brother, neither do I." Paul glanced to the side of the building and there was a small outcropping. It looked like something from a dryer vent perhaps, or from the heating system.

"All right then, listen up, chump, and listen good. Unless you want both of us to fall to our deaths you need to let me go. See that metal vent sticking out of the bricks? Well, get your ass over to it and hold on. Once I'm up on the roof again we'll talk."

"But you'll just leave me there and I'll fall when I can't hold on anymore!"

Paul gritted his teeth. "Well sucker, we're both gonna fall in a minute if you don't do what I say, so make up your damn mind!"

The man weighed his options and realized he had no choice, so with a tentative hand, he let go of Paul's waist and reached out for the protrudence. Immediately, Paul felt a hundred percent lighter and he swung his other arm over to the edge and latched onto it. With his right hand now holding on, too, he was able to lessen the weight on his other hand; the one with shallow cuts on it.

He sucked in a few breaths of air and with a grunt and a yell, he pulled himself up like he was doing a chin-up. His arms trembled with the effort, as he was already taxed to the breaking point, but his iron will saw him through, and when he was high enough, he swung his left leg over the edge, now taking the weight off his hands and arms by more than half. Breathing for a few seconds, he waited for the spots to leave his vision and with one last grunt of exertion, he pulled himself up and onto the roof, rolling a few feet away and laying on his back.

The sun beat down on his closed eyes and his chest rose and fell quickly as he sucked in those precious lungfuls of fresh air. His arms felt like wet noodles and his left hand was throbbing from where it had been sliced, but before he could do anything else, a voice called up from over the edge.

"Please help me! Please. I'm sorry, please don't let me die!"

With a moan that rivaled the undead, Paul rolled to his feet and crawled to the edge of the roof, gazing down at the man. The man's wide eyes looked up and a few tears dropped down his face to fall to the street below.

A long fall at that.

"Give me one reason why I shouldn't just let you fall, you bastard. You nearly killed me," Paul said as he sucked in more air.

"Please, I've been trapped in that shack for weeks and if I hadn't had the pigeons to suck their blood I'd be dead already. That was my wife you pushed off the roof and I loved her dearly. I just went mad when I saw you desecrate her body."

Paul stared at the man's face, trying to read falsehood there, but he could find none.

"Where's her head?" Paul asked.

"What?"

"Her head, man, her damn head wasn't with her body, it was gone," Paul said as he felt his strength returning with each lungful of air he took in.

"Oh, uh, it's gone; been gone for a while now. You killed that zombie right?"

Paul nodded.

"That was my friend. He had me trapped in the shack, now please. For the love of God, I can't hold on anymore!"

Paul knew he needed to make a decision, and at the end of the day, he was still a cop, so he reached across the roof, picked up his Winchester from where it had fallen and hung it over the edge so the man could grab the shoulder strap.

"Here, grab this and I'll pull you up. But so help me, brother, if you try anything..." Paul trailed off, his warning clear.

"I won't, I won't, just let me up, please!" the man shrieked.

Paul let the man grab the strap of the rifle, and when he was secure, he used his shoulder muscles to slowly bring the man up. It was a strain, but Paul was the larger man and he didn't slide on the roof, and in seconds the smaller man was wrapping his hands on the edge. Once this was accomplished, Paul set the rifle aside, made sure behind him was still clear, no foes to deal with, and he grabbed the man's wrists, pulling him onto the roof again.

The man slid over the edge and collapsed onto the roof, breathing heavily, a few sobs of happiness filling his throat.

Paul was on his knees, hands on his thighs, and he reached out for the Winchester, then he stood on wobbly legs. The blood rushed to his head and he needed to wait a moment, but when his vision was steady and his head was clear, he began walking away from the man.

"Wait. Where are you going?" the man asked, his white face was covered in sweat and nervousness.

"I have a friend at the other end, on the helipad. I want to make sure she's all right. Just stay away from us and I'll leave you alone, but if you even try..."

"No I understand, I won't bother you," the man said in a soft voice like a dejected child.

"Are there any more of those things on this roof with you?" Paul inquired as he looked around again.

The man shook his head as he rolled onto his side

"No, my friend was the only one."

"Good, that's real good," Paul said and turned away. He only glanced back to make sure the man was still where he was supposed to be. He wasn't stupid enough to turn his back on another man that might do him harm, but his gut told him the small guy was harmless, as long as he kept an eye on him.

Strolling away, he left the man to lie alone on the roof.

* * *

Francesca was waiting for him in the pilot's seat, anxiousness covering her face. The baby was awake, fussing in her arms while her other remained on the control stick. She was not getting caught unawares like on the hospital roof. One look at a ghoul and she was prepared to go...as soon as Paul would return, of course.

Paul waved to her, then drew his right hand across his neck, then pointed to the rotors. Francesca nodded, then cut the engine, the rotors beginning to cycle down almost immediately, the whine slowing to a dull drone which would stop eventually.

Knowing Paul would never tell her to cut the engine if it wasn't safe, she opened the door to the helicopter and stepped onto the helipad.

By the time she was on both feet, Paul was only a few feet away.

"You all right?" he asked brusquely.

"Yes, fine. You?" She took in his disheveled state, the cut on his hand and knew something had happened.

He glanced down at his hand, seeing her staring at it, and shrugged the wound off.

"It's nothing, Francesca. I can clean it later. We still have that antiseptic left." Then he saw her eyes go wide and her mouth open in mild surprise. Turning with the Winchester ready, he stopped from squeezing the trigger when he saw it was the man from a moment before.

The man stood at the edge of the helipad, looking very pathetic. Under his right arm he carried a Styrofoam cooler, like what picnickers use on a day at the park when they bring a packed lunch.

"Who's that?" Francesca asked, gently rocking baby Shaun in her arms. She had a holster on her hip with a .45 in it and the rifle was slung over her shoulder. It was an odd combination, guns and baby, but it suited her to a T.

"No one. Some dumb bastard who got caught up here thanks to that zombie I took out earlier." He grinned sheepishly. "Sorry about gettin' blood on the helicopter."

She glanced back to see the red splatter, like specks, covering the rear of the helicopter.

"It's fine, Paul. It'll wash off when it rains." She gestured to the man on the edge of the helipad with her elbow. "What's his story exactly? And why is he standing there like that?"

Paul quickly filled her in on what had happened, leaving most of it out. He was a stoic man and never went in for bravado. But when he was finished, Francesca's eyes were slits, her jaw set tight.

"So what do we do now? We can't just leave him there like that, Paul. He's still human. He's still alive like us and for all we know we're the only ones left in this entire city. We have to take him with us when we leave here."

Paul frowned, not liking where she was going with this, but realizing she had a point. The time to kill the man had past. And if he wasn't planning on doing it in the future, he might as well try to be friendly. After all, the man had apologized. Unfortunately, the man had knocked him off the roof first.

When Paul looked back at everything leading up to him hanging by one hand twenty stories up, he realized the entire situation had been a giant misunderstanding.

"Fine, Francesca, but I'm still keeping an eye on him," Paul grumbled as he stared down at her. He stood nearly a foot taller than her, but she wasn't the slightest bit intimidated. After all the time they had lived together in the office complex, he was like family to her.

She only nodded for a reply to his statement.

With a long sigh, Paul turned around and waved to the man.

"Come on; she says you can join us when we leave."

"Really? You really mean it?" the man asked, stepping forward hesitantly.

Paul nodded brusquely. "Yeah, I really mean it."

"Hi, I'm Francesca and this is Paul, if he didn't introduce himself to you yet," Francesca said with a wan smile. The baby cooed in her arms and she gently rocked him.

"Uh, no, we never did introductions," the man said. "My name's Stavin, Thomas Stavin." He didn't try to shake anyone's hand, especially as it was holding the cooler.

Paul eyed the cooler and gestured with the barrel of the Winchester.

"What's in there?"

"Oh, uh, nothing. Just what little food I managed to save on top of eating the pigeons," he said, his eyes shifting back and forth like a rat.

"Pigeons?" Francesca asked, not understanding what the man was talking about.

Paul waved her question away.

"Another time, Francesca, it doesn't matter."

Francesca let it go, her attention back on the baby.

"Well, why don't you come over to the helicopter? We have some supplies if you're hungry," she said. She was referring to the cans of corned beef in the rear storage compartment of the helicopter.

She idly remembered when they had first arrived at the office complex. There had been four of them then. The canned corned beef had been their first real meal together. She smiled wanly as she remembered Richard, teasing her when she complained about the food only being canned corned beef.

"You got a can opener on you for that?" Richard had asked her wittily.

"No, I'm afraid I don't carry one with me," she'd replied.

"Then don't complain," Richard had said. "The can has its own key so you can open it easily wherever you a."

Then Paul and Richard had taken off on some harebrained adventure to see what they could find in the office complex. The two had acted like a couple of five-year-olds left alone in a candy store.

"All right, then, so let's get to it," Paul said. "I'm pretty hungry myself. Hell, even corned beef sounds good right now."

With Francesca leading the way, Paul escorted Thomas back to the helicopter. As the two men walked, Thomas stayed on his right side with the white Styrofoam cooler still under his right arm, so Paul really couldn't see it very well.

If he had, he might have noticed the cooler jump ever so slightly in the man's arm, as if something inside was alive and wanted to get out desperately.

Chapter 16

Frank barely glanced at the signs over the doors lining the different hallways as he followed Duane through the building. He had when he'd first made the City County Building his home, but not now.

Signs for the City Clerk, Human Relations, Park and Recreations, the Finance Department and finally near the middle of the building on the second floor, the Mayor's office, all blurred past as he dashed upstairs and through hallways like a rat in a maze searching for cheese.

Duane still was in the lead and the man dashed along the hallways, surefooted and knowing exactly where he was going.

People living in the enclave glanced up as the four men and one woman dashed down the corridors, some asking what was wrong, but they were ignored. With no way of knowing what was happening, they went back to whatever errand they were on.

All were armed, mostly with low caliber handguns, but a few carried S&W's, Magnums and large Colts, .357's mostly. One or two had rifles and shotguns strapped to their backs because even in the supposed safety of the building, no one wanted to take chances.

Only a few children were living in the building, and at the moment they were in a room on the third floor, at school. Frank thought it was a good idea to try and keep their lives as normal as possible. Well, as normal as one could make it in a world where the dead walked and fed on the living.

In no time, Duane was leading the party into the large room where Sharon was hanging out the window. Frank had a brief glimpse of the room, seeing it was one single room with green cubicles separating each worker's area. Desk phones were silent and scattered paper littered the floor and desktops, the workers probably long dead or walking the earth as the living dead.

The area around the window had been cleared of desks and cubicles so the men could work when they had to raise and lower the decoy.

Frank slowed as he approached the window. There were four men already in the room. There was Marc, Ronny, and Alex, all under thirty years of age, and there was Bob, Sharon's husband.

When Frank entered the room, Bob was yelling at Marc, telling the man to pull his wife up or so help him he was going to put a bullet in the man's head.

Marc was arguing, trying to explain to Bob how he couldn't; that Sharon was stuck on something.

Charging into the situation, Frank placed his hand on Bob's shoulder as he moved to the frazzled man. He noticed in passing where there should have been two ropes played out of the window, there was now only one, and he saw the frayed end of the other, shortened by dozens of yards lying impotently on the floor, the opposite end still tied and secured to a desk.

"What the hell happened here?" he snapped at the three men and Bob.

Alex answered, looking like a kid who'd been caught sneaking cookies before dinner.

"We don't know. We think the rope had a thin spot and it gave out from rubbing the windowsill too many times."

Making an annoyed face, Frank moved to the open window, Frank peered out and down, frowning and muttering a string of imprecations when he saw the condition of Sharon.

When one of the ropes holding the swing she'd been perched on had given way, the woman had begun to fall. Reaching out for something other than the remaining rope, she had tried to grasp the side of the building.

But there had been the protrudence of an old flag pole on the side of the structure, about six inches worth of wood still there. Sharon had swung straight for it and the tip had slid into her like a spear, impaling her as good as any true spear would have. The only thing saving her life was that the broken flag pole might not have, by a miracle, punctured any vital organs.

If they could get her back inside the building safely, she might live to see another day.

"We need to get her up here now, Frank!" Bob yelled, moving next to him as he stared down at his wife.

"Hang on, baby, we'll get you up, just hang on!"

Sharon was barely responsive. At first she had screamed in pain when the flag pole had punctured her side, but now shock was setting in. Drops of her blood seeped from her wound to fall onto the faces of the ghouls only a few feet below her. They reached up and opened mouths, drinking greedily. Flies filled the air and the incessant buzzing was just one more distasteful item to ignore.

Bob turned to Frank. "Damn it, Frank, what the hell are we gonna do?"

Frank didn't have an answer for him. He was getting one though. His hope was that another person could be dropped down with another line and grab the woman, then both could be hauled back up.

He was about to run his idea by the others and get them into action when Sharon let out a shrill scream that chilled the blood of every man in the room.

Bodies crowded to the open window to see what had happened, and after a second, Frank grabbed Marc and Alex by the collars of their shirts and pulled them out of the way so he could see. Neither man argued, deferring to the leader of the enclave.

It had been taken to a vote months ago and Frank had won. He hadn't wanted the job, but had taken it anyway, knowing at least in his own hands he might not see himself and the others killed.

Looking out and down again, he saw things had changed drastically for the suffering woman.

Sharon had somehow managed to dislodge herself from the flag pole, the tip now coated in red, and she had slipped down so she was hanging over the ghouls.

She was less than a foot from them and already they were trying to grab her, just coming inches short with each attempt.

"Jesus Christ, get my wife up here!" Bob screamed as he pushed men out of the way and grasped the remaining rope.

Frank saw what he was doing and jumped to help, yelling at the other men as well.

Below, they could hear Sharon's screams reach a frightening crescendo, and Frank could only wonder what had happened to make her cry out like that.

As one group, they began pulling her up, one foot at a time.

"Don, go get Timothy, he'll need his medical bag, too," Frank told the man.

Don nodded and took off at a half-trot, his legs moving as fast as they would allow. Timothy was a nurse, but was as good as the enclave could do. Doctors had been one of the first casualties when the dead had risen. Hospitals had been deathtraps and almost every doctor in the city had been at one hospital or clinic, trying to help the suffering victims of wounds or bite marks. When the wounded had finally died and had then risen again, the best food for them was the doctors and nurses, and a few orderlies, for quick snacks. But Timothy had been out that day, helping his mother with the flu. It had saved his life and then Frank and the others had found him and taken him in.

Bob was yelling for the others to pull faster, but Frank knew that might not be such a good idea. If the woman was bleeding badly then each jerk of the rope could be opening the wound more. But then, if she was bleeding badly, they needed to get her back inside and stabilized fast.

Ronny was near the window and he yelled that she was almost to the windowsill. It was Bob who made sure the others had hold of the rope and ran to the sill, wanting to be the one to bring his wife inside.

Reaching out, he called to the others to stop pulling, and with Ronny's help, he managed to get his wife under the armpits and lift her to the windowsill.

She was perched on the frame, like she was sitting on the edge of a swimming pool and her head hung low like she was asleep. Frank prayed she was only unconscious.

Then what seemed like a half dozen things happened in the same moment in time.

The first was Frank's eyes went to the large two inch hole in her right side, the wound now seeping only a little blood. The second was her right fingers began to twitch, slowly at first, but then with more alacrity.

Bob had his wife's face cradled in his hands and he was gazing up into her closed eyes, trying to get her to open them.

And then she did.

But where once a beautiful woman named Sharon had lived, loved and breathed, now there was something dead, foul and evil.

"Sharon? Oh my God, you're all right," Bob breathed as he stared at his wife's open eyes. He hadn't realized the light, the twinkle of life that had filled his wife's orbs was now gone, and there was only a dead space inside her head.

But he found out soon enough.

Before anyone in the room could do anything about it, Sharon opened her mouth wide, practically dislocating her jaw in the process, and clamped her teeth down over Bob's nose. There was a subtle crunching sound, like when a diner patron rips a lobster in half, and then Sharon's head snapped back, a bloody protrudence sticking out of her mouth.

Bob screamed, pushing away from the dead woman who was once his wife and both his hands went to staunch the flow of blood shooting out of his nose like a broken fire hose. He had the mother of all nose bleeds and, sorry to say, if he tried to just tip his head back it wasn't going to work.

Sharon sat on the windowsill, chewing on her husband's nose like it was a large gummy worm, and while she did, chaos erupted in the room. Ronny screamed; falling away from the window and Marc stood stock still, his hands still holding the remaining rope. Dale and Lucy were also caught off guard, no one expecting a ghoul to pop up instead of a wounded woman.

But Frank had been prepared, and though he had kept his thoughts to himself, he was ready for the eventual outcome.

Just as Sharon prepared to hop off the windowsill and try to attack one of the others, there was the reverberating echo of a single gunshot.

A neat, black, hole blossomed on Sharon's forehead and the head snapped backward from the impact. Already balancing on the windowsill, the body lost its precarious position and tumbled from sight to fall into the crowd of ghouls below.

"Holy shit! You fucking shot her!" Dale gasped as he stared at the now empty window. It was Lucy who regained her composure an instant quicker than Dale.

"He had no choice, Dale, she'd turned," Lucy said, reasoning. Her automatic weapon was in her hands, but there was nothing to shoot, at least not yet.

Slowly, she turned to face Bob who was in a corner of the room holding his nose. He had a handkerchief over the opening and he had actually managed to staunch the blood flow a little, forcing the cloth into the orifice. The once white handkerchief was a bright scarlet and already plasma was dripping onto his shoes and the floor.

With wide, pain-filled eyes, Bob whimpered as he saw Lucy turn the muzzle of her rifle towards him. At first, he was too lost in pain to fully understand what had just happened, shock overwhelming his consciousness. But as each second passed, he came to the realization that his wife had died, revived and had bitten his nose off, thus dooming him to die painfully while the infection took hold and eventually killed him.

Timothy charged into the room and was about to run over to Bob when the man raised a blood-soaked hand.

His voice was muffled and nasally now, like he had fingers squeezing his nose closed, but that was now impossible as he didn't have one any longer.

"Stay away from me, Tim, don't waste your time, damn it! I'm fucking dead anyway! What's the point? Even if I lived, my wife is dead and she was the only thing keeping me going these past few months."

"Bob, I'm so…" Frank began to say, but Bob stabbed a scarlet finger at him accusingly.

"Don't you fucking say it, Frank, don't you goddamn say it!" He glanced to the others and then back to Frank. "You know damn well you're not sorry. She was one of those things and you killed her, that was it. Fuck!" He screamed louder. "It's not fair! We survived all that time and now this has to happen?" His eyes were filled with madness, grief, loss and his own inner pain. "You should have left us in our apartment, at least then we would have died together!" he screamed at Frank.

Timothy was trying to edge closer to the man, hoping once he was, some of the other men could tackle him and he could try to staunch the blood flow. The man must have lost a pint of plasma already and Timothy believed it was only the man's rage and adrenalin still keeping him standing.

Then, before anyone could stop him, he pushed Timothy away from him and charged for the open window.

Frank realized a second too late what the man was doing and yelled out to the others.

"Jesus Christ, someone stop him!"

But Bob was determined to reach his destination unchecked.

Ronny was the only one near him and Bob shouldered past the man, like they were playing football. Frank watched the tableau like it was in slow motion. Ronny was knocked to the side where he sprawled onto the floor and then Bob was lunging for the window. With one hand still holding the handkerchief, the other was out in front of him like he was going to dive into a pool of water.

The man soared through the window, his shoes just touching the windowsill, and then he was gone.

Dale, Lucy and Frank dashed for the open window and gazed down below. Where Bob had landed there was no sign, but there was a mass of bodies, all leaned over and clumped together. As he watched, Frank spotted bloody appendages and internal organs in the hands of the ghouls as they tried to move away from the large crowd. It was when he spotted Bob's detached and severed head, the handkerchief still shoved into the exposed orifice of his sinuses that Frank knew it was over for good. Nearby, Sharon's body was already in pieces, the ravenous ghouls attacking like starving animals.

The ghouls were feeding well today, and after banging an angry fist against the wall just on the side of the window frame, Frank stepped away from the window. He turned to Marc, Ronny and Alex and pointed to the blood and disarray in the room.

"You three, get some stuff and clean this shit up as best you can. We still need this room and I don't want the next person we use as a decoy to see any of this. If anyone asks, just say Bob and Sharon killed themselves. Say they couldn't take living like this, like we all do. Hell, it's not that far from the truth, I think, sometimes." He scanned the faces of Timothy and the others. "You guys all got this? What happened here stays in this room. It has to for the good of the rest of the people living here."

There were murmurs of agreement and nods of heads.

"Good, that's good. All right, let's get to work, and remember what I said."

He turned and left, Dale and Lucy by his side. Don had finally arrived, huffing and puffing, and he slowed, his eyes wide, wondering what was going on. Dale moved closer to the war veteran and whispered into his ear.

"Oh, shit, no," he gasped as he stared at Frank, the open window, and the others.

Don was about to walk over to Frank, wanting to console him when Frank held up his hand to stop the veteran.

"No, Don, not now. I think I need to be alone for a while," he said, and without a backward glance to the others, headed down the corridor to the Mayors office. He hadn't wanted to make that place his sleeping quarters, but the others had insisted, saying that was where the man in charge ruled from, even if he ruled over a pitiful group of ragtag survivors in a city of the dead.

So with a weary heart, Frank left them, the others watching him go, and once he had turned a corner and was lost from sight, they all returned to the grim task of covering up what had happened.

Chapter 17

Francesca was sitting in the rear seat of the helicopter again, breast feeding baby Shaun. The side door was open and a cool breeze wafted in, foretelling of a coming winter.

On the helipad right below her, sat Thomas, and only a few feet away, Paul was sitting on his haunches, ever wary of the man.

Next to Thomas, sat the white Styrofoam cooler. Paul noticed the man never let it go far from his sight, and with the exception of when Thomas had attacked him, the cooler seemed like a part of the man.

Thomas was munching on a piece of canned corned beef, acting like it had been his first real meal in months.

And from the story he was weaving between bites of corned beef, it seemed that was so.

"Go 'head, Thomas, finish your story, I want to hear it," Francesca said from inside the helicopter. Her coat was covering the baby while she fed, her modesty getting the better of her. Truth was, it wouldn't have bothered her much if Paul happened to get a glimpse of her breasts. She had always been an open woman about nudity and breast feeding was a natural thing, but Thomas was another matter. She had already caught stolen furtive glances from him when he thought she wasn't looking.

As long as they just stayed glances, she would leave it alone. Plus, she knew Paul was on edge. The tall ex-cop had his Winchester in his hand, and his finger was never far from the trigger.

Thomas swallowed the corned beef in his mouth and then continued his story.

"Okay, so I told you how we hid in the bakery and then made it to this building, right?"

Paul nodded.

"Okay, so the guy you killed, the zombie? His name was Ted, Ted Johnson, and both he and my wife worked together. So when I went to work and got her, Ted came with us, as he had no other family. So after we stayed in the bakery and decided it wasn't safe, we took off in my car. We made it a mile before the streets were so choked with stalled cars there was no hope to go further by vehicle. So we left it in the street, and when we got out, we saw there were so many of them on the streets you could barely walk. Some just wandered around like drunks, but others, well, those were the ones that scared the hell out of me. They would look at you and then never turn away. They'd chase you, this stumbling, half jog, and they never seemed to tire." He took another bite and then talked while he chewed, spitting bits of corned beef onto his lap.

"So we were running and then there were others at the other end of the street. We were trapped! Ted thought we should duck into this building so we did. There were a few of them in the lobby, and one attacked my wife, but we made it to the stairwell alive. It was a long climb up here to the roof, but we made it. Ted thought we should go on the roof so we could signal the police or someone for help when they came looking for survivors."

His face became downcast.

"But no one ever came for us. It was then I found out my wife had been bitten by one of those things. At first, we didn't know what was happening to her. She began to get sick like she had the flu or something. I tried to make her as comfortable as possible, but within three days she died. Ted said he would deal with it, knowing how broke up I was and it was while he was getting ready to wrap her in an old tarp he'd found on the roof that she came back as one of them. Ted didn't expect that, hell, who would? She bit his arm and then he pushed her away. There was a large piece of sheet metal near him and when she came for him he panicked."

His voice grew quiet, so Paul and Francesca had to strain to hear him.

"He used the sheet metal like a large knife and he actually chopped my wife's head off. It didn't go in smoothly, but after the first slice he knocked her to the roof and finished the job. He was so distraught from what he'd done; he left her there and told me she was gone. I guess he couldn't bear to tell me he'd just chopped off my wife's head. Kelly was her name, did I tell you that?"

Paul shook his head back and forth. "No, brother, you didn't."

"Oh, well, it was, Kelly I mean. So okay, little did I know that my wife had managed to bite Ted in the upper arm. He hid the bite from me, don't know why. We still hadn't figured out that a bite will kill you in days. How could we? We'd been isolated in the bakery and then on the roof. By the way, we did manage to secure the roof door. After the first day we did hear pounding on it from the other side, but so far they can't get through it. I haven't heard any in a few days, but sometimes they come back. I think they actually remember I'm up here."

He popped another piece of corned beef in his mouth, chewed and swallowed.

"So, three days later, Ted is dying and I'm dealing with it all over again. This time, Ted dies at night, while I was sleeping, and then he came back as one of them. I woke up to see him standing over me. You saw him, he's bigger than me and I only just got away with my life. After that I was running and hiding, trapped on the roof. I would stay in the bird shack someone built up here. Ted couldn't get inside. Sometimes he would wander away and I would sneak out. That's when I found my wife and knew what he'd done to her. Then I would go back to the shack. The pigeons still called the shack home so I managed to live on them, sucking their blood for sustenance. It was distasteful, but I didn't want to die, so there you have it," he said in a jumble, like one sentence. His eyes were wide and manic as he relived his tragic tail of survival, a corner of his mouth curved up and then down, a tick he never knew he had from the stress of surviving so close to the edge of death.

"You poor man," Francesca said. "I'm so sorry for you, your wife and your friend."

Thomas didn't answer, but only stared at the helipad. Paul noticed idly while he talked the man placed a hand protectively on the cooler next to him, as if for comfort. The gesture seemed odd, but he left it alone.

The sun was finally beginning to set, casting the rooftop in a wan glow that would soon diminish to the point of blackness. Gazing out over the rooftop, the city sprawled before him, Paul felt a chill slide down his spine.

Where there would have once been lights appearing in the building's windows, now there was only blackness.

No street lamps came on and no artificial light cut through the encroaching darkness. It was all too eerie. When they had been at the office complex, the power had never diminished. Paul assumed it had to be nuclear or solar, but whatever power lines had routed that power to the complex had been untouched or buried underground, but the ones for the city had either been damaged or destroyed, leaving Pittsburgh a dead city in more ways than just its residents.

Standing to his full height, Paul stretched.

"We should get some rest, Francesca. It's been one helluva day and we should get moving in the morning."

"What about me? Can I come with you?" Thomas asked, hopefully. There was an unsettling gleam in his eye that Paul failed to notice, as if the man being trapped alone on the roof had caused something inside him to crack slightly.

Though Francesca had told Paul she wanted to take the man, Paul had yet to broach the subject.

Paul frowned deeply. "Shit, brother, I'd like to take you, but we're low on fuel, we're on fumes as it is. That reminds me, I need to check that tank over there and see if there's anything in it. I'm gonna do that now actually." He glanced at Francesca. "You'll be all right while I'm gone?"

She nodded. The baby had finished eating and was sleeping again. She had covered herself and removed the jacket. Her rifle was on the seat next to her.

"Sure, Paul, go 'head, I'll be fine. Thomas can keep me company."

"Watch yourself, man," Paul said curtly to Thomas, his voice deep and hard, and then he moved off.

As he passed him, Paul flashed Thomas a glare that warned the man to be cool, and Thomas nodded quickly, his head bouncing up and down like a bobblehead.

*   *   *

Paul walked across the helipad and rounded the tank and a massive air conditioning unit. As he studied the tank, he saw a mishmash of debris scattered around it. There were empty buckets, some filled with stagnant rainwater, old boxes and rusting tools. Moving to the tank, he rapped it with his knuckles. A hollow sound reverberated back and he frowned.

Well, what did he expect? A full tank of fuel just waiting for him? He continued tapping, moving from the middle to the bottom, the same hollow sound following each time his knuckles connected with the metal.

It was when he was literally down to the last four inches that he heard a distinctively different sound. Instead of an empty echo, this time the sound was more muffled, as if something was behind the metal.

Moving to the hose, he tried the nozzle, but with no power there was no way to pump the remaining fuel. He gave his situation some thought and then an idea struck him as he studied all the debris on the roof with him.

There was an old crowbar and a rusting hammer nearby. He went to them and picked them up, his left hand stiff from the bandage on it. Then he grabbed an overturned plastic bucket, one that hadn't been filled with rain water.

With all these items in his hands, he returned to the tank, lined up the tip of the crowbar to the exact bottom of the tank, and with the hammer, whacked the tip into the metal.

The metal was thick, but not so thick it could withstand the flat out vandalism he was attacking it with. The instant the crowbar penetrated the metal, a clear liquid shot out, the odor assaulting his nose.

He dropped his tools and shoved the bucket under the small stream of fuel, and while it was filling, he went back to get another bucket. It wasn't much, but the small amount he was recovering might be just enough to get them to their destination, wherever that might be.

As he continued working, feeling heartened by his luck, he put the dead world out of his mind for just a little while, enjoying the simple task of manual labor.

* * *

While Paul was busy retrieving the fuel for the helicopter, Francesca and Thomas sat quietly together on the helipad while baby Shaun slept the sleep of the innocent.

Baby Shaun was lying on the rear seat, sleeping, and Francesca was eating from an open can of corned beef.

The darkness was almost complete and the newly appearing stars flickered in the night sky. With no ambient light on earth polluting the atmosphere, the stars seemed to twinkle even brighter than normal.

A few times she had sat on the roof of the main building of the office complex with Shaun, the two sharing a few tender moments alone. But they never stayed long. While they would have the roof of the building to themselves, the stench of the walking dead below and their constant moans was distracting and usually after only twenty minutes they would go back inside.

She thought of Shaun now as she gazed up at the stars, still trying to take in the realization that it had only been a day since Shaun had died.

It was then she caught Thomas staring at her like a love sick puppy and she turned to look at him, confronting him as he turned his eyes away.

"You keep looking at me, Thomas, is there a reason why?"

"I'm sorry, Francesca, it's just...well, you remind me of my wife, that's all. She was very pretty, also."

"Oh, well, thank you, I guess. I didn't know. I'm so sorry again for your loss, truly I am. I just lost my baby's father, too. I know how you must feel," she said softly.

Francesca expected Thomas to answer in the same soft tone, but instead his voice grew in pitch and his eyes flared anger.

"Don't tell me how I must feel, damn it. No one knows how I feel!" His fists were clenched by his sides, his neck muscles taut.

Taken aback by his sudden outburst, Francesca shifted uncomfortably against the landing strut.

"Thomas, please, you'll wake the baby, lower your voice," Francesca said sternly, like a mother would to an unruly child.

Thomas' eyes seemed to calm and he nodded slightly.

"I'm sorry, Francesca. Really I am. Since my wife died sometimes I just get so full of anger. I loved her dearly."

"That's all right, Thomas, just please, keep your voice down."

There was a pounding floating over the roof and Francesca looked up, her eyes searching for the disturbance. Thomas saw her looking and he waved a hand in dismissal.

"Oh, that's just more of those things trying to get onto the roof. They pound on the roof access door every now and then. So far it's held. I'm sure it'll make it until we leave in the morning."

Francesca listened to his explanation and relaxed slightly, but only slightly. She had seen too much and been through far too many close calls to let herself and her baby be caught off guard now.

Thomas stood up and walked closer to her, the cooler under his arm as always. The darkness was almost complete, but there was still enough light to see his face.

When he was only a few feet away from her, she could smell the ripeness of him. The man hadn't bathed in months with the exception of when it might rain, and he was almost as bad as the ghouls walking the streets of Pittsburgh.

Unlike Thomas' body odor, when he moved closer to her, he was able to detect the sweet smell of Francesca's hair, and the perfume she was wearing. The office complex had more soaps and perfumes than she could have used in a hundred lifetimes in the executive bathrooms.

"You smell good, Francesca. My wife used to wear perfume, too."

Francesca smiled wanly, still trying to be polite.

"Oh, that's nice, Thomas." She glanced over her shoulder in the direction Paul had headed off in. "You know, Paul should be back any second. He's been gone for a little while now."

She took a step away from him, beginning to feel threatened. For the moment, she was trying to be nonchalant about it, still wondering if perhaps she was mistaken, or could Thomas pose a threat to her and the baby?

Across the rooftop, more pounding could be heard, growing louder now.

Her eyes went to the rear seat of the helicopter, her rifle and sidearm lying on the floor of the helicopter. She had taken her .45 off, the weight of it uncomfortable and she figured at least while she ate her food she could feel normal, without the weight of the gun on her hip. Now she was regretting it and she vowed if she could get to the gun, she would never take it off again.

Hell, she would sleep with it.

Glancing where Paul had headed again, she debated if she should call out. After all, if he heard her call out, he would come running, but would it be too late to help her? Thomas wasn't a big man like Paul, but he was still taller and stronger than Francesca. He could do a lot of damage quickly if he had an inclination to. And then what would happen to her child?

It all didn't make any sense. If Thomas hurt her, he would be trapped on the roof forever with no chance of escape, so why would he want to hurt his only escape route?

When she backed away from him, towards her baby, Thomas would take a similar step towards her, and she was beginning to become scared.

"Thomas, please stop moving towards me. Stay there." She said this nicely, willing her voice to remain calm, but inside her veins the adrenalin was pumping and her fight or flight instincts were kicking in. In the gloom of the falling night, Thomas' face seemed wild, his eyes filled with instability.

"You don't believe me, do you? About my wife," he said in a cold voice. "You think I'm just some crazy man who's been alone on this rooftop for far too long, is that it?"

"No, Thomas, of course not. I don't know what you mean," she replied, trying to stall for time. "The thought never crossed my mind." The longer she kept him talking he might not do something they would both regret.

He still had the cooler under his right arm, the white cube an extension of his body. He had managed to come between her and the helicopter so she decided she needed to at least get him away from her baby, so she backed up a few more feet, acting like she was just moving away casually.

He followed her step for step, the cooler scratching under his arm, sometimes she thought she could hear an odd, scratching sound, like when a fingernail is scraped on a chalkboard. But the sound was faded and soft. She almost thought it was coming from inside the cooler, but that would be ridiculous. What could be in there that would make sounds? Anything alive would be far too big to fit in there.

"No, I can see the doubt on your face. Fine then, I'll prove it to you," he said and stopped moving towards her. She watched silently as he set the cooler down and took off the top, his right hand reaching inside to take something out.

She didn't know what she expected him to take out of there. A live pigeon perhaps, one he'd been saving to eat later? Some pictures of his late wife, salvaged from his personal affects after arriving on the roof. Perhaps even something she had worn like a shoe or a hat?

So when he took out a decapitated head and held it up for her to see, she gasped in shock and disgust, tasting bile in her mouth.

The head was from a female, there was no doubt. The long blonde hair, now matted with blood and gore, lay flat on the top of the skull. Francesca was utterly shocked to see the milky eyes moving back and forth, as if they were searching for something. Then the mouth slowly opened, the jaw sliding from side to side. The lips were peeled back from death and Francesca could see the moving mouth had no teeth. Only bloody gums were visible and a blackened tongue that reminded her of those big, juicy slugs she used to find under rocks in her backyard when she was a girl. The tongue seemed to be swimming in a black ichor, residue from the open wounds where teeth had once been. Even from a few feet away, the redolence of decay was overwhelming. The skin on the head was pulled tight across the skull, making the dead woman's face look like a facelift gone horribly wrong. The eyes had sunk into the sockets, the forehead now protruding, and the orbs jumped back and forth like two white marbles until they locked onto Francesca. Then they stared at her, never blinking, never moving.

Francesca felt a shiver crawl down her spine as she stared into those dead eyes.

"Meet my wife," Thomas said. "Isn't she beautiful? I managed to find her head and save her. She's kept me company all these months. And other things, if you know what I mean."

Then, while Francesca gaped in abject horror, Thomas raised the head to his own, lining up the toothless mouth with his. Then he pushed the dead face against his, the mouths locking in a dead embrace. Francesca felt her stomach preparing to heave as she watched Thomas' tongue flicking in and out, wrapping around the black tongue passionately.

After a long kiss, Thomas pulled the head away, a slime-like ooze still connecting their mouths. When he moved the head, the string of ooze snapped, falling to the helipad.

"What's wrong with you? Aren't you afraid you'll become infected?" Francesca asked as she desperately tried to keep her lunch down. The head was staring at her again; the eyes locked onto her body, and even in the falling darkness she could see those orbs penetrating into her soul.

"Not at all. That's why I pulled her teeth out. This way I can kiss her." He rubbed his crotch as he eyed Francesca. "She and I still have sex, too. Well, oral anyway."

Francesca's eyes went wide when she realized what he meant and she almost vomited, only her will to keep her dinner down preventing her from spewing her insides all over the helipad.

"I still love her you see, and if this is the only way I can be with her, so be it."

While he was talking, she began moving closer to the rear seat of the helicopter, wanting her gun.

Thomas made no move towards her, but instead gently placed the head back into the cooler and closed it again.

It was as he lovingly set the head in the cooler and she saw the look on his face that she realized the man was utterly mad from everything he'd suffered, and up until now he'd been putting on quite an act.

She'd heard from many of the news anchors that insane people knew how to fool others of their true state of mind, but up until now she had never believed it was truly possible.

She was almost to the helicopter and was already working through scenarios in her mind when Paul appeared at the edge of the helipad, only his shadowy form moving through the almost complete darkness.

He took in what was happening immediately and he set the two buckets of fuel down and moved away from them, already drawing his Colt.

"What's going on here, Francesca?"

With a sigh of relief, Francesca reached in, grabbed her rifle and closed the door of the helicopter, thus protecting baby Shaun. Then she stepped away as Paul moved next to her. She quickly filled him in on what had happened, and finished by pointing to the cooler.

Paul stared at Thomas, finding it hard to believe what he'd just heard, but knowing better than not to believe Francesca.

"Well, I've got to see this for myself," he said and gestured to Thomas with the Colt. "Open it so I can see it."

"I will do no such thing," Thomas snapped back, defensively.

"Fine, I'll do it myself," Paul said and crossed the helipad in a few quick strides. When he was a few feet away, Thomas lunged at him, wanting to stop him, but Paul was ready for him this time and punched the smaller man in the jaw. Thomas rocked with the punch, sprawling across the helipad as he groaned in pain.

"Stay," Paul ordered him while he aimed the Colt at Thomas' chest.

The man knew what would happen if he moved, so he obeyed, his face a mask of angst.

Paul gazed down at the cooler, and with his right foot, he kicked it over, the top falling away and the contents rolling out like a soccer ball. The mouth still moved up and down, no sound emerging. None could ever leave that mouth as there was no air or lungs to allow this. The eyes were open, looking around, and even in the darkness, Paul could see the dead eyes turning to look up at him. He could almost imagine the silent hiss the mouth would make while the eyes glared at him.

He raised his boot into the air, prepared to step on the abomination and flatten it to mush when he was stopped by Thomas' pleas.

"No! Don't touch her!" Thomas screamed as he jumped to his feet, crossing the space between him and Paul in an instant. But if Paul thought he was going to be attacked again, he was wrong.

Thomas leaned down and scooped the head in his hands, running away a few feet like a spoiled child who wouldn't return a purloined kickball.

"Don't you hurt her!" Thomas screamed loudly, hugging the head to him in a lover's embrace

"Man, what the hell's wrong with you? That damn thing is dead!" Paul yelled at Thomas, waving his free hand in the air.

"No, she's not dead. See?" He held the head up so Paul could get a good look at the pale, white face. The mouth shifted and the eyes rolled, the black tongue sliding out of dry lips. "She still moves. She's still my wife and she's all I have left!"

Paul glanced to Francesca who was holding her rifle. She was standing near the helicopter, her eyes on the baby who had miraculously remained sleeping so far. Across the roof, more pounding could be heard as the roof access door shook on its hinges. Neither Paul nor the others noticed, too wrapped up in the present situation.

"Francesca," Paul said. "Go get those buckets over there and be careful. I managed to get some fuel out of the very bottom of the tank."

She nodded, slung her rifle over her shoulder and crossed the helipad, picking up the buckets and carrying them back. Each one was about half full, a few gallons at most.

"Okay, done," she said from next to the helicopter.

"Good, Francesca, okay, now get something to use, like a cup, and see if you can manage to get that shit into the tanks of the copter." He turned to Thomas just as the man acted like he was going to run. "Don't move, brother, or so help me I will cut you down where you stand."

Thomas stopped, and stood straight up, knowing to move was to die.

Francesca looked around for a moment and then an empty corned beef can caught her eye. With a stray rag, she cleaned the inside of the can and bent one end to make it more like a spout. Then she opened up the fuel hatch, and after propping the small backsplash tab open, she slowly began filling the tank. It was slow work and a lot was missing, spilling out and onto the side of the aircraft, but it couldn't be helped and she made due with what she had.

With the Winchester in his hands, Paul kept Thomas away from them, the man hugging the head and talking to it soothingly like it was a baby the entire time.

Almost an hour later, Francesca had finally finished, the last of the fuel now either inside the helicopter's fuel tank or splashed on the helipad in a small pool of spreading liquid. It had been a sloppy job, and now that she was finished, she quickly went to the rear of the helicopter and grabbed some antiseptic and pieces of a sheet. It was from one that Paul had sliced up to use as diapers for the baby.

"All finished, Paul," she said as she wiped her hands clean. She smelled like a dock worker now, and the memory of when she and Shaun had first arrived at a refueling station looking for fuel and had found a woman dead on the ground, and two in the office, their heads blown partially off, came flooding back to her. She pushed the memories away. Now was not the time.

Suddenly there was a loud noise from across the roof, resembling if something heavy had fallen. It was Thomas who was the first to react as Paul and Francesca both looked around in the darkness for what had made the odd sound.

"Oh, no, that's the roof door; they managed to break it down finally!" Thomas screamed as he hugged the head to him like a life preserver.

Not believing his bad luck, Paul turned to Francesca.

"Francesca, get in the copter. We're leaving right now."

She didn't need to ask questions, it seemed in the past twenty-four hours all they'd been doing is roof hopping from one place to another. And she was still weary. She had given birth just that morning and she needed to rest, though sleep and rest seemed like a distant memory.

Climbing into the pilot's seat, she began flicking switches, powering up the engine. Once the rotors had begun to spin, she climbed out, picked up baby Shaun and jumped back into the pilot's seat, preparing for lift off. The rpms were building slowly, but it would be a few minutes before they were at the proper cycling rate to lift off.

"What about me? You said you'd take me with you," Thomas begged as he took a step towards the helicopter. The eyes in the severed head rolled around, like the head was dizzy or drunk. There was a slight breeze and the matted hair flowed around it like a wispy cloud.

"Fat chance, chump, not after what I've just seen."

For an instant, Paul was tempted to just shoot the man and save him from being killed by the zombies, but in the end he couldn't do it. He was not a murderer.

A memory of a fellow cop named Jimmy he had shot months ago flashed through his mind, but he pushed it down. He wasn't a murderer then either. The man had been out of control and needed to be put down like a rabid dog, slaughtering women and children. He did what he had to do and he would do it again if it ever came to pass.

The ghouls were coming, their moans floating across the roof, all the more ominous in the darkness. Shadowy shapes could be seen silhouetted against the dark sky, the frail frames of the zombies moving like a parade of drunken men and women.

When Francesca was satisfied with the engine speed, she called out to Paul, telling him to get on board.

Paul backed away from Thomas, the Winchester never wavering. He was expecting the man to do something reckless, to try and attack him in a desperate gambit to get on the helicopter, but he did nothing, merely standing on the helipad with the severed head of his wife in his arms.

"Please, don't leave me here. I can't do this anymore," Thomas pleaded, a remnant of the sane man showing through the madness.

Paul hesitated for a fraction of a second, almost as if he was going to change his mind. But then he saw Francesca looking at him and the baby wrapped in her jacket and realized he couldn't take the risk. They were his responsibility now.

Without a word, Paul backed up to the helicopter and climbed on board, taking the rear seat so he had more room for his long legs. The landing skids touched off the helipad, slowly rising.

From the opposite end of the helipad, more than a score of zombies slowly moved closer.

Baby Shaun stirred in her arm and Francesca rocked him gently, trying to focus on flying. As the helicopter rose into the air, the rotor wash blew away the empty corned beef cans, cups and anything else littering the roof.

Though night had fallen, Paul could still see the shapes of Thomas and the zombies, the larger group of shapes moving closer to the stationary one.

"Think he'll survive till morning? He could go back to his shack," Francesca said as she, too, gazed down on the darkened helipad.

Paul shrugged. "I don't give a damn what he does, Francesca. He had his chance and he blew it; the sucker was crazy. Better we find out now than later when we would've all been trapped in this machine together."

She said nothing in reply, though she had to agree with his wisdom. She glanced down one last time to see the larger group of shapes surrounding the single one. She thought she saw the single shape, who she believed was Thomas, fall to his knees as the other zombies moved in, closing the trap with their greater numbers. Even if the man changed his mind it was already too late to escape.

She looked away, her eyes checking the dials, the glow of the gauges illuminating her face.

"So where to now?" Francesca asked.

"Good question," Paul replied. "Just fly west and look for another rooftop, preferably one that's uninhabited." He said this with slight sarcasm, like it was her fault that each time they set down the undead were there.

Ignoring or not picking up on his words, she nodded, and with the baby in her left arm, her right on the control stick, she banked the helicopter north, heading deeper into the city.

"How's the fuel level?" Paul asked.

"Not much better, but still better than it was before we added what you found," she replied, her voice morose. Without fuel they were doomed, as sooner or later they would run out and have to set down. Both knew their odds if they were on foot. They had to get to someplace safe before that happened.

There were more than 150 high-rises and hundreds of other buildings in the city of steel, surely one of them would be safe to land on until morning.

Chapter 18

Frank strolled through the City County Building with a heavy heart.

How many people had he lost in the span of half a day?

Too damn many, that was for sure.

He stopped in the hallway as an older couple passed him. Both smiled to him and he returned it, putting on a happy face for the people who looked up to him.

There was a closed window to his right, so he moved over to it, gazing out into the street. Night was falling, and within another twenty minutes it would be dark, the moans of the living dead always sounding just a little more ominous in the dead of night.

A man came walking down the hall from the way he had just come and he realized it was Dale. The younger man was taciturn as he waved slightly and then crossed the remaining distance.

"Hey, Frank, sorry to bother you, but the guys wanted to know if you still wanted to light the signal fire tonight."

Frank was exhausted and he was fed up with all the shit he had to deal with every day and night. At this moment in time, when he was feeling the weight of lost lives bearing down on him, he just wished someone else would take this mantle of responsibility from his shoulders and let him just be him for just a little while.

But he knew that wouldn't be happening anytime soon.

For better or worse, he was the leader of their little enclave and he would remain the leader as long as he was standing upright and breathing, though that particular analogy didn't mean what it once had before the dead rose.

But he was aggravated and short tempered, so when Dale asked him the question, he wasn't in the mood.

"No, not tonight, Dale. Save the gas for when we might need it."

Dale looked perplexed. The one thing that would happen every night on the roof of the building was there would be a small fire built in the hopes some aircraft would see it and know there were survivors inside.

"Oh, please, Dale, don't look at me like that. We've been setting that damn fire for months and nothing has flown by. Whether we want to believe it or not, I think we're alone in the city. Well, except for Carver and his people."

Dale was going to reply, but he opened and then closed his mouth, deciding Frank made some sense.

"Okay, so what about a watch? Do you still want someone up there all night?"

Frank nodded he did. Saving fuel was one thing, but having a man up there was just smart. From the roof, the guard would have a good view of the area and if an aircraft did fly over it would be short work to build a bonfire.

Frank told Dale as much and the man nodded, then headed off to relay the orders.

Frank watched him go, wishing he still felt the hope the younger man did. Just before Dale turned the corner at the far end of the hallway, Lucy appeared waiting for her man. She saw Frank at the opposite end and waved. He nodded curtly to her and Dale reached her, wrapped his arm around her and the two disappeared.

Frank turned away and gazed out the window again.

The dead were out en mass as always, pushing on the barricaded windows and doors of the first floor. More than one had pieces of meat in their hands, bones covered with gristle, blood and muscle. Blackened teeth tore at the remains of his friends and chewed merrily, swallowing the fetid mush. What would happen to the human meat after the ghouls had devoured it was a running subject in the enclave. Though almost every ghoul had a bloated abdomen, no one truly knew whether the food was actually digested or if it just lay in their bowels like sludge from an old sink.

From his vantage point, all he could see were heads, hundreds of heads, all shifting and swaying like a living ocean.

No wait, check that.

An undead ocean.

On a whim, he raised the window and pulled his Glock, sighting a few heads moving back and forth as each ghoul tried to gain the upper hand over one another.

One zombie he noticed immediately. The ghoul had once been a woman, with bright red hair and a heaving bosom. But now both breasts were missing and only one eye remained. Her lips were gone, her perfectly white teeth reflecting the light of the day. Maggots squirmed within the empty eye socket, a few sliding down her cheek and into her gaping mouth. Even with all this damage she still was relatively attractive, which made Frank wonder what the hell was wrong with him to think such a thing.

He prepared to fire, wanting to send her and a few more of the abominations of life back to the Hell they had crawled out of, but just as his finger tensed, he stopped himself, realizing the futility of his actions.

You couldn't think of them as human. There was no revenge in killing them. They were mindless beasts who only wanted to feed. And though many of his people liked to call them evil, in reality they were merely a force of nature, a simple instinct of hunger driving the creatures on. They were human in form only. Whatever had made them a part of mankind was gone, lost in whatever quagmire of despair that had birthed them in the first place.

No, all he would end up doing is wasting bullets and causing a stir when others heard his gunshots.

With a sigh, he closed the window and holstered his weapon.

Deciding he had seen enough, he turned and walked away.

He was hoping for just an hour or so of downtime, when no one would knock on his door and bother him. He knew that wouldn't happen. He was consulted in everything that happened in the enclave, whether he wanted to or not.

With his boots echoing off the stone walls, he strolled deeper into the building, his thoughts still filled with dark images of loss and death. While he walked, the moaning of the undead followed him, haunting him as it had done for every day since they had risen.

Chapter 19

Marc Wachowski stood watch on the roof tonight and he strolled back and forth, bored out of his mind.

All around him were the dead remnants of finished cigarettes, the small filters blowing in the wind. Far below on the ground surrounding the building, the undead wailed and moaned, sounding like a scratched and broken record.

He leaned against an old ventilation unit and closed his eyes, imagining the wailing was music. It rose in pitch and then faltered, like a giant guitar with only one string left and that one out of tune. He could almost imagine one of the ghouls, acting like a maestro, waving a small stick in the air as he directed the ghouls in harmony.

No wait, not a stick, an arm.

A severed arm, with bone sticking out of the end where it would have been attached to a shoulder with droplets of blood flipping every which way.

The maestro ghoul would wave the arm majestically and the zombies would all be standing one behind the other in neat rows, like a choir.

Yeah, he liked that.

A choir of the dead.

That was pretty good. He'd have to tell Ronny and Alex when he got back inside after his watch was over. He checked the Rolex on his right wrist to see he had more than two hours left to go. He admired the Rolex, remembering where he'd found it.

The salvaging team had been scavenging near a convenience store on Fifth Street and there had been a man lying dead on the floor, just inside the door. Half the man's head had been blown off and black and crusting brain matter had spilled out to coat the floor a dark maroon.

The man had been wearing a rich, three piece suit and a black leather briefcase had been near his feet. Marc had checked the briefcase, but all it had contained was a rotten banana, files and a bunch of papers that now meant nothing unless he needed something to start a fire with or wipe his ass after taking a dump.

But the withered corpse had worn the watch just under the sleeve, and though the band had sunk into the bloated flesh of the limb, Marc had taken it anyway. After he had picked the dead flesh from between the gold bands, he had himself a very expensive timepiece.

That it was from a dead man meant nothing to him. The guy was dead, it's not like you could tell time in Hell.

Suddenly he heard an odd sound coming from the distance and overheard. It floated on the air and was originating from the inner city. After months of never hearing anything on watch but the moans of the dead, it took him a second to realize he was hearing what could only be an airplane.

No wait, not an airplane, a helicopter.

Holy shit! It was a friggin' helicopter!

His eyes scanned the darkness enveloping the city, remembering all the lights that used to fill every window in every building, and at first he couldn't see a thing.

But then, slowly, he saw the tiny blinking running lights of the helicopter and knew he wasn't imagining it.

There was a goddamn helicopter flying over Pittsburgh!

At first he panicked, not knowing what he should do, but then he came to his senses and quickly ran to the unlit campfire.

Knowing there was no time to get anyone to help, he shot his gun three times into the air, hoping the people below him, inside the building, would hear the shots and come to investigate.

After all, what the hell could he be shooting at on the roof?

The small, red metal gas can sat to the left of the unlit fire pit and he quickly poured some of the fuel on the wood and cardboard and other miscellaneous flammable debris found while they were scavenging for food and supplies.

Picking up a piece of newspaper dated six months ago, he lit it with his small Zippo and tossed the flaming paper onto the gas soaked debris.

With a massive whoosh, the flames jumped to life, reaching seven feet into the air. Standing too close to the flicking flames,

Marc felt the hairs on his arms curl so he moved away. He gazed out into the night sky, his eyes searching for the helicopter.

After he blinked the white spots from his vision, he spotted the small running lights and, yes, the helicopter was heading right for him.

He began jumping up and down; waving his hands over his head happily as the aircraft slowly grew closer, the excitement growing with every passing second.

*   *   *

Francesca was the first of the two of them to see the fire flash to life from almost a mile away.

One second there was nothing but darkness in every direction, and then there was a small light coming from the rooftop of one of the buildings near the river.

"Paul, look over there, is that a signal fire?"

The ex-cop looked over her shoulder, his gaze immediately spotting the fire.

"Sure looks like it," he replied.

She waited for him to continue, but after almost ten seconds of silence she realized he was finished talking.

"Well, what should we do about it?"

Paul's jaw was set tight as he considered her question. Should they ignore the signal? Or should they see if they could set down on the roof. A controlled fire like that meant more survivors, but after leaving Thomas, he was wondering if that was such a great idea.

First the bikers, then Thomas, and who knew what next?

"How's the fuel?" Paul asked, needing the information to make his decision.

"Not so good, Paul. We're a little better than when we left the complex, but not by much. Flying around with nowhere to go is foolish. We need to set down somewhere."

He frowned deeply. They were low on fuel and had nowhere to go. They were right back where they were that morning.

"What do you think, Francesca? You want to go over there? See what's what?"

Though he was the man in charge, he still wanted her opinion. He had grown to respect her over the months together and knew she was a bright woman. He valued her opinion greatly.

"What choice do we have? We either pick a roof at random or we set off for somewhere away from the city." She glanced at Paul over her shoulder from the pilot's seat while she hugged baby Shaun. "Frankly, Paul, I don't want to be walking around down there. Even if we do leave the city, this helicopter is our only chance to make it somewhere safe. We can't waste fuel flying around aimlessly."

He nodded curtly. "Fine, then go 'head. Let's just hope it's better there than the last two places. And when we land, you stay in the copter. At the first sign of trouble, you leave. With or without me. You got it?"

"Paul, I can't..."

"No, Francesca, you can. Think of the baby. Any sign of trouble you leave. Either that or we try for someplace else."

"Okay, Paul, but if you see something that looks bad, you get your butt back in here, fast. You got that?"

He chuckled, the sound resembling a subtle growl thanks to his deep voice.

"Yeah, I got that."

With a slight grin she turned forward, and after repositioning the baby in her arm, she banked the helicopter towards the signal fire.

They didn't know who was waiting for them on that rooftop, but they were truly out of options

* * *

Ben Carver stood on the rooftop of the City County Building, a set of binoculars raised to his eyes.

Next to him was Lynn, the woman getting upset she was being ignored. The two of them had gone up to the roof to be alone, wanting to make love under the stars, but now he was preoccupied with something in the distance, towards the part of the city Pearson and his group lived.

"Hey, Lynn, it's a fuckin' helicopter. Would you believe it?"

Lynn shrugged, but realizing Carver wasn't looking at her, she spoke up.

"So, what's that got to do with us? What can one helicopter do for anyone?"

He lowered the binoculars and stared at her, her face shrouded in darkness. "What are you an idiot? It could be a search party checking to see if anyone's still left alive."

"Is it coming this way?" she asked.

Carver shook his had. "Fuck no. It's heading straight for Pearson's camp. Shit, they lit that damn fire again and it looks like the chopper is gonna go right for it."

Carver held his gaze, tweaking the focus on the binoculars. There was the helicopter, a blurry shadow in the sky. Only the running lights outlined its true form. He could barely see it, but he did see the chopper heading directly for the fire on the rooftop. If it wasn't for the fact there were no other lights in the city, and that Carver's building was built on slightly higher ground, he would never have been able to see Pearson's building at all.

He lowered the binoculars when he was absolutely sure the chopper was going to land on Pearson's rooftop. Lynn stared at him, waiting for him to say something.

"Well? Where did it go?"

"Just like I said? Weren't you listening? Christ, Lynn, the chopper landed on Pearson's roof."

"Yeah, so what are we gonna do about it?"

Carver shook his head. "I don't know yet. But if we could get our hands on that chopper we could get out of the city in style. You can cover a shitload of land in one of those compared to driving."

Lynn snickered. "Oh, okay, baby, and are you gonna fly it, too?"

Carver frowned, Lynn barely seeing the gesture.

"Shit, I didn't think of that. You're right. Damn thing is worthless if we don't have someone to fly it."

"And what about the others?" she asked. "Are we gonna take them too? How many can you fit in a helicopter? Three, four?"

Carver scowled. "Fuck them all, baby. It's only you and me I'm worried about. They can fend for themselves for all I care." Then he grinned in the darkness and he reached out, pulling her to him. He wrapped his corded muscled arms around her, hugging her tightly. She squealed at first, taken by surprise, and then she melted into his arms.

He kissed her fast and hard, his tongue dancing over her soft lips while his strong hands kneaded her soft buttocks. When the kiss was finished, he pulled away, but still held her in his arms. He was already getting excited and he could feel his pants growing tighter in the groin area thanks to her soft body so close to his.

"It's just you and me, baby. That's all that matters to me in this goddamn world. And don't you forget it."

She said nothing in reply, but instead jumped into the air and wrapped her legs around his butt. He held her easily, cradling her in his arms. Then, with a sly smile on his face, he carried her across the few feet of roof until he reached a small blanket with pillows. Setting her down gently, he began to remove his shirt, feeling the cool night air on his bare skin.

She stretched like a cat, and he reached down and slowly raised her shirt to expose her glorious breasts.

She squealed again and he stopped, hoping he didn't somehow hurt her.

"No, baby, it's all right, your hands are cold, that's all."

He chuckled at that and leaned over her, his body only an inch from hers. She was already sliding off her pants, kicking them to the side and soon her hands were working on his belt buckle. In seconds, her deft fingers had his pants open and she was sliding them down over his hard buttocks, her hands pausing to squeeze each cheek playfully.

He could see her eyes reflecting the small, almost ambient light from the sky, and as he lay on her, nuzzling her neck; he slid inside of her, causing her to gasp in pleasure.

With the brisk night air caressing his exposed skin, he began a slow rhythm that soon picked up in speed as he neared orgasm, time seeming to slip away as if it never existed. It was only her and him and the rest of the world was irrelevant. Beneath him, Lynn's eyes were closed and her mouth was open, her face locked in perpetual ecstasy. He grinned to himself. While he wasn't a ridiculously huge man, he was larger than average when it came to the size of his penis and he had learned to use every inch to pleasure a woman to fulfillment.

He had heard a saying one time. "It's not how big you are it's how you use it." Well, that was something men with small dicks said. He was big and goddamn he knew how to use it well, and the testament was Lynn's gasp of pleasure as she began to shake beneath him. Her pelvic muscles clamped and suddenly the warmness grew tight, holding him like a vise. The unexpected feeling caused him to release himself and he filled her with his seed as he grunted over her, his eyes closed, his head back and sweat covering his body in a thin sheen.

He dropped onto her, unafraid of crushing her, and she slowly wrapped her arms around his shoulders. He moved his head to the side and kissed her cheek.

"I love you, Ben," she said softly as she basked in the warm glow of after-sex.

"Me, too, baby, you're my world." Then he rolled off her and stretched out on the blanket, relishing the after effects of his exertions. After doing push-ups on top of her for ten minutes straight, his muscles stood out, the pronouncement more so thanks to the sheen of perspiration reflecting the luminance of the night sky.

Lynn rolled over to him, wrapping the blanket around her and the two lay quietly, staring up at the night sky and enjoying the company of one another.

"So, what're you gonna do about that helicopter?" she asked as she laid her head on his chest, her left finger twisting and curling the small black hairs on his chest.

"Nothing right now. Right now it's just you and me. If it's still there in the morning, we'll deal with it then."

Then he closed his eyes, and like most men, drifted off into a light sleep. Lynn lay on his chest for another four minutes, and then moved off him, curling up next to him as, she too, drifted off to sleep, enjoying the feeling of the night air on her body.

The only thing to ruin it was the subtle odor of death floating up from the living dead below and the soft moans they made as they struggled to gain entry into the building.

Chapter 20

Frank was sleeping in his office, what was once the mayor's office, and it was a restless slumber.

Visions of Sharon's face came back to him, taunting him with her dead eyes. In his dream, she was still on the window frame, only now she was half-naked. From the waist down, she wore nothing, and from the belly up her shirt was open, exposing her generous breasts.

She had been a beautiful woman in life and Frank had admired her from afar as did many of the other men in the enclave. But they had all managed to remain civilized and respected that she was married to Bob.

But in his dream, where his subconscious could go wild, she only had eyes for him. Over the time since she had joined their group, he had dreamed about her and had sometimes pleasured himself to her memory as he lay in the darkness of the office.

But now, all those memories were jumbled together.

From the neck down she was still voluptuous; a woman any man would want in bed, but from the neck up, she was a blood drooling ghoul with sunken eyes and lips that had withdrawn in emaciation, exposing her teeth in a grim rictus of death.

On his bedroll, he tossed and turned, but in his dream he moved closer to her, reaching out with both hands to cup each soft breast in his palms.

Mucus dribbled from her nose and mixed with the blood from her mouth, making a viscous, jelly-like substance. But he kept his attention aimed downward, his eyes only for her lower form.

But then something happened that most definitely shouldn't have.

As he cupped each breast in his hands, they popped off, making small sounds like when a suction cup is removed from a glass wall.

Like two bags of jelly wrapped in skin, the breast sagged in his hands, the nipple of each one seeming like a pink eye, accusing him of...something?

He knew what, though he didn't want to admit, even to his own subconscious.

He had killed her. Perhaps it hadn't been his idea to send her down on that swing, but he was the one who had the final say.

In the end, it was he who had sent her to her doom.

He tossed in his bedroll, his body becoming wet with sweat as he struggled with his nightmare.

She was balancing on the window frame and then she reached her left leg out and caressed his groin with her bare foot. Deciding the breasts were irrelevant, as there were plenty of other areas on a woman to please, he tossed the breasts over his shoulder, the two bouncing and rolling like two flattened tennis balls.

He reached down, and with a sly smile began to caress her calf. That is until the leg popped off at the hip, right at the junction of her thighs.

"Oops," she said in a playful tone, but then began finding him with her other foot.

Frank tossed the leg aside and began massaging her remaining leg. That is until that one popped off like a cork from a bottle.

"Whoopsie?" she said around the blood in her mouth.

Frank shrugged, and tossed the leg away, where it slid to a stop next to the breasts.

Sharon reached out with her left hand and Frank took her hand, cupping it gently. It was when she moved to reach for his lump in his pants that she over extended and the arm dropped off like a balloon had popped.

"Oh, wow," she said. "I just can't seem to keep myself together today."

Frank merely shrugged, and as he reached for her, he moved in closer, taking her last arm in his.

But no sooner did he do this then the arm popped off, like a toy action figure with worn parts.

She only smiled weirdly, her dry lips making the grin look like something out of a monster movie. Frank chucked the arm away and moved so close to her he was a mere inch away.

She still had uses, and as he dropped his pants and prepared to enter her, he looked down just as his penis dropped off. Like a dead leaf on a branch at the end of the fall season, it seemed to just slough off his groin to fall into his pants sitting at his ankles. He opened his mouth to scream, but as he did, his tongue slid out of his mouth to drop onto the floor.

A rat from a hole in the wall dashed out, snagged the tongue in its jaws and ran away, Frank watching in amazement.

Then, as he stood in amazement, his left arm fell off, then his right, followed by both his legs sliding loose, falling to the sides as his torso dropped straight to the floor with a dull thump.

"What's happening? I don't understand?" he asked in a garbled voice thanks to no tongue. He lay on the floor, now nothing but a torso and a head.

Sharon just laughed at him, and with a twist, pushed off the window frame and landed on top of him.

That was when he got a really good look at her face, finally having to stare at that grisly countenance.

"Don't worry, baby, it'll only hurt forever," she said in a rasping voice, and as Frank tried to struggle to escape, her teeth dove in and began chewing as she feasted on his flesh like a starving dog.

Frank screamed long and loud, the sound still garbled thanks to no tongue in his mouth, and as he felt her teeth severing his jugular, he felt himself slipping into death.

As he did, he could hear his heart pounding. Thump, thump, thump.

Then he knew no more.

* * *

Thump, thump, thump.

Frank opened his eyes in the gloom of the office, fleeting images of his nightmare coming back to haunt him, and as he shot furtive glances around the darkened room, he heard the noise again.

Thump, thump, thump.

It was as he came to full wakefulness that he realized the sound wasn't his heart, but was the door to his office.

Someone was pounding on it.

As he snapped awake, he could now hear voices. Don and Dale were calling for him to open the goddamn door.

Sitting up, drenched in sweat, he glanced at his limbs, relieved to see they were still attached. With a groan, he climbed to his feet and stumbled to the door.

He idly noticed it was now fully dark, and after checking his wrist watch, the dials glowing in the dark, he saw he had been asleep for more than three hours.

The pounding never ceased, and when he opened the door, Don and Dale charged in, Don holding a flashlight aimed at his face.

"What the hell?" Frank snapped as they forced their way inside.

"Damn it, Frank, we've been banging for what seems like hours," Don yelled. "There's a helicopter flying around outside. Marc lit a fire and it looks like the pilot has seen it and is coming straight for us!"

"Seriously?" Frank asked

"Yeah, Frank, seriously." It was then that Don got a good look at Frank and saw the flushed look, the sweat drenched hair and bloodshot eyes.

"You all right? You don't look so hot," Don told him.

Frank waved it away. "It's nothing, I'm fine, just didn't sleep so well."

"Are you two old farts gonna talk all night or are we gonna get to the roof?" Dale asked as he moved from foot to foot anxiously.

"Huh? Oh, shit, yeah, of course," Frank said. He reached out to the nearby desk and retrieved his Glock still in its holster. Then he followed the two men into the hall while quickly attaching the holster to his belt.

Upon reaching the stairwell, Frank could hear the sounds of more footsteps and talking as people moved upward from below. Not wanting to wait to see who it was, anxious to get onto the roof, he charged upwards, Don and Dale next to him. Don's flashlight bounced as the man climbed the stairs, throwing the circular light ring every which way.

But it was still more than enough to navigate by, and in less than thirty seconds the men charged onto the roof, all breathing heavy from their rapid climb.

Marc was there, standing near the fire, and he immediately shouted and pointed at the oncoming helicopter.

Frank ran closer and the man gestured excitedly.

"Holy shit, Frank, it's a real helicopter. Shit, man, I didn't think we were ever gonna see one of those again!"

Frank didn't reply; there was no need. He knew what the man meant, though. After more than five months without seeing a single aircraft fly over Pittsburgh, he had truly believed they may have been the only ones left.

On the street below, the living dead moaned and wailed, agitated at the sound of the approaching helicopter.

More people came out of the stairwell door, everyone talking animatedly amongst themselves. Lucy shoved her way through the crowd and went to Dale, who wrapped his right arm around her.

Frank glanced to the helipad where some miscellaneous boxes and other debris had been tossed. He spotted Ronny and another man and got their attention.

"You two, get that shit off the helipad so that bird can land!" he snapped.

The two men obeyed immediately, realizing what Frank said was true. Running across the roof, he climbed the small platform that was the helipad and began kicking the items off the pad, some falling to the ground below.

"Here it comes!" someone yelled, the crowd echoing the comment.

Frank turned and saw the helicopter was now within easy viewing, the moonlight and stars enough to make out the markings and color of the aircraft.

Gray and white were the predominant colors, and as the aircraft banked to the left, he saw the logo of a television station on the side.

Everyone was waving, clapping, and cheering as the helicopter slowly came closer. It hovered for a few seconds, and Frank figured the occupants were studying him and his people. He thought they were going to leave, but then the helicopter started to drift to the helipad and slowly began to land.

Evidently the pilot liked what he saw, Frank thought, as he watched the aircraft slowly touching down. It wasn't a perfect landing and the landing skids bounced once when the pilot over-compensated. But Frank knew nothing about helicopters, so barely noticed.

All around them, debris was washed off the roof and the fire began to spread, sparks bouncing across the rooftop, looking like small stars had fallen to earth.

Some men and a few women immediately ran to the spreading flames, stomping them out with their boots and shoes and a few with nothing but bare feet.

No one was taking chances. If the building somehow caught on fire, there would be no fire trucks or firemen to put out the flames.

The rotors of the helicopter began to slow in pitch and Frank could feel the rotor wash slowing as the engine cycled down to idle speed.

At first, the twenty people on the roof began to move forward and it was Frank who realized this couldn't happen. Whoever was in that bird would be overwhelmed with people, questions, and strange faces.

No, he needed to regain order quickly.

Moving around to block the path of the first men and women in line, he reached the stairs for the helipad.

Blocking the stairs, he waved his hands in the air, getting everyone's attention.

"Now hold on a damn minute, people! This can't happen like this! You all need to get down below with the exception of Don, Dale and Lucy and a couple of others who are armed!"

"But we want to see who's in there!" someone called out and a few tossed in their agreements.

"I know you do, but there's too many of you up here. Look, tell you what, go downstairs to the main lobby on the first floor and when I've talked to whoever's in there, I'll bring them down to the rest of you!"

There were mutinies of dissent and a few flat out refused, but then Don moved up next to Frank, his rifle in his hands.

"What the fuck are you people still doing standing here? Didn't Frank just give you an order?"

The tone of his voice was firm and told all who made eye contact with him he would brook no arguments. At first no one moved away, but then by twos and threes the group shuffled back to the stairwell door for the roof.

Dale and Lucy remained behind along with Marc, Ronny and the other man who had helped clear the helipad.

"You want us to go, too?" Ronny asked.

Frank shook his head. "No, you guys stay in case there's trouble. But stay back here."

Ronny nodded and moved to the side, Marc and the nameless man following.

Dale, Don, Lucy were now at the stairs with Frank and he glanced to Don and the others.

"Why don't you guys hang back a little, too, but keep me covered. The chances these people are hostile is slim, but I don't want to take any chances."

"So then let us come with you," Dale said.

"No, Dale, we don't want to spook these people. For all we know, they're a rescue party or something. Let me do this alone. Anything happens, you know what to do, right?" He glanced at Don also as he said his last words.

"He's got a point, Dale, let the man go alone," Don said.

Not liking his orders, but giving in, Dale nodded. "Fine," he said.

Frank smiled wanly, admiring the younger man's loyalty to him, and then with a last glance at Don, the veteran grinning back, Frank began walking to the helicopter, making sure to keep his hands far away from his body, and especially his sidearm, his eyes on the helicopter the entire time.

Chapter 21

With a sigh of relief, Francesca took her hands off the control stick, relieved she was once again on solid ground, even if it was the roof of a building.

She was still so new to flying she was on the edge of her seat the entire time the helicopter was in the air, but she knew to force her fears down and concentrate on flying.

Baby Shaun stirred in her arms and she knew he would need to be fed soon, but at the moment that wasn't an option. There were more than a dozen people on the roof and as she set the helicopter down, she saw almost all of them leave, one man seeming to make them disperse.

"Should I turn off the engine?" she asked Paul as he watched the people moving about on the roof.

"No, leave it on. If anything happens I at least want a chance we might be able to get out of here."

"All right, but remember we don't have a lot of fuel left."

He didn't reply, his eyes only for the men on the roof a dozen yards away.

"So what do we do next?" Francesca asked, as she too, studied the men on the roof.

"Nothing yet, let them make the first move," Paul told her.

One man had his back to them and he was talking to a couple of others.

To Francesca it looked like they were discussing something.

But then one of the men, the man who had his back to them, turned and began walking towards the helicopter, his hands held out and away from his body.

"And there it is," Paul said. "This guy's smart. He knows not to crowd us, and he's keeping his hands away from his body so that the chances of him reaching his gun are slim if we decide to shoot him. He's letting us know he trusts us not to do that."

"Why on earth would we do that?" Francesca asked, rocking the baby in her arms.

"Because things are different now, Francesca," he said simply. "'Sides, it's irrelevant. Why the hell would we set down if we're gonna shoot him? And if we did, his friends would take us out about a half second later." He gestured to the men and one woman near the stairs. Francesca followed his gaze and realized that though the people looked relaxed, all had fingers on the outside of trigger guards and their weapons were just barely pointing downward.

It would take them nothing to bring them to bear on the helicopter. Francesca felt a shiver crawl down her spine and she hugged baby Shaun harder. She prayed they hadn't made a grave mistake by landing on the roof of this building.

For all they knew, the people who lived here were blood-thirsty killers, no better than the military faction that had attacked the office complex less than two days ago.

"He's almost here," Francesca stated as she watched the man move closer. He was of medium height and build and from a casual observation seemed like a normal enough man that she would have met on the street in Philly while she had been on her way home or out for lunch with some of her girlfriends.

"Well, I might as well get out and talk to him. After all, we did land on his roof," Paul said as he opened the door to the helicopter, his Winchester in his hand.

"Be careful," Francesca told him as he was about to step out.

He grinned laconically. "Hey, after everything we've been through, I think I can handle whatever this guy wants. You just be ready to get out of here if there's trouble."

Without a backward glance to Francesca, he stepped out of the helicopter to greet the man moving towards him.

* * *

Both men walked towards one another and stopped when they were no more than four feet separating them.

Frank took in the tall man's demeanor and immediately took him for either a cop or a soldier. His eyes played over the Winchester rifle in the brooding man's arms which could be brought up to aim at his chest in an instant. He studied the firm set of the jaw. The deep brown eyes gazing back at him were hard, and Frank was just starting to wonder if he was about to be killed when the man lowered the rifle so the barrel was pointing down at the helipad.

The man said nothing, his face emotionless as he stared at Frank.

Swallowing the lump in his throat, Frank held out his right hand, and with a slight grin, introduced himself.

"Welcome, friend, name's Frank Pearson. I don't know who you are, but it's nice to see a new face, especially when it arrives in an operational helicopter." Frank had to look upwards at the silent man to make eye contact, as he was almost a half foot taller than Frank.

The man stared down at Frank for almost ten full seconds, his eyes then moving past him to study Lucy, Dale and Don and the others. Frank was beginning to think this was a bad idea again when the man's placid demeanor cracked and he smiled wanly.

Holding out his right hand as he shifted the Winchester to his left, the man took the proffered limb and shook it heartily.

"Names Paul Washburn and it's good to see you, too. Especially if you're friendly." The tone implied he wasn't sure what the answer was just yet.

"Of course we are; why wouldn't we be? Shit, we've been praying for someone like you to come for almost six months."

"Someone like me?" Paul asked, perplexed. Just who did these people think he and Francesca were?

"Why sure. You're a rescue party, right? When you leave, how long will it be before they come and get the rest of us?" Frank asked, his face filled with excitement.

Paul held up his hand to calm the man down.

"Whoa, Frank, I don't know who you think I am, but that ain't it. Shit, I'm just a guy trying to get by, that's all."

"You are? So then there's...."

"'Fraid not. Far as I know, there's no one left that ain't one of them. At least not from what I could see from the air." He turned slightly and pointed to Francesca. "The pilot is a woman. She had a baby this morning if you'll believe it. We've been on the move ever since we had to leave from where we'd been. Took a chance and flew to the city. Philly was already bad when we left six months ago. I'd hoped Pittsburgh might have been better seems it's a little smaller. Shit, guess I was wrong on that count, huh?"

"Yeah, I'm sorry to say you are," Frank said and sighed. "Well, you're welcome to stay if you want. The woman, too. We got food and shelter and this place is boarded up tight. You're as safe as you can be nowadays."

Paul considered Frank's words and decided he didn't really have a choice. Besides, if they had wanted him dead he figured he would have never made it across the helipad.

"Thanks, Frank, that sounds great. Let me go get Francesca and the baby and have her lock down the copter."

"Sure, take your time. We got all day," Frank joked.

Paul ignored the man's last words and jogged back to the helicopter while Frank turned and waved the all clear to Don, Dale, Lucy and the others.

All of them visibly relaxed and Frank turned and waited for Paul to return. He heard the rotors change in pitch and saw them begin to slow as the pilot turned off the engine. Then he watched as a beautiful woman in her late twenties or early thirties stepped out of the pilot's seat with a small bundle in her arms.

With Paul in the lead, the tall man led Francesca back to Frank. She smiled wistfully and Frank leaned forward slightly, wanting to get a better look at the baby.

"Well, I'll be damned. A real baby," he said as he looked at the sleeping infant. "I haven't seen another baby in months now."

"Francesca, this is Frank, he's in charge of the people who live here," Paul told her.

"Hello, Frank, it's nice to meet you," Francesca said as she held out her hand while the other cradled the baby.

"Charmed, I'm sure," Frank replied. He stared at Francesca's smooth complexion, dark brown hair, and admired the curve of her neck. She was a beautiful mother. Hell, she was a beautiful woman.

"You folks ready to go inside?" Frank asked. "There's a lot of people who can't wait to meet you, and the little one."

Don, Dale and Lucy chose that moment to cross the helipad and introduce themselves while Marc and the others hung back.

Frank went through the introductions quickly and Paul shook each person's hand. When he got to Don, he sized the older man up. He wasn't sure whether the older man was a soldier or a cop, but he knew the posture and the way his eyes took in everything there was to see of Paul and Francesca.

Lucy was the most animate as she ooed and ahhed over the baby. She and Francesca moved a few feet away and began talking, Lucy chatting like a school girl while she played with the baby.

Dale asked a few questions of Paul, and in quick, terse words, Paul filled them all in on where he and Francesca had been. He left a lot out, deciding there was no need to tell everything, but when he was finished, only a few minutes had passed and Frank and the others seemed satisfied.

"Wow, that's some story. Sounds like you've been through a lot, as much as any of us has," Frank said. "Still, sounded nice in the complex, too bad it didn't work out."

"Yeah, guess so," Paul said.

"Well, you're here now and you're welcome to join us. Hell, that copter alone makes you more valuable than any one of us. Come on downstairs and we'll get you some food and something to drink." Then he paused and pointed to the Winchester in Paul's hands. "You know how to handle that?"

Paul merely nodded, not needing words to reply.

"That's good, once you're integrated with the group; you'll need to go out on scavenging duty with the rest of us. We all pitch in around here; it's the way we've survived for this long."

"That's fine, Frank, I've got no problem with pulling my weight, for Francesca, too."

Frank nodded, pleased with Paul's answer and turned and lead Paul off the helipad and back into the building. Seeing the men leaving, Lucy escorted Francesca, fawning over the baby the entire time. Paul cast Francesca a look and she grinned back, enjoying the companionship of another woman. For more than six months she had no one to talk to but men, and it was a welcome change.

As they approached the door that would lead the group back into the building, Paul paused and turned to Frank.

"Hey, Frank, I got a question for you," Paul said.

"Shoot," Frank replied in a jovial mood.

"You got anyone in your group that knows how to fly that machine?" He gestured to the helicopter.

"No, 'fraid not. Back when we all got together we did an inventory on who knows what. We got a machinist, a welder, a baker and a whole bunch of traders, but no, no ones a pilot. Why?"

"No reason," Paul answered, but what he was really trying to find out was if he was in danger of one of their group jacking the helicopter and leaving him and Francesca trapped in the middle of Pittsburgh. "Just want to know who everyone is."

Frank chuckled at that, but when he realized Paul was serious, he stopped. Then he gestured for Paul to go first, and as the group descended into the building, Lucy and Francesca bonded with the baby between them.

*　*　*

The next two days passed quickly for Francesca and Paul.

Francesca was left alone by the enclave, as she had the baby to take care of, but after the second day, Frank had placed Paul in the roster for standing watch on the roof of the building.

Paul didn't mind, and though he wasn't used to being told what to do, he found having a purpose, a duty, comforting. It reminded him of his time back on the police force, and though he wasn't on a standard shift, it was close enough.

While he was on watch, Dale had come up to visit him. The young man had tried to chat Paul up, but soon found the tall, taciturn man wasn't a big conversationalist. Paul wasn't rude, he just didn't talk unless it was necessary, so after fifteen minutes, Dale finally gave up, said his goodbyes and left.

Paul had politely told the man thanks for the company and had then gone back to being alone.

Wandering the edge of the roof, he gazed down to the street. Almost a hundred zombies milled about, each in disrepair and decay. One dead man stumbled around blind, his eyes sockets nothing but blackened holes, dried blood crusted to the sides of his face. Another, a cheerleader, still wore her uniform, only now it was covered in gore and grime. Her once blonde hair was a tangled mess and spiders had made the scalp their new home. Another man wore construction attire, right down to the yellow hard hat.

Paul was able to see the man clearly in the light of the day and when the zombie bumped into another, the hat was knocked off his head. The brain was exposed, showing a deep scalp wound that had probably killed the man, but wasn't enough to kill him. If Paul had gotten the man under an x-ray machine, he would have known the man had died when a nail gun had gone off and the nail had punctured a fraction of the zombie's brain. The man had bled out, but the brain had still been intact enough for the man to reanimate.

A frumpy housewife with faded makeup and a clear negligee stumbled around, her ponderous breasts swaying back and forth like lazy pendulums. He also saw more than a dozen were completely naked and one still wore the shower cap donned before the shower. A slip in the tub and crack to the head had killed that particular ghoul.

Deciding he had seen enough death, he stepped away and wandered over to the helicopter. Images of Richard and Shaun floated back to him and he pushed them down.

Christ, after more than six months and Richard's death was still fresh, like an open wound that was constantly picked at.

He couldn't help but wonder how things might have turned out if the man hadn't been bitten. Would they have managed to protect the office complex from the military faction? Hell, they could have let the people be and after they'd departed, they could have taken the complex back. They'd done it once; they could have done it again.

Lighting a cigarette, he flicked the Zippo, Richard's Zippo, and sucked in the smoke, letting it out slowly. The cloud caught on the breeze and drifted away, and Paul followed it as it floated and dispersed.

Sometimes he wondered if Richard and Shaun were the lucky ones and he and Francesca were the losers.

With a weary sigh, he strolled across the helipad and back to the edge of the roof. He wanted to leave, to go back downstairs, but he couldn't. Though he was restless he knew there was nowhere to go.

Even if he and Francesca climbed into that helicopter, where on earth would they go?

As far as Frank knew, there were no other settlements left in the city or surrounding towns and the amount of fuel in the helicopter was severely limited.

Finishing the cigarette, he flicked the butt over the edge of the roof and lit another. He only had so many, but it was the only thing he could think of to keep occupied.

So with another lit smoke in his mouth, he continued to patrol the roof, images of his late friends constantly flashing through his mind, whether he wanted them to or not.

*   *   *

An hour later Paul was relieved of his watch by Ronny who tried to make some small talk with him the same as Dale had. Paul merely told the man thanks and left, wanting to get back inside and check on Francesca.

It had been a long four hours on watch and he was concerned about her.

Though he knew she could handle herself, now with the baby to worry about, she was more vulnerable than ever.

They had been given a small room on the third floor. It had once been used for Park and Recreations, but now it was just another room used for living space.

With his Winchester over his shoulder, Paul walked down the stairs on the cold stairwell, his heavy boots echoing off the walls.

Upon stepping out into the small, side hallway, he proceeded onward. This part of the building was relatively empty, most of the enclave living on the second floor, but Paul liked it that way. He had asked to be somewhat segregated from the others as he didn't know who he could trust just yet.

Frank seemed like a good man, but that still didn't mean Paul could put his life in the guy's hands. Don also seemed competent and when Paul had found out the man had been to Vietnam and had survived a full tour there, it had only made him respect the grizzled veteran slightly more.

Don was someone Paul could relate to, and with Richard gone and no one else with any sort of police or military experience, Paul had decided if he was going to befriend anyone, it would be Don.

Walking down the deserted hallway, he slowed when he heard the sound of voices accompanied by footsteps.

He stood stock still, his hand on his Colt, the Winchester slung over his shoulder, when three men rounded the corner of the hallway and strode up to him. All three men were white and all had a rather redneck look to them. One man had bright red hair and a large wart on his chin. Red Head was the loudest of the three and he gestured to Paul, chuckling as he spoke.

"Well, looky who we got here. It's the new guy who flew in on a whirly bird like he was one of those rich assholes who used ta live in one of those fancy penthouses."

The second man giggled; his voice high and nasally. He had a green baseball cap on his head and a dirty tank top covering his torso.

"Yeah, he came in with that good lookin' brunette. Man, that's a nice piece of ass. Hell, even if she's a mom, I'd do her," Baseball Cap said with a lecherous grin.

The third man said nothing, but nodded his head like it was attached with elastics. He had a skinny mustache and big eyes. Mustache was the follower, who would do whatever the other two did.

Paul had seen his kind countless times.

The two men continued to talk, trying to get a rise out of Paul.

"What's the matter, there, Mexican man, you don't got a tongue? Tell you what; I give you permission to talk."

Paul's jaw was taut as he tried to keep his anger in check. Red Head was goading him, he knew that, and what was amusing was that the man was almost a foot shorter than Paul. Hell, all three were. But evidently, Red Head and Baseball cap thought their greater numbers were superior to Paul's added height.

Then Baseball Cap noticed the cigarettes in Paul's breast pocket and he gestured with a dirty finger, the rest of the hand just as filthy.

"Hey, give me those smokes and we'll let you go without knocking you around too much," he said as he grinned widely. The man was relatively fit, his arms corded with muscle. So was Red Head. Mustache was slightly smaller, but as he wasn't the main threat, Paul wasn't too worried about him.

He could already see it was the two men talking to him that looked liked they were going to be the real problem.

"I don't think so, now why don't you boys keep moving before something bad happens," Paul said, his voice cold.

Baseball Cap snickered. "Yeah, to you. Case you can't count, there's three of us and only one of you."

Red Head reached for the cigarettes in Paul's pocket, and before the man's hand was halfway there, Paul snatched the hand out of the air with his right palm. Using his weight, Paul twisted the man's arm and there was a soft crack as three of Red Head's fingers snapped like dried twigs. The man howled in pain and yanked his hand away, Paul's face still impassive.

The three digits were now bent the wrong way, the skin already turning purple. Red Head spit curses while he hopped around in agony. Baseball Cap was caught off guard at first, but after a second had passed, he realized what had happened to his buddy and now he wanted revenge.

Mustache was right behind Baseball Cap and both men pulled knives from their person and charged at Paul, lips curled into snarls of anger.

But Paul was ready. As a police officer, he knew how to handle himself and had done so countless times on the streets of Philly.

When the two men came at him, he was already moving.

Baseball Cap was slightly in the lead, so he received the first blow. Paul had spun on his left leg and kicked up, planting the sole of his boot into Baseball Cap's stomach. The air whooshed out of the man like he was a punctured hot air balloon.

But Paul never stopped moving. Dropping his foot, he went to his knees and sent his left fist pummeling upwards directly at Mustache's chin, while his right blocked the knife coming for his body.

The blow would have been damaging in of itself, but Mustache had been licking his lips in anticipation of the fight and as Paul's fist pushed upward on his jaw, the man's tongue was sticking out. Upper and lower teeth slammed shut, severing the tip of the man's tongue. The man had a glass jaw and as he saw stars, he dropped to the floor unconscious, rivulets of blood seeping out of his half-open mouth. If he had landed on his back, he probably would have drowned in his own blood, but he had fallen onto his side and so would live another day.

A woman appeared in the hallway and she let out a soft screech at the sight of a man lying on the floor in a pool of blood and the bared blades in the other two men's hands.

"Get out of here, bitch! This ain't your concern," Baseball Cap snapped. The woman spun around and backpedaled from where she'd just come.

By now Red Head wanted some revenge and he waved a large, nine-inch Bowie knife he had pulled from a sheath on his belt. With his remaining working hand, he waved the blade back and forth in the air while Baseball Cap, now recovered, tried to flank Paul on his other side.

"You're gonna die now, spic, I'm gonna see how red your blood is in a minute," Red Head hissed as he moved closer to Paul.

Paul said nothing. There was no need. His eyes creased in concentration as he tried to watch both men at the same time.

Baseball Cap was giggling, his eyes twinkling with glee. Both men were enjoying this and Paul knew if he didn't watch himself, he just might end up joining Mustache on the floor.

Paul took a step backward, but then stopped when his back came up against the wall. Baseball Cap barked laughter and with a glance at Red Head to make sure his buddy was ready, Baseball Cap charged in, while Red Head did the same.

With nowhere to go, Paul chose his only option.

He dropped to the floor like he had been shot and then kicked out his legs, sweeping both men off their feet. Red Head went horizontal for a moment and then dropped straight down, his back connecting with the stone floor with crushing force, the man's shoulder blades taking the brunt of the fall.

Baseball Cap wasn't as lucky. Though horizontal in the air, the back of his head came down first with concussion-sized force. The man landed hard and immediately fell into a daze, his vision blurry from the sudden trauma of his brain.

Jumping back up, Paul moved towards Red Head, and before the man could move, Paul's boot connected with the man's chin.

Red Head spit blood and teeth as he mercifully fell into unconsciousness, his eyes fluttering and then closing.

Paul was still moving; his right hand clenched into a fist. Spinning on his heels, he leaned over Baseball Cap and punched the man twice in the face, the inside of the prone man's cheek becoming cut by his teeth as the inner cheek sliced against enamel.

Blood formed in the man's mouth and with an annoyed sigh, Paul turned the now unconscious man's head to the side so he didn't drown in plasma.

Blood was pooling on the floor and collecting under the bodies, and with a weary groan, Paul stood up and gazed down at the three men who had attempted to roust him and had paid the price for their ignorance.

Paul looked up at the sound of more footsteps and remained still, his arms at his sides, fists clenched as he prepared to battle whoever came next.

Don came rushing around the far corner of the hallway, a handgun in his hand, moving at a fast clip towards the four men, but he slowed as his eyes took in what had happened at a glance.

The men were all moaning now, while consciousness attempted to get a foothold on their befuddled minds. Paul took a step away from them, careful not to step in any of the blood on the floor.

"What the hell happened here, Paul?" Don asked; his voice short and powerful. Paul recognized the tone and knew the man was falling back on his military training. The two had talked a few times and both were fellow souls, used to battle and danger.

Paul shrugged his wide shoulders and gestured to the three men.

"Don't know. I guess they tripped or something."

Don frowned. "Tripped, huh? Sally came and got me. She said she saw these men attacking you and Bert was already on the floor, bleeding from the mouth like a stuck pig."

Paul was impressed. The woman had seen all that in an instant. And she had run off to get help. He would never tell her, but he owed her his thanks. If things hadn't gone in his favor, if the three men had been better brawlers, he may have been glad Don had arrived when he did.

Paul remained silent.

Don chuckled, knowing Paul wasn't going to say anything.

"You know, Paul, these three assholes trip a lot, but usually it's the guy they find that ends up on the floor. It's nice to see them get a taste of their own medicine."

He glanced at the men and then back to Paul. This time he lowered his voice so only Paul could hear him, the three men out of earshot. "If it wasn't for the fact we're short on manpower, we would have kicked these shitheads out a long time ago, but even though they're idiots, they're needed. You get me?"

Paul nodded. "Yeah, Don, I get it, only too well." He turned slightly, stared at his handiwork and then back to Don. "That's why I didn't kill them."

With Don watching, he reached into his breast pocket, took out his pack of cigarettes and took out three of them. Moving closer to the three moaning men, he flicked one cigarette onto each man's chest, the small white stick falling off the bodies to land in the pools of blood, the pain-covered faces glaring back at him.

Paul began to walk away and Don reached out and grasped his arm, halting him.

"What'd you do that for?" he asked Paul.

"They asked me for a smoke and I figure they could use one more than I can now," he said and then freed his arm and strode away down the hall.

Don watched the tall man walk away, and after he was gone, he turned and moved closer to the three bleeding men.

"Looks like you idiots picked the wrong man to fuck with this time," he said casually as he reached down to help them up.

Neither of the men replied, but merely moaned louder as Don pulled each one to his feet.

Don eyed Red Head's hand, seeing the shattered fingers and shook his head.

"Jesus, Doug, what the hell? Go see Timothy and have him get a splint or something on that hand before your damn fingers swell and fall off." He turned to Mustache who was swaying on his feet. The man's mouth dribbled blood and his eyes were glazed. He looked like a drunk who'd had way more than his fill.

"And you, too, Bert. Get to Timothy and see what he can for you before you friggin' bleed to death." He pointed to Baseball Cap. "You, help them both as you look in the best shape."

The man assented, and with one wounded man on each arm, Baseball Cap led them away, a small trail of blood appearing behind them as they walked, like a leaking garbage bag being taken to the curb on trash day.

Don stood and watched the three men hobble away, and when they had turned the corner and were headed for the stairwell, he spun around and moved off to find Frank.

Whenever disturbances like this happened, Frank always wanted to know, and especially if it had anything to do with Paul. Don had been told to keep an eye on the tall man, as he was a lifeline to the helicopter.

Plus, after six months in the building, trapped by the living dead, cabin fever was a problem.

As the man moved away, he made a note to get someone back there to cleanup all that blood in the hallway before someone slipped and killed themselves.

And that would definitely be bad. All the survivors in the enclave knew to be on constant guard of each other. If someone passed away in the middle of the night from a heart attack or an aneurism, they would revive and attack the first human they found. One more constant threat to add to an already perilous existence.

With a shake of his head, Don moved away, a few flies already finding the congealing plasma and feasting heartily.

Chapter 22

Ben Carver was frowning deeply as he gazed out into the dead city, the light breeze gently blowing his hair.

Next to him, Lynn waited silently, her blonde hair fluttering in the same breeze.

After more than five minutes of silence, she spoke up.

"What're you thinking about?" she asked and moved up against him, sliding her right arm through the crook of his left arm.

"Huh? Oh, sorry, baby, I was just thinkin' about that helicopter. You know, if we could get to it, take the pilot hostage, we could fly away from here."

"Oh, really. And where would we go?" she asked as she leaned her head against his shoulder. Under his light jacket she could feel his muscles, his power, and it made her feel safe.

"Where? Hell, who knows? But it's gotta be better than waiting here to run out of food and die."

"You don't mean that," she said, looking up into his hard eyes.

"Yeah, I do. There's only so much food left in this city and we've been picking what's left of it clean for months. A lot of stuff is either spoiled or has been destroyed by looters and fires. No, baby, there's only so much time left to stay in this city and that's running out." She was about to reply when he stopped her. "Yeah, I know what you're gonna say, and I know there's still plenty of food, but sooner or later we will run out, and when that happens, I don't wanna be around here. No, Lynn, we need to get that chopper and fly it the hell out of here."

She merely nodded, and laid her head back onto his shoulder.

"Whatever you want to do, you know I'm with you," she said. He turned and reached out with a callused palm, brushing the errant hair from her face.

"I know that, baby, and I wouldn't want it any other way. If it wasn't for you, I don't think I could take all this shit."

She chuckled. "You're just saying that so you can get into my pants."

He grinned like a schoolboy on his first date.

"So what if I am?"

"No reason, it's just that you don't have to, you know, say anything. You can get into my pants anytime you want."

He wrapped his arms around her and pulled her close. Pulling her lips to his, he kissed her passionately, his tongue exploring her warm mouth. She pressed against him, sighing in pleasure as they were lost in the carnal pleasure of their lust for one another.

When they finally broke free of the embrace, Lynn was breathing heavily and Carver had a distinct bulge in his pants.

"You want to go inside and finish what we've started?" he asked.

She nodded, and with her hand holding his, the two headed for the door to lead them back inside the building, where they would spend the next hour loving and laughing together as only two people in love could.

*   *   *

One hour and twenty minutes later, Carver rolled off the bed-roll the two shared and began getting dressed.

Lynn rolled over, one shapely thigh visible, the rest covered by silk sheets acquired from a small store in downtown Pittsburgh.

Suddenly, there was a knock on the door and Carver, already up, crossed the room in his bare feet and opened it enough to see who was there. It was one of his men, a small portly man by the name of Porks, because he looked so much like a pig.

Porks was like a gopher, and would do and go wherever he was sent. Right now he was reporting a message for Carver from O'Hara. Lynn watched from across the room as Porks whispered to Carver, then when he was through, Carver closed the door and padded back to her, but instead of sliding into the bedroll next to her, he began finishing getting dressed.

"Where're you going?" Lynn asked.

"I'm, gonna go find O'Hara, Sherman, and the others," he said. "David says one of our scouting parties followed Pearson's people to a warehouse at the docks that's still filled with canned food and dried goods. He says no one's been there since all this shit started. There's enough food in there to keep us fed for months, maybe longer. The only bad thing is there's a shitload of zombies wandering around the area."

"Does that mean we don't have to leave the city?" she asked.

"Maybe, we'll have to wait and see how much is really there." He frowned deeply and Lynn saw his change in composure.

"What? What is it?" Lynn asked.

"Nothing, baby, it's just that I hope my scouts following Pearson's people didn't fuck it up and get spotted. But if they did, it's a real possibility that Pearson's gonna find out that we know about the warehouse, too. I don't really know for sure and it sucks. Either way, his scouts would have taken off once they found the stash of food in the first place; wanting to get back and tell Pearson so they could come back with bigger trucks."

"So, what do you want to do?" Lynn asked.

"Simple," Carver told her. "We need to get there first and get all we can, then hold the place so Pearson can't get in there and take what's rightfully ours."

She jumped up, the sheets falling away, exposing her glorious body. For a heartbeat Carver wanted to scrub everything and make love to her for another hour, but he knew the warehouse wouldn't wait. No, he needed to get in there and lock the place down before Pearson and his assholes did it before him.

"I'm coming, too," Lynn said as she got dressed.

Carver smiled and reached down, handing her the shirt she'd discarded when they had stripped one another in their lust for each other.

"Wouldn't have it any other way, baby."

With a seductive smile, she took the shirt and slid her arms into it, and after finishing, she grabbed her weapons and followed Carver out of the room.

She knew time was an issue and would be damned if she would slow her man down for even a second.

Carver saw she was behind him, and with his shotgun in hand, went off to find his men. They had to move fast, and he planned on leaving at first light, which was just a few hours away.

And then they would have more food than they would know what to do with, and if Pearson and his people starved because of it, well, tough shit for them.

* * *

Baby Shaun fussed in his bedroll and Francesca moved next to him, picking him up and carrying him to one of the large windows in the room she and Paul shared.

The moon was high in the sky and bathed the room in an anemic pale-yellow glow. Turning to the side, she opened her shirt and let baby Shaun begin nursing.

She was so preoccupied with feeding the baby, she never heard Paul move up behind her, his shadow falling across her.

"Oh, Paul, I'm sorry, did we wake you?"

In the dim gloom, Paul's tan skin made him appear to be even more a part of the shadows.

"Nah, I wasn't really sleeping anyway." He gestured to the baby, who was nursing happily. "How's he doing?"

"He's fine, Paul. He's like his father."

"Is that a good thing or a bad one?" Paul asked laconically.

Francesca grinned, both of them sharing a playful jab at the man they both cared for.

"It's a good thing," she finally replied, Paul nodding in agreement.

A soft knock came to the door of the room and Paul's head swiveled towards it. Turning, he paused long enough to pick up his Colt and then moved to the door. According to his watch, it was a little past three in the morning and no one should be calling at this hour, unless there was trouble. The three hicks came to his mind and he wondered if one or all of them would be stupid enough to try and get even after suffering their humiliating beating from him.

Moving to the door, he stopped with his hand over the doorknob.

"Yeah?" Paul called softly.

"It's me," Frank's voice said through the door, muffled. "I took a chance you might be up. Can I come in?"

Paul glanced at Francesca, her body silhouetted from the wan light seeping through the window. "Is it okay with you?"

"Sure, it's fine, Paul. Go 'head and let him in. It must be important if he's coming now."

Paul opened the door and Frank stood with a small candle in his hands.

"Hey, sorry to come so late, but it's important," he said as Paul moved aside and Frank entered the room.

He saw Francesca nursing and immediately averted his gaze.

"Oh, sorry, I didn't know," he said bashfully.

Francesca smiled, his politeness endearing to her. "That's okay, Frank, I'm covered," she said, gazing down at the nursing baby. Frank looked back at Francesca and watched her, admiring her beauty in the moonlight.

"So what do you want that it can't wait till morning?" Paul asked, pulling the man's attention back to him.

It worked and Frank turned to face Paul.

"One of our scouts just got back about an hour ago. He and two other guys went to the docks to see if there was anything salvageable we could use. They found a warehouse full of food. Mostly canned and some dried, too. It's the haul of a lifetime and we need it badly. With Carver always taking everything he can get his hands on, and the rest either spoiled or destroyed by the fires, well, it's getting mighty tight to find supplies."

"Who's Carver?"

Frank waved the question away. "No one important, just another man with mouths to feed."

"Okay, and how does that apply to me?" Paul asked, impatient for the man to get on with it.

"I want you to come tomorrow and be on the salvage team. From what Don told me, you can handle yourself and we need men like you. So what do you say? You need to do more around here than just stand watch, surely you knew that."

Paul nodded, his face grim. "Yeah, I know, don't worry, I'll be there. Ready to go."

Frank looked pleased and reached out his right hand. Paul stared at it and then took it with his own, the two men shaking three times. Frank considered telling Paul more about Carver, but decided against it, Paul being the new recruit.

"Good, Paul, excellent. Don't worry; these excursions usually go down smooth and fast. As far as my scouts saw, the place is empty, only a bunch of zombies to get rid of. We can be in and out of there in a matter of hours with enough food and supplies to get us through the winter."

Paul said nothing and Frank realized the conversation was over. Scratching the back of his head nervously, he moved to the door.

"Okay, I'll see you at first light, someone will come fetch you." He turned to Francesca. "You keep that little guy safe, all right? He's our future."

Francesca smiled. "Will do, Frank," she said. She had switched breasts, the spicket dry on the first one. Baby Shaun ate greedily, cooing softly, his small hands reaching into the air.

Frank left and Paul closed the door. He walked back to Francesca who gazed up at him silently. The only sounds were the baby eating and the moaning of the undead floating from ground level. By now it was only background noise, barely noticed by either of them.

"So what do you think?" Francesca asked.

Paul shook his head, his face still almost invisible in the darkness. "I don't. I do what I'm told now, Francesca. If we're gonna stay here I have no choice. But Frank is right. These people need food and so do we. If he needs my help, then so be it."

"You just be careful," she told him as she finished feeding the baby. She brought him up to her shoulder and began patting his back gently, rubbing him.

"Don't you know it," he replied and then baby Shaun let out a belch three times larger than his small form.

"Oh my goodness!" Francesca said as she began to laugh. It was contagious and Paul began to laugh also, his rich baritone voice filling the room.

The baby looked at both of them with wide eyes, as if he somehow knew what was happening and was wondering just what the hell was so funny?

Chapter 23

The sun had barely touched the tip of the sky as the three vehicles headed away from the loading dock and out onto the deserted street. The moving van was in the lead, followed by Dale's Camaro, and a pickup truck brought up the rear, the back loaded with three men, Ronny and Marc and another man with sandy brown hair and freckles who went by the name, Mouse, because of his rodent-like features.

With the convoy away from the enclave and safe, the decoy was pulled back inside the building, what had happened a few days ago the stuff of rumors. Everyone in that room had remained silent about what had happened, but all it took was one wrong word said to the wrong person to begin the rumors and gossip.

In the cab of the moving truck, Frank was in the driver's seat with Don and Paul, the leg room at a minimum.

Paul's Winchester was held between his legs and he watched the road as the van plowed down the street, knocking ghouls left and right as the large grille served as a battering ram.

Paul stared at the buildings and empty cars, the first time he had really seen the destruction since leaving the office complex. From the air, inside the helicopter, the damage just didn't seem so bad.

They rounded a corner where a line of storefronts could be seen. There was a small convenience store, a burned out diner and a three-story office building with the sign, *THE MASTER VISION* on the front door.

As the convoy drove by, Paul was able to see the zombies moving about on the street. Out of the doorway of the building with the sign, a zombie with white hair and large coke-bottle glasses stumbled into the light of the morning. The ghoul's hair was a matted mess of gore and the skin hung on its head like dried leather. There was a slick sheen to the corpse, and the skin sagged to the point it seemed to slough off the bones. The glazed look of death in the ghoul's eyes followed the convoy, and as the last vehicle passed it by, the ghoul stumbled onto the street, tripping over the remains of a maggot-infested corpse strewn in multiple pieces across the sidewalk. The zombie's head jerked foreword and the glasses flew off the face to fall to the asphalt. The ghoul, its white eyes covered in cataracts, stepped on the glasses and continued onward, never the worse for wear.

Paul shifted uncomfortably in his seat as he stared at the devastated city.

"It's really somethin', huh?" Frank asked as he swung onto Beaver Avenue.

Ahead of them was the Allegheny River and the massive steel bridge that spanned it. The arcing, half-circles of steel that made up the sides of the bridge seemed to beckon to Paul, to remind him of what was gone, and taunting him with an uncertain future.

"Yeah, somthin'," Paul said. He didn't want to talk. Seeing the city like this had him remembering some unpleasant images from his own past. Such as the first time he had met Richard in the basement of an old tenement house. The two had been wary of each other at first, but had soon become fast friends.

When they had found more than two dozen zombies in the basement of the building and had to dispose of them together, it had only sealed their growing bond of friendship.

Don and Frank chatted a little as Paul remained silent between them. He hoped Francesca was all right and she had assured him she would be fine when he had left her that morning. She had her sidearm and her rifle with her and had agreed not to go anywhere without them.

She had bonded with a few of the other women in the enclave and they were seeing to her this morning as Lucy was with Dale in the Camaro.

The moving van plowed through the city, sometimes knocking empty cars out of the way, and in no time they were pulling onto the docks.

Seagulls flew overhead, hoping for a meal, a few seeming to already be dining that morning.

The feast of the day was dead and rotting corpses, more than a score of bodies floating near the edge of the docks. The bloated and saturated bodies were constantly pushed against the docks, only to be pulled back out again by the current. The seagulls dove in and snatched what they could of the fetid meat. Where once the gulls had relied on man for handouts and had fed well at the city dump, now they chose to feed on the discarded corpses of the humans themselves. Food was food and the gulls weren't picky.

Unfortunately, the rotten meat was filled with deadly bacteria and more than fifty gulls lay on the edge of the docks and floated in the water next to the corpses.

The other seagulls ignored them and kept right on feeding, continuing the cycle.

As the van slowed in front of the correct warehouse, Frank checked the small scrap of paper in his hand, not wanting to make a mistake and go to the trouble of breaking into the wrong building.

Outside on the docks themselves, the zombies were moving towards the vehicles, their moans carrying on the ocean breeze.

"This is it," Frank said as he pointed to the sign near the large bay doors.

"So how do you want to do this?" Don asked as he eyed the approaching ghouls. There were more than twenty-five already and more were appearing from around crates and from between buildings.

"Tell Dale to draw them away from us and once the area's empty, we'll get the loading doors open. Then he can double back and join us. We'll pull the van and pickup in, load them with everything we possibly can, and then when we leave we'll just open the doors again and drive right through 'em."

"Sounds good," Don agreed.

He picked up the two-way radio sitting on the dashboard and called Dale. After a second or two, Dale answered and Don filled him in. Two seconds later, the Camaro peeled away to shoot across the dock, heading for the edge where ships would normally moor. At the moment, there was nothing, only the old car tires tied to the side to protect the hulls of the ships from becoming damaged when the currents would push them against the dock.

When Dale was far enough away, Lucy climbed out of the Camaro and sat on the sill of the door while Dale pressed the car's horn, yelling as loud as he could out his open window. With the van and pickup remaining still with engines off, Marc and Ronny hiding behind the cab, the ghouls soon lost interest and began moving towards the greater noise disturbance.

Frank waited until almost all the undead were gone and then he started the engine and floored the gas pedal, driving straight for the loading dock. Ronny, Mouse, and Marc had to fend off a few ghouls who had decided they were the better choice to go for, but when the pickup began moving again, they were left behind.

No one wanted to shoot a gun, the noise would instantly draw the ghouls back to them.

With the van in front of the two large, bay doors, Don jumped out with Paul behind him. Don had a set of bolt cutters, the large tool up to the task of any standard-sized lock.

Reaching the doors, he cut each padlock off, while Paul guarded his back. A zombie came from around the truck and Paul cracked it in the forehead, sending the body tumbling to the ground with a fractured skull, stopping it before it could get too close to Don.

"Thanks, I didn't see that one," Don told Paul when he saw how close he'd come to being lunch for a zombie.

"No problem, just get finished so we can get inside." He didn't like being out in the open like this, so exposed. After months in the office complex, the large buildings like a fortress, he now felt vulnerable. And it was a feeling he didn't relish.

Don worked quickly, and in no time the bay doors were opened and Frank began backing the moving van inside. At the same time the pickup truck was driven in and parked. There was still more than enough room for the Camaro.

Ronny and Marc were already at the bay doors, making sure no zombies took an interest in them, but unfortunately once the men were walking around it didn't take long for the undead to see them and begin moving toward them.

Frank saw this, reached inside the cab and called Dale back to the loading dock.

While he was doing this, the rear sliding door of the moving van was raised and seven men and women climbed out. Alex, Jeff and five others all jumped down onto the cement floor, happy to finally be out of the back of the moving van. It was uncomfortable inside there, and though they had jury rigged the door so it could be opened from the inside while a person was in there, they knew nothing about what was happening outside.

Frank moved to the loading bay doors while Dale shot across the pavement outside. Behind him, more than fifty ghouls were following, but it would be a few minutes until they reached the warehouse again.

Frank pointed to Dale where to park and the Camaro slid into the bay, then the door was closed with a clang. The other door was also being rolled down, Don pulling on the manual chain and sealing the three vehicles inside the warehouse.

Paul was standing near the large swinging doors leading into the actual warehouse. As none of them knew what waited beyond those doors, they had agreed to go in together. Paul was just making sure nothing came through from the other side until they were ready to go. With the bay doors now closed, the loading dock was cast into semi-darkness, only a few slits of light slipping in through the sides of the metal doors.

The loading dock was one level, with the large swinging doors leading into the main warehouse. To the side of the doors was a small shack, three by three in diameter, and inside the shack were bills of lading and sign-in sheets. This would have been where the man on watch in the dock would have coordinated everything for this side of the building.

There was another loading dock on the opposite side, but as this one had been the easiest to access, so Frank had chosen it as their point of entry.

Dale and Lucy climbed out of the Camaro and ran up to Frank, Don and the others. Most were silent, waiting for what would come next, but a few others were talking amongst themselves.

"Man, that was awesome!" Dale yelled as he stepped in front of Frank. He was pumped up from playing tag with the zombies and his adrenalin was flowing.

"Great job, Dale, now I need you to dial it down a little and focus," Frank told the younger man. Dale nodded, took Lucy in his arms and both seemed to calm a little.

Paul was waiting for the others to get it together and he was beginning to grow impatient. If there had been anything waiting for them inside the warehouse, all the time Frank had taken to get organized would have given their position away in an instant and given the opposition time to prepare for them.

As nothing had happened, Paul was fairly confident the warehouse was empty.

"All right, boys and girls, if you're ready, then let's see what we can get. The rest of our people are waiting for us back at the County Building and they're relying on us, so let's do this and get back to them safely."

Everyone agreed, and with Don, Frank and Paul in the lead, the group stepped through the large, swinging double doors and into the warehouse.

Paul was the first through, his Winchester leading the way and the first thing he spotted was a forklift parked to the side of the doors. It was parked with the two blades on the front in the up position, as if the owner had just run off for a coffee break and would be back in a second. There was a yellow hard hat sitting on the seat, another testament to the brevity of the driver.

The second thing Paul noticed, as well as the others in the group, was the massive twelve foot piles of crates stacked from end to end in neat rows. The warehouse was massive and there was more food than the group could take in one trip. They had found the mother load.

"Jackpot!" Dale said, elated, as he gazed out at all the food and boxes of stores with greed in his eyes. The others agreed and there was clapping and pats on the back as everyone congratulated each other for the wonderful find.

"All right, enough, let's get moving. The sooner we're loaded and gone the better," Frank told everyone. He was thinking of just a few days ago at the supermarket where he had lost good men. If he could help it this time, he would lose no one.

He quickly organized the men and women into groups of twos and threes, and with everyone using flat dollies four feet squared; he began sending them out to retrieve supplies. Dale and Lucy headed off in their own direction and Frank asked Paul and Don to stay with him.

Paul complied and the three men grabbed a dolly and began moving through the warehouse.

Boxes of crackers, canned vegetables, flour, cooking oils, including shortening, were stacked three high and the men began filling their loads onto the dolly. From all around them men and women were calling out to one another as each found something new to add to their collection.

Frank and Don chatted happily, while Paul remained mostly silent. He had never been a talker and preferred to let his actions speak for him.

Frank and Don barely noticed, both men having eyes only for the food.

It took almost three hours to get the moving van so stuffed with canned food and other necessary items that the door could barely be closed. The plan was for everyone to ride back in the pickup truck. It would be tight, but they would all fit.

Everyone was standing in the middle of the warehouse, admiring all the food still left behind and Frank was discussing how they would be returning the next morning for more when a shot rang out and a small man in their group was knocked to the floor. It was Mouse, the man dropping to the floor like he had been slapped by a giant.

At first no one understood what was happening, that is until a brown-haired woman gazed down at Mouse and saw half his head was missing. She screamed loudly just as more bullets filled the air like angry bees.

Paul was the first to move, pushing both Don and Frank to the cement floor. Bullets whined over their heads, a few missing by inches.

"What the hell!" Frank snapped as he searched for their attackers. His eyes finally stopped at the rear of the warehouse.

Ben Carver stood in the middle of the wide aisle, a sniper rifle in his hand. Next to him was his woman, his lover, Lynn, and she stood with legs spread and her own gun aimed at Frank and the others. All around Carver, men were swarming into the warehouse, firing at will across the empty floor, spent shell casings tinkling to the floor like spare change. Paul was already moving and had taken cover behind a large crate.

"You two, move your ass or get it shot off!" Paul yelled at them. Frank and Don did as instructed and crawled towards Paul. Behind Frank, the rest of his group was doing the same.

When the aisle had been cleared, two of Frank's people lay in pools of blood on the cold floor. It was the man called Mouse with the head wound and a woman with gray hair and small glasses. She had been struck in the neck and had bled out almost immediately when her carotid artery had been severed. She twitched on the ground as she breathed her last and Frank had to look away.

Her name had been Mildred and she had been a mother of two, both boys back at the County Building.

But he would have to worry about informing her children that they were now orphans later, that is if there was a later.

Carver's men were spreading out and cutting off their retreat. Meanwhile, bodies were going down on both sides of the fight. A man on Carver's side received a round to the chest, the back of his shirt exploding outward to bathe the wall in scarlet. He actually looked down and saw the small hole in his chest, pushing his index finger into the hole like a child plays with clay.

In his mind, it didn't seem so bad, the small hole wasn't really that big, but if he had been able to see the fist-sized jagged hole in his back, he would have realized he had seconds left to live. His eyes fluttered, his gun dropped to the floor and he followed it a moment later. On Frank's side, Ronny was firing from the hip, but the man hadn't taken cover as well as he should have and he screamed when a bullet took off his right ear. Ducking down, he realized he should be dead now and decided not to take anymore stupid chances.

Another woman on Frank's side of the fight, a girl almost barely seventeen, took a bullet to the shoulder. The frail, skinny frame spun from the impact and she dropped to the ground. Only she fell the wrong way and landed in the aisle, now exposed. No sooner had she fallen then another shot rang out and the girl's face exploded, teeth shooting across the area like white shrapnel.

"Jesus Christ, how the hell did he get here?" Frank yelled as he fired at the opposing force.

"Who the hell is that?" Paul growled, firing his Winchester at a man as he tried to gain a better firing position. The man received a round in the leg and he spun in the air, coming down hard, face first. His nose was bleeding profusely and when the man tried to get up and keep moving, another round struck him in the back, dropping him to the floor like a sack of potatoes. Paul didn't know who had fired the killing shot, but he was pleased. Now he could focus on another target. Frank was searching for one target in general, namely Carver. The man was killing his people and there was more than enough food for both of their enclaves. But as he knew in the past, the man couldn't be reasoned with.

So he knew if this was ever to stop, Carver had to be taken down for good.

"Cover me, I'm gonna try and get closer!" Frank yelled to Paul and Don, who both assented.

The air was filled with zinging bullets and the hairs on the back of Frank's neck were at attention as he waited for the bullet that would find him. But it didn't come and he managed to get to a better position. Behind him, Paul and Don were firing at the opposing force, keeping their heads down. For the moment, the casualties on both sides seemed to have stopped as everyone was now keeping their heads down, not wanting to get it shot off.

Bodies were everywhere and Frank already knew what would be happening any second. Then there would be two attacking groups to deal with. One living and one undead.

Inching as close as he could go, he was rewarded when he saw Carver's head and shoulders through a small opening between two crates while the man moved back and forth behind them. He was ordering his men and was waving his arms in the air, angry that he hadn't taken the warehouse yet and destroyed the opposition.

Licking his lips in concentration, Frank lined up the man's head in his gun sight, and when he was as sure as he could be that he had a killing shot, he fired off a round.

At the last second, Carver moved to the side, the bullet missing him by a mere inch, but the round continued onward and Lynn was there to stop it. The woman was standing next to Carver, never far from his side, and as the man gave orders to his men in loud growls, he suddenly heard Lynn gasp in surprise.

At first Carver didn't understand what had happened, but when he turned to look at her and ask her if she was all right, he saw the small, nickel-sized hole in her neck, both sides to be precise. Blood was squirting out of the wound on either side and he reached for her, catching her as she slumped to the floor.

"Baby? Lynn, what the fuck? What happened? Oh, shit, oh, Christ, Lynn, no, not you, not now, you can't die, hang on, baby, hang on!" He turned to Sherman standing near him. "You, give me a damn rag so I can stop this bleeding!" he snapped. Sherman obliged and Carver snatched the material from the man's hand. He tried to staunch the blood, but her jugular had been nicked and there was no way to apply pressure without strangling her.

Lynn's mouth was opening and closing as she tried to speak, but only blood spilled out in a red, bubbling froth.

"Hang on, Lynn, please hang on," Carver pleaded as he stared down at the woman he loved. Hell, the only thing he loved in this goddamn world.

She reached up with a blood covered hand, her eyes jumping back and forth in their sockets. He could see the terror in her eyes and he wanted to scream. Her left hand touched his cheek, caressing it softly with one finger, then the arm dropped away and was limp, leaving a small streak of vermilion on his face.

"Lynn? Lynn? Baby? No, no, no. No, this can't happen! No, you can't fucking die! I won't let you!" He cradled her in his arms, rocking her back and forth while all around him the gunfight continued. He was oblivious to it. His hearing seemed to fade away and his limbs went numb as everything became muffled, like he was underwater. He held Lynn for what seemed forever, but was in fact merely minutes, and when her lifeless body began to stir again, he reached down to his hip, pulled his hunting knife that was strapped there and slid it out of its sheath.

He leaned back and gazed down at the woman he loved and watched her eyes open. The eyes moved left, then right, then looked up at him. But where the terror and pain was there moments ago, now there was a deep emptiness, a void that could never be filled.

With tears in his eyes, he raised the knife to her left ear, placed the tip just so, and when she opened her mouth to try and bite his arm, he slid the blade deep into her brain, twisting when the hilt touched her hair. She bucked once in his arms and remained still.

He slowly pulled the bloody blade out and slowly closed her eyes forever. He stared at her face for another minute, his eyes never blinking, the tears running freely. The blood streak on his cheek was now diluted from tears and when he wiped his face, the blood was gone. Gently resting Lynn onto the floor, he stood up, sucked in a deep breath, and screamed as loud as he could. His cry of anger and loss filled the warehouse, chilling all who heard it to the bone.

"*KILL THEM ALL!*" he roared, now wanting nothing but vengeance for his lost love.

With a rallying cry, his men and a few women rose up and charged forward, firing a steady barrage of gunfire at Frank and his people. With the onslaught so forceful, all Frank, Paul and the others could do was keep their heads down and ride the wave of death, hoping they could get their licks in once it had slowed down in its fury.

Don was ducking low, but he was peeking out from the side of a crate and as he watched the attacking force. He saw two dead men and one woman in the middle of the aisle twitch as they were pulled back from death's embrace.

He glanced to the left and right of him and everywhere a body had fallen, the corpse was in similar signs of reviving with the exception of the man who had been head shot and the teenage girl with no face. Across the warehouse, he could see more corpses slowly coming to their hands and knees as each dead warrior was now reborn for yet another team.

"Frank? We got more trouble," Don called out when Frank had made his way back to safety after shooting Lynn. He didn't know he'd killed the woman, but he did know he had missed Carver.

Frank looked to his friend and wondered what exactly could be worse than what was happening now? And then he saw the first zombies moving towards them and realized what Don meant.

"Oh, shit," he said and then had to duck down as a staccato of bullets chewed up the crate inches from his head.

Glancing around himself, he realized Paul had disappeared, as well.

That was odd, after getting to know the taciturn man; he never would have pegged him for a coward.

Chapter 24

Frank realized he was in deep shit, to put it bluntly.

Carver's people were slowly moving through the warehouse, leapfrogging from crate to crate. It was obvious they had superior firepower, and while one reloaded, the others would keep forcing Frank and his people to being able to do nothing but stay down or risk being shot.

Ronny was a few crates over and Frank got the man's attention.

"Get to the van and take as many people with you as you can! Get that food back to the County Building! Don and me will hold Carver off until you're gone!"

"But what about you and Don?" Ronny replied. "You'll be slaughtered!"

"Don't worry about us, damn it, just go!" Frank ducked lower just before the crate he hid behind took a fusillade of rounds. Holes appeared in the wood and a red, sap-like substance leaked out, making the crate look like it was bleeding.

There was a small pool near his knee and he reached out, touched some to his finger and tasted it.

Ketchup. The crate was full of cans of ketchup.

Dale crab walked next to Ronny and Frank could see Lucy, Marc and a few others behind him.

Frank told Dale the same thing, and after a brief refusal to leave, the younger man relented.

Frank counted to three and came up firing, emptying half a clip in less time than it would take to spit. As he returned fire, the rest of his people dashed for the loading dock, weaving in and out of the crates. Bullets whined around them and an older man in his fifties went down hard like he'd been pushed from behind. The hole in his back was small, but the explosive rounds Carver's men were using blew half his chest open. Dropping to the floor in a tangle of limbs, he was instantly surrounded by the newly revived zombies. He saw faces that were once his friends as they leaned down and plunged hands into the open wound. The man would have died anyway, but it would have been from blood loss and the trauma he'd sustained from the gunshot. But instead of quietly falling into oblivion, he died in utter agony while his internal organs were pulled from his body, his lower intestine becoming a meal for a dead woman he'd once called a friend.

Eventually he expired, but the ghouls continued feeding.

Dale and Lucy raced for the docks, followed by the others.

Dale glanced over his shoulder one time to see Don and Frank firing at Carver's people, then he rounded a bend in the aisle and they were lost from sight. But the staccato of bullets being shot at each group still filled the warehouse, gun smoke hovering around the ceiling like fog.

Upon reaching the loading dock, Dale jumped down and ran to the moving van while Lucy went to the pickup truck. She climbed inside, the keys still in the ignition while the rest of the survivors climbed into the rear bed. Another man Dale only knew as Fred climbed into the cab next to him, taking the passenger seat as his own. Dale didn't say anything, it was fine with him.

A man ran to the bay doors and pulled on the chain, opening the doors wide. If the man hadn't been in such a rush, he would have realized that was a bad idea.

He had barely raised the main door more than four feet before he had to run away. The zombies outside were on their knees and had immediately swarmed into the loading dock, wanting the humans within. The man reached the pickup truck and was helped onboard while Dale revved the moving van's engine.

The doors were only open about four and half feet, but there was no option but to go straight through them.

With the engine reaching the red line in rpms, Dale took his foot off the brake and sent the vehicle straight into the bay doors. There was a crunching sound of tearing metal and the van's windshield cracked and spider webbed as the door bounced off it, but the safety glass held.

Decaying bodies were thrown in all directions as the moving van plowed through them. Some were knocked over to fall under the churning wheels, their torsos becoming pulverized by the weight of the large tires. Blood and gore shot out the back of the tire wells like red slush as Dale powered through the worse of the undead crowd, the steering fighting him every step of the way.

And just as quickly as it had begun, it was over and he was driving on solid ground, the zombies left behind him. He glanced in his driver's side mirror to see Lucy was still behind him, the pickup truck bouncing over a few fallen bodies. There was a ghoul on the hood of the pickup and as Dale watched, he saw someone in the back of the pickup lean forward and shoot the zombie off the hood.

The body tumbled away with half a head and the truck was free.

Swinging around the wide open area near the warehouse, he slowed near the water's edge, the waves crashing against the pylons.

Lucy slowed next to him and he looked down at her from his superior height in the cab of the moving van. She smiled wanly and her eyes reflected his concern.

"Did you see Paul anywhere?" Dale asked her.

She shook her head. "No, I thought he was with you."

"He must still be inside with Frank and Don."

"Hope so," she replied as she gazed back to the destroyed loading door of the building. The zombies were swarming inside the bay as they entered the warehouse, attracted to the gunshots coming from within.

Don, Frank and Paul were still inside the warehouse with a shitload of zombies now flooding in. On top of that, Carver's men would be closing the vise trapping the three men like rats in a cage.

Dale shook his head, realizing he had probably just left his leader to die.

And it probably didn't matter who got a hold of him either. Whether it was Carver or the living dead, Frank and the others were going to die hard no matter what.

With the truck idling, he decided he would stay for as long as possible, praying Don, Frank and Paul would soon emerge so they could all escape together.

* * *

Carver slowly moved closer, only revenge on his mind. His woman was dead and Pearson was the reason. He would see the man skinned alive if it was the last thing he did.

With each step he took, he and his people were closing in on the position of Frank and a few others of his group. He had seen the others run for it, but they could be gotten to later. After all, he knew where they lived, so to speak.

In the past few minutes, the amount of return fire had reduced drastically, but there was still danger. Already he'd lost two men and a woman from enemy fire.

But he would reach Pearson soon and then he would get his vengeance.

* * *

"I'm out, cover me while I reload!" Frank yelled to Don, who only nodded and sprayed the area in front of the crate they were behind with automatic fire. The rifle was hot in his hands and he was beginning to worry about failure.

Don, too, was looking for Paul. He knew the tall man hadn't left with the others, but he was nowhere to be seen. Don shook his head as he slapped in a new clip in an experienced instant. The quiet man hadn't struck Don as a coward and he didn't understand where Paul could have gone to. It didn't seem to be in Paul's character to run away and leave his fellow companions to die.

But he had been wrong about people before and he could only assume this was one of those times.

Spraying round after round at Carver's men, Don put Paul out of his mind. There was a battle to fight, and if they made it through alive and he met up with Paul again, he would deal with the coward then.

Don and Frank turned at the sound of metal tearing behind them and knew that was the moving van making its escape.

Frank nodded to himself. Good, at least most of his people would live to see another day and the food in the back of the moving van would keep them fed for months to come.

It was a shame he wouldn't be there to see them enjoying it, but that was the way it was. In truth, he should have been dead months ago and it was only dumb luck that had seen him this far.

Firing the Glock again and again, he knew he had only two more clips and at the rate he was shooting, either the gun would overheat or he would run out of bullets. Then he would be at the mercy of Carver and his men.

Well, perhaps the man would show mercy to Don and him and maybe even let them go. Frank chuckled under his breath and Don glanced at him, wondering what his leader could find so amusing at a time like this.

Frank was chuckling because he knew the last thing Carver would show was mercy. When his men finally reached him and Don, they would both die. The only question was: would it be hard or quick?

"I'm sorry about this, Don, I really am," Frank called to the old veteran between a break in the shooting. His back was against a crate and his butt was on the cold floor.

"It's okay, Frank, I'm an old man anyway. At least I get to go out in battle."

Don flashed him a smile and a quick nod and Frank returned it with one of his own. Then the two men spun back around, jumped up, and began firing again, while with each second that passed Carver's men inched just a little closer.

Unknown to Frank or Don, the loading dock was filling with the undead and they were slowly entering the warehouse. In less than three minutes, the first ones would be upon them and there would be no escape but death, and even that was a tenuous prospect in a world where the dead walked.

* * *

Paul wasn't running away, in fact, he was heading straight for the enemy.

When he saw Carver's men begin charging forward, spraying Frank and the others in his group without mercy, he'd fallen back and had decided to try and circle around Carver, wanting to flank the man and his people.

He had made it to the next aisle, the crates blocking him from view when he was blocked by five zombies.

He recognized three of them as part of Frank's group, but the other two he didn't know. Either way they were now all the enemy. With treacle-like movements they surrounded him and it was only their numbers that made them dangerous.

Paul raised the Winchester, wanting to even the odds when he stopped. If he fired at the ghouls, the gunshots would alert Carver's men he was there and that he couldn't do, so with his rifle in his left hand, he punched the first ghoul in the chin with his right. The head rocked to the side by the blow, dislocating the zombie's jaw, but the dead man was barely fazed. Spitting out teeth like they were sunflower seeds after the flavor was gone, the ghoul continued forward. Spinning on his left foot, Paul kicked with his right, knocking a dead woman off her feet. She fell back and crashed against a box, only the staccato of gunfire filling the warehouse hiding her fall. Her hand punched through the box and white rice poured out, the bags inside the container ripped by the woman's hand.

Paul punched two more ghouls in the body and face and then he was past them, running towards an uneven stack of crates and boxes. With the ghouls right behind him, he climbed onto the first crate and then ascended until he was on top of the aisle. The ghouls tried to follow, but they could only hop up the few inches to reach the first crate, their muscles now not up to the task.

"Tough luck, suckers," Paul said under his breath as he ran across the crates, keeping low so he wouldn't be spotted from below.

He stopped at the middle of the warehouse and gazed down at the fight below. From his vantage point, he could see Don and Frank trapped behind their pockmarked crates; the bullets making them look like pincushions. He gazed to the opposite end to see Carver and his men moving slowly forward. From where Paul was, he could see Frank and Don were vastly outnumbered. Paul dropped prone on the crate and prepared to start picking his shots at the opposing force when he spotted the first of the zombies entering the warehouse from the loading dock.

They shuffled into the warehouse, their heads looking every which way, but they all moved in the same direction, namely right for Frank and Don. Both men didn't know what was coming up behind them as the sound of gunfire overrode the moans of the undead.

Paul quickly realized whatever plans he had to even the odds with Carver were meaningless now. Even if he killed Carver and his people, there were still dozens of zombies to deal with.

No, he needed to find a way to save Frank and Don, and then get them all out of the warehouse alive.

His eyes played over the area and then he spotted the forklift sitting alone to the left side of the building. An idea began to form in his mind and Paul jumped up and ran across the crates, his destination now the forklift.

He knew his idea was risky, and if the forklift didn't start then all was lost before it began, but he knew he had to try.

If he didn't, then Frank and Don were as good as dead.

* * *

Frank fired again and again at Carver's people, and when his clip went dry, he dropped back down to change it. He was on his last one and he knew the fight was almost over. Next to him, Don fired his second to last clip for his rifle, as well, and the man's face was grim.

As Frank dropped down behind the crate, he turned around and his mouth dropped open when he saw the wall of undead coming towards him and Don. They were about thirty feet away and as he gazed around for an escape, he saw there was none. The ghouls were splitting up, some heading toward Carver's men and already Carver had to stop firing at Frank and begin shooting the zombies or risk being overwhelmed himself.

Carver's screams of rage at the distraction overrode the gunshots and Frank had to wonder just why the man wanted him so badly.

"Don, behind you!" Frank shouted, and the veteran turned and began spraying the ghouls with round after round. Bodies danced a jig of death and most fell to the ground with head shots, but Don had rushed his shots and most missed.

Cursing his bad aim, he popped out the empty clip and slammed in his last one

"Jesus, Frank, how the hell are we supposed to get out of this?" Don asked as he fired in single shot, trying to save ammunition.

"I don't know, I really don't," Frank replied while shooting an old woman in the head, her skull snapping back where she dropped to the floor, her open cranium now leaking a black vicious fluid that had once been blood.

At first, he didn't hear the sound of the small engine, but as it grew closer, he realized that was what it was. Focusing on the engine through the noise of the gunshots, he could hear it coming closer with each passing second. Then he heard the squeal of rubber on the cement floor and he yelped in surprise when the crates to his right exploded outward, knocking their contents across the floor. Canned vegetables and bags of rice went everywhere, some getting under the feet of the ghouls and causing them to trip.

Frank had turned away when the crates had exploded outward, but now he turned back and was shocked to see Paul in the driver's seat of the forklift.

The man had used it like a plow and now he spun it towards the approaching ghouls.

Hydraulics whined as the two blades of the forklift rose to stomach height and then Paul drove straight into the crowd of walking corpses. The blades weren't razor sharp, but they were more than a match for the rotting bodies before him and the blades bit deep into abdomens and chests, spearing each ghoul as he made his way through the crowd.

The zombies he missed tried to reach him and he punched and kicked at them, then pulled his Colt and shot a few in the face.

When he had moved through the crowd, he had six zombies on each blade, the ghouls trapped like speared fish. Raising the blades a few inches higher, the ghouls kicked their legs ineffectually.

Paul spun around with the forklift and then began to head back into the deepest crowd of ghouls yet again. Frank watched and had no idea why Paul would do this when he heard the hydraulics whine and the blades began to move together again. With the ghouls twitching helplessly in the air, the blades closed until they had connected to make one blade in the middle of the forklift, and when this happened, the ghouls were cut in half like a hot knife through butter.

Torsos fell one way and lower halves dropped to the floor to flop around. Blood gushed across the concrete and organs plopped into the pools of plasma like a baseball into a puddle of water.

Paul never slowed.

With the blades now free of bodies, he headed back into the fray, spearing twelve more corpses like fish in a barrel. Once he had his catch, he closed the blades again, severing bodies in half. He repeated this process three more times and when he was done, there was an unbelievable stink of death permeating the air, the redolence of rot so strong it overrode any stench of decay the zombies carried with them on any given day.

With a large part of the zombies down and out, Paul jumped out of the forklift, letting the machine keep moving. The blades speared three more ghouls and then crashed into the far wall, the ghouls flopping around like rag dolls.

Paul never noticed.

Running to Frank and Don, he pointed to the exit.

"I think it's time to go," he said, his voice low and calm.

"Yeah, I think you're right," Frank replied. He didn't know what to say to the visceral sight he had just witnessed and he was still in mild shock. The way the bodies had been sliced in two, the top halves still crawling around as the organs and intestines slid out behind them like long snakes was hard to see, even after all the months of death he'd witnessed. There was what seemed like gallons of black and semi-red blood covering the floor now and the only way to the exit was through that gore pond.

"Then let's get the fuck out of here," Don said as he grabbed Frank by the arm and began pulling the man along.

Paul was right behind them, and as the three men splashed through the pools of blood, their boots and legs became soaked in gore and gobbets of flesh. The upper halves of the ghouls tried to reach up and grab their legs, but they had no leverage. Paul kicked a few in the face who were too close and the three men made a run for the now mostly empty loading dock.

Any ghouls that were too close got shot or kicked out of the way. All three men knew the goal was to escape, not to kill every zombie in their path.

Powering ahead, the three men ran.

* * *

Carver fired at the approaching ghouls, yelling at the top of his lungs. He was losing his chance at vengeance and as he shot yet another zombie in the face, he lost sight of where Frank was.

Then he spotted Paul driving around with the forklift and he had tried to shoot him, but every time he tried to line up a shot the damn forklift would turn suddenly. There was no chance to get a good shot in without having more time to aim and a moving target was even harder.

Plus, the zombies were everywhere and he was quickly realizing it might be time to retreat, however distasteful that would feel.

Then he saw the tall man jump off the forklift and run back to the crates. A second later he saw Frank and another man, along with the tall man, running to the far exit.

He lined up a shot, wanting to kill Pearson and get his revenge for Lynn when a zombie stumbled in front of the escaping man. Carver fired anyway and instead of the bullet finding Pearson's back, the bullet found the zombie. The ghoul spun on its feet and dropped to the floor, splashing blood everywhere.

Cursing, Carver tried to line up another shot, but it was too late. Pearson and the others were at the loading dock and were disappearing through the swinging doors.

Screaming his rage and anger to the ceiling, he shot a ghoul in the mouth, blowing the top of its head clean off, then turned to his people.

"Let's get the fuck out of here! They're gone!"

As one group, the men and the few women remaining began a controlled retreat, firing at the approaching ghouls as they went. But their superior firepower easily outmatched the stumbling dead bodies and it wasn't long before Carver was back at the rear of the warehouse again.

Slinging his weapon, he leaned over and picked up Lynn's still body, cradling her gently in his arms. He brushed the hair off her face and wiped the blood splatter from her cheeks with his thumb, then he moved through the exit and out onto the back alley where his men were waiting with the vehicles. All around the three trucks, bodies were strewn about. The men had been busy guarding the vehicles, taking out any ghouls who came too close.

Gently, Carver set Lynn in the back of one of the trucks and then climbed into the driver's seat.

All around him was motion as the rest of his people boarded the vehicles and prepared to leave.

Turning over the engine, Carver drove off, not caring if his people were following him. They were, but he was in a world of his own. With Lynn lying dead behind him, he felt hollow. There was now an empty hole in his heart that he knew could never be filled.

Well, maybe one thing might fill it.

Vengeance.

With his jaw taut with anger and loss, he headed back to the enclave.

There would be time to take care of Pearson later, but for now he needed to bury his woman.

* * *

Frank, Don and Paul dashed into the loading dock, pushing zombies out of their way like linebackers.

"There! Dale's Camaro!" Frank yelled as he shot a dead man in the face and ran for the driver's door of the car.

Don and Paul were right behind, and after shooting the closest zombies, all three men climbed inside. The keys were in the ignition and Frank turned the engine over, the powerful eight cylinder motor starting on the first try.

Without asking if the other two were ready, he floored the pedal, knocking bodies away from the car and more than one corpse rolling over the hood to fall away. Then he was out into the daylight and he breathed a breath of freedom.

Across the lot, he saw the moving van and pickup truck and he frowned, but then he saw Dale and Lucy waving and decided what they did was fine. They just wanted to make sure Frank and the others had made it out in one piece.

Frank drove towards the moving van, but he didn't slow down. As he approached the two vehicles, he flashed his headlights and beeped the horn, then sped by on his way back to the County Building. Dale swung the van around and followed, Lucy following in the rear position with the pickup.

In the driver's seat, Frank leaned back and glanced at Paul, who was cramped in the back seat, his long legs not having enough room.

"I got worried there for a minute, Paul. I thought you'd taken off on us," Frank said. Frank was looking in the rearview mirror and Paul's cold eyes gazed back.

"Even if I had considered that, Frank, I wouldn't leave without Francesca or the baby. You should've known that."

"Yeah, guess you're right, sorry," he said as he maneuvered through the deserted streets of Pittsburgh.

Paul leaned forward, staring at the side of Frank's face.

"You said these runs go smoothly, that wasn't smooth, what else aren't you telling me," he growled with anger. "Who was that guy leading those raiders, was that Carver?"

Frank didn't reply, his jaw tight.

"Hey, Paul, it's not his fault," Don said, defending Frank. "Yeah, that was Carver, and he's been a thorn in our side from day one."

"So then you knew we might get attacked by that guy and you didn't tell me? Why the hell not?" Paul snapped.

"Because you didn't need to know, that's why. Look, I fucked up and people died, get over it," Frank said coldly, his own anger seething within himself for the people he'd lost; good people who had relied on him to keep them safe.

Paul's jaw went taut, but he didn't reply. Instead, he leaned back and rested his head on the back seat. He closed his eyes and let out a deep sigh.

Frank watched the man for another second in his rearview mirror and then pulled his attention back to the road. He glanced to Don who only nodded in reply. The man was already checking his weapon, making sure it was still in working order.

Frank's brow creased as he thought about everything that had happened. The more he thought about it, the more he realized it wasn't his fault, it was Carver's fault. Evidently, he couldn't ignore the man anymore. Something would have to be done about him sooner or later, preferably sooner.

As if to echo his own thoughts, Don reached out and touched his arm.

"Hey, that wasn't your fault back there. Next time we need to plan a little better," Don said softly so Paul wouldn't hear.

Frank only nodded in reply and then concentrated on driving, weaving in and out of the derelict cars and shambling corpses that littered the streets of the steel city.

By a miracle of fate, the three of them had managed to survive certain death, and though they had lost a lot of good people today, they had found enough food to feed the rest for many months.

It wasn't a perfect day, but it wasn't the worst.

So hoping to get his spirits up, and resolving to make things better the next time, Frank popped in an eight track tape of Styx, then leaned back to let the music clear his mind.

Behind him, Paul snored as the tall man drifted off to sleep, only his battle-hardened nerves from years as a police officer allowing him the will to calm down enough to get some rest.

Chapter 25

Like an ebony cloak, darkness enveloped the city of Pittsburgh, hiding the desolation like a sheet over a cadaver.

On the roof of the City Courts Building, Ben Carver stared at the body of Lynn Hopkins, the woman he had loved more than life itself. Next to him stood David O'Hara, his leather biker jacket zipped up to stave off the cold wind gusting over the rooftop like an icy hand.

Behind O'Hara, seven more people all stood silently watching. Fred Sherman, Dax and five of the closest friends Lynn had were all waiting for Carver to send her off to whatever waited in the next life.

In the middle of the roof was Lynn's corpse, now cleaned and dressed in her favorite outfit. Her hair had been washed and styled, her face adorned with makeup, and the bullet holes in her neck were hidden by a red scarf.

The hole in her ear where Carver had plunged the knife into her brain was covered by her hair, and from a casual glance she looked like she was just sleeping.

Her body lay on a pile of wood and cardboard and the errant smell of gasoline could be detected if a person was standing downwind of the funeral pyre.

In Carver's right hand he held a burning torch, the flames flickering in the wind.

He walked the few feet separating him from his lost love, and when he was standing over her, he leaned over and gently kissed her still lips. One lone tear rolled down his cheek to fall onto her closed right eyelid and when he stepped away it looked just like she was crying.

Without looking back to the others, he lowered the torch and set the kindling ablaze.

With the gasoline soaking the wood and cardboard, the fire surrounded the body in an instant. Carver stood back, the heat singeing the hair on his arms and watched his love burning.

Her hair went first, turning to ash and then her skin began to char. Soon her clothes were aflame, cooking the flesh beneath and the sickly sweet smell of charred meat filled the rooftop.

He stared mournfully as the skin on her face was burned away, revealing the skull beneath. He never moved as the organs inside the body bubbled and cooked, the heart and kidneys popping like firecrackers as the moisture inside them expanded and exploded.

As the minutes passed by, the others slowly moved away, heading back down into the building. But Carver never moved, never so much as blinked while he watched Lynn's still body become nothing but ash.

Eventually the fire waned and he watched the skull slip to the side, falling off the pyre to roll and land near his feet.

Reaching down, he picked up the blackened skull, ignoring the pain in his hands as the searing heat burned his palms. He stared at the empty eye sockets where her glorious blue eyes had once been, at least until they had popped and oozed out of the skull from the heat of the fire.

Without saying a word, he walked back to the dying pyre and set the skull back where it belonged.

When he was finished, he turned to see O'Hara still standing exactly where he had been before the fire had been lit.

"You didn't have to stay," Carver said in a cold voice.

"Yeah, man, I know, but I did. She was my friend, too."

Carver nodded and then glanced down at his seared palms, the lines of the skull now indented into his flesh. Already bubbles could be seen where the skull had burned him. He raised his hands to his face and then squeezed them, popping the blisters and causing the fists to weep as the moisture slid between his fingers.

"I want Pearson dead, Dave, and everything he holds dear. When I get through with him, everyone he loves will die in the flames of Hell when I bring everything down on his head." His eyes flared with hatred as he spoke and O'Hara knew to remain silent and listen. When Carver seemed to be finished, Dave spoke up.

"Okay, I'm all for it, but exactly how are we gonna do it? That building they're in is as barricaded as ours. If it wasn't, we would've done something about them before this."

Carver nodded, his jaw firm while his mind raced with how he could kill his mortal enemy.

Then his face lightened as an idea caressed the forefront of his mind. He began to smile, slowly at first and then wider until his teeth flashed in the moonlight.

"I got it, Dave, I know what to do. Go get Dax, I need him. And then get the others together. When we go, I want every damn person in this building with us. This will be an all or nothing assault and if anyone says they won't be a part of it then toss their ass out into the street. This is for Lynn, and most of all this is so we can end this shit once and for all."

Carver's eyes reflected the last remaining flames from the funeral pyre and O'Hara thought the fires of Hell were burning inside his head.

"When we get through with Pearson, only one group will be left standing and I'm gonna make damn sure it's us."

"Okay, when do we do this?" O'Hara asked.

"Now, damn it, right fucking now. We start now and I want to be ready by morning, before the sun comes up. I want to hit them when they're the most vulnerable." He checked his watch. "Do you know what time the sun comes up?"

O'Hara shrugged. "Not exactly, about six or so, why?"

"Good, then we hit them at five-thirty, just before it becomes light."

He turned and gazed back at the charred corpse of the woman he loved.

"By dawn tomorrow, Pearson and the rest of his people will be nothing but ashes." He began moving back to the door leading downward and O'Hara followed. "I'm gonna get my payback for Lynn, Dave, and anyone who gets in my way is gonna fry, I swear on my life."

"We're all with ya, brother, you know that," O'Hara replied, the determination on his face apparent. He'd loved Lynn like a daughter and he would be damned if her murderer was going to get away with it.

Carver nodded, and with the flames of the funeral pyre flickering out for the last time, Carver and O'Hara left the roof, the charred body now alone with nothing but the night for company.

* * *

The moving van slowed when it reached the outskirts of the City County Building and Dale called in on the two-way radio to let the men on guard know they were back. A decoy was dropped down over the side of the building and the woman began screaming at the top of her lungs.

As the zombies wandered away, the three vehicles shot across the parking lot and into the loading dock.

The stray ghouls were dispatched and in no time all three vehicles were safely ensconced inside the bays with the doors closed once more. The decoy was pulled back up and for once everything went smoothly with no loss of life.

With the sounds of clapping and car doors opening and closing, Frank climbed out of the Camaro, and before he took two steps, Lucy jumped into his arms, almost bowling him over as she gave him a big kiss on the cheek.

"We thought you guys were goners," she said as she hugged him tight. Dale moved up next to them, and after shaking Don's hand and slapping Paul on the back, he shook Frank's hand.

"So, just how the hell did you manage to get out of there, Frank?" Dale asked.

Frank gestured to Paul who stood on the fringe of the group. The activity inside the loading dock was hectic as men and women began off-loading the supplies from the moving van. Ronny was led away to Timothy who would get his ear patched up.

"It was all him," Frank said, gesturing to Paul. "He saved our asses and then some."

Paul shrugged. "It was nothin'. I did what I had to do. Hell, you guys were my ride back here. If you died then I was walkin'."

That elicited a bout of laughter and everyone moved up to the door leading into the building.

Paul looked up to see Francesca at the door and he strode over to her while others slapped him on the back and congratulated him.

"Are you all right?" Francesca asked while she cradled baby Shaun. She could see the blood splatter on his clothing and the dirt covering his face and arms. He looked like he'd been through a war and had barely made it out alive.

"I'm fine, Francesca, really. Some shit went down on the run and I don't think it's over, just stay sharp, okay?"

"Okay, just tell me what to do and when."

He nodded then changed the subject.

"So, how are you and the baby doing? You okay?"

She grinned. "We're fine. Timothy is a nurse and he checked out Shaun to make sure he's all right. He says he's fine. Shaun's perfectly healthy. And a few of the women have been really great to us. One even took Shaun for a while and let me get some rest. She even stayed in the room the entire time, knowing how protective I am of him."

Paul smiled, staring down at the sleeping baby. "That's good, Francesca, really."

She took his hand with her free one. "Come on; let's get you cleaned up and into some new clothes. Are you hungry? I got some canned food from the kitchen and it's all ready for you."

He nodded and followed her.

Thinking about the food she had prepared for him, he couldn't help but comment on it.

"You remember when you told me, Richard and Shaun that you weren't gonna be our den mother? That you wouldn't be just the maid, cooking and cleaning all day? So what happened to change your mind?"

Francesca shrugged while she walked slightly in front of him. She stopped and turned, gazing up at his taciturn face and she glanced down to the baby in her arms.

"This happened, Paul. That's all. I'm still me, but I'm bending some more, that's all. If I can't go out and fight with you, then I can still do other things." She smiled again, a twinkle in her eye. "At least until he's old enough to be on his own. Then I'm right back with you."

Paul smiled; his teeth white in the gloom of the hallway. "Wouldn't have it any other way, Francesca." She spun around and continued on to their room, while behind them, the supplies were offloaded and people felt uplifted. True, they had lost many of their group this day, but with their sacrifice the rest would live for many days to come.

It wasn't a perfect world, but it was all they had left.

* * *

It was just a little before five A.M. when Carver and the rest of his people headed out to attack Pearson's enclave.

It had been a long night of working on the two vehicles Carver had wanted to use for the attack.

The first one was a massive cement mixer that had been parked only a block away in an abandoned construction site. It hadn't taken long too jump-start the battery and get it running again while keeping off any zombies trying to attack. The cement inside the large bowl of the cement truck was now hard and useless, but the vehicle itself was still massive and would serve well for what he had in mind.

Next to him in the passenger seat, David O'Hara rode in silence. It had been a long night banging out the plan Carver had finally settled on and the man was tired.

But despite this, he was ready for what would come next. Lynn would be avenged and so too would Frank Pearson's enclave be destroyed. When the sun rose in a few hours, there would only be Carver's people left in the city and whatever supplies they found hereafter would now only be theirs.

Behind the cement truck, in the transit bus that had been found parked and empty a few streets over from the cement truck, rode the rest of Carver's people. They had been told what was going down and all were onboard, realizing if Pearson's group wasn't taken out, then they would always be fearful for their lives.

Zombies were one thing, but no man or woman wanted to have to worry about getting shot every time they went out on a foraging mission.

In the first seat of the bus was Dax and next to the man, in a wooden crate, was all the dynamite he had been saving in the armory. On top of the dynamite he had blasting caps and he knew they were integral to Carver's plan. If Dax didn't do his job, then the entire operation would go down in flames. The bus was packed with men and women with bleary eyes, grim faces and every firearm from the armory.

All knew what was to come and all were ready.

When they reached Pearson's enclave there would be nothing less than all out war. A war that would see only one side victorious. There would be no compromise and there would be no mercy shown.

The cement truck plowed through the city streets, crushing zombies like they were made of paper. By the time Carver was a mile from the City County Building, the front of the cement truck was covered in red, brown and black ichor, gobbets of flesh catching in the serrated grille. Flesh steamed on the radiator causing the inside of the cab to stink. Carver rolled his window down and continued onward.

The cement truck crashed through the streets, nothing short of a tank on wheels, and cars were pushed to the side in a rending crash of metal as if they weighed nothing. The transit bus powered along behind, the two vehicles headlights slicing through the darkness.

Twenty-five minutes later, they had reached the edge of the parking lot leading to Pearson's building. The City County Building was in a secluded part of town, surrounded on three sides by asphalt, while the last side had two more one-story buildings which were used for storage and office space.

Carver had to give the man credit for where he had decided to hole up. The County Building was as good a place as any and Carver could see the place looked well barricaded.

"Dave, hand me those binocs, will ya?" Carver asked.

O'Hara handed the black binoculars to Carver who raised them to his eyes. Focusing them into the night, Carver could see how the first floor was securely barricaded and see the metal and wood over the main doors of the building. He also saw all the bodies moving about the building. There were a lot of them, but not so many he would stop his plans.

Just one more obstacle to be dealt with.

He picked up the two-way radio and called the transit bus.

Fred Sherman answered. He was driving the bus. He once did a stint as a school bus driver and was comfortable behind the wheel of the large vehicle. No one had objected so he got the job.

"Go 'head, Carver," Fred said through the radio.

"Put Dax on now," Carver said impatiently.

There was a pause while Carver assumed Dax was getting the radio and then Dax came on.

"Go ahead, Carver, this is Dax."

"Good, Dax. Okay. So you know what to do, right?"

"Yeah, Carver, I got it," Dax replied.

"Well tell me one more time. I don't want you fucking this up."

Dax sighed into the radio and then began to talk.

"Okay, so after you crash through the front of the building, I wait while some of the other guys take out any zombies that are too close. Then I get inside with the guys I picked and I'm gonna strap the dynamite to the foundation of the building. Then, when you tell me, I'm gonna blow the sticks and cause the building to collapse in on itself."

Carver waited for more and when it didn't come he nodded. "Good, Dax, just make sure you do it to the letter, no fuck-ups."

"'Kay," Dax replied.

"Put Fred back on," Carver said into the radio.

A second later Sherman was on the radio again.

"Yeah, Carver?"

"You got all that, right?"

"Yeah, man, we're ready here."

"Okay, make sure everyone does what they're supposed to do. And remember, no one kills Pearson, he's mine."

"Got it," Sherman said.

Carver tossed the two-way back to Dave who placed it on the dashboard. The man had an automatic rifle in his hands and extra clips strapped to his body. He also wore a large Magnum on his hip.

Carver had his shotgun and on his hip he wore Lynn's .38. If all went as planned he hoped to kill Pearson with it.

Surging the engine, he placed the transmission in first and began rolling towards the building.

With each yard he crossed, the truck began to move faster. It was a ponderous beast, but the ground was level and the engine was powerful. The cement trapped inside the bowl only added to the weight, making the cement truck one massive battering ram.

"Hold on, this is gonna get rough," Carver told O'Hara who placed his hands on the dashboard for support. Behind them, the transit bus followed, but from a safe distance. The plan was for Carver to crash through the first floor of the building and then the transit bus would stop near the opening and everyone would rush into the building and attack all they found, killing them easily as they would all be sleeping.

The cement truck's engine growled under its hood and Carver floored the pedal, shifting to a higher gear. They were moving at a good forty miles an hour with more speed gaining with each passing second.

And then the large vehicle was entering the crowd of zombies as they turned to attack the cement truck. Bodies flew off in all directions as the bumper and grille swatted them off their feet like flies. Heads were snapped off shoulders and arms and legs were crushed under the massive tires, leaving human road kill in their wake. The radiator steamed with the generous coating of blood on it and Carver winced at the odor.

Then the building was in his windshield and he braced himself for the impact. Just before the front tires jumped the curb and the front bumper of the cement truck impacted with the building, he thought of Lynn and silently wished she could be here to share in his victory.

Then he was thrown against the steering wheel as the heavy vehicle plowed into the first floor lobby of the building.

The barricaded doors and windows were no match for the thousands of pounds of steel and the cement truck drove into the main lobby easily. Pieces of stone, metal and miscellaneous debris flew everywhere, and inside the cab, Carver and O'Hara were tossed about like rag dolls.

When the cement truck came to a screeching halt, the radiator was hissing steam and differential fluid was spilling out of the undercarriage like blood.

Carver was dazed for just a second until he slowly forced himself to come to his senses. The front windshield had exploded upon impact, the cab bending and twisting like a child's plastic toy truck. Both door windows were shattered and Carver could taste dust.

A dead, pale face popped up where his driver's window once was and a growl issued from the blackened mouth filled with rotting teeth. Carver picked his shotgun up from off the floor and shoved the barrel into the ghoul's mouth, breaking off the front teeth like they were made of glass. He pulled the trigger at the same time as he pushed the weapon into the fetid orifice.

The top of the zombie's head disappeared in a spray of blood, bone and brain matter, and the remaining lower portion of the head swayed back and forth. The tongue was still there and it flopped upward like a dead fish until the body toppled over to the debris strewn floor of the lobby.

"You okay?" Carver asked O'Hara as he prepared to get out of the cab.

O'Hara nodded. "Yeah, man, let's get this done," He had a small cut on his forehead, but he didn't know it was there and Carver wasn't about to tell him. It was a small wound and the man would live.

Opening his door, Carver stepped out of the cab of the truck, the gloom pervasive to the point he could barely see. By some miracle, one of the headlights still worked and the unbroken lens bathed the lobby in a soft glow. Carver looked behind him to see more zombies spilling through the large gap the cement truck had made, but he also saw the transit bus. As he watched, the bus' door opened and his people spilled out, shooting down any ghouls they could see. He saw Dax come running towards him, three men behind him.

Carver knew the men and also knew they would look after Dax.

"Get moving, Dax, and don't fuck it up," Carver snapped and then shot a dead woman in the face as she tried to crawl out from under the cement truck. Half her face disappeared in a brilliant spray of blood, the pink plasma particles hanging in the air like a fine mist.

"I won't," Dax said simply and headed for the stairwell leading to the basement. It was easily marked and it took only seconds for

him to find and get through the door, the other three men right
behind him. A few zombies followed them, but once they reached
the door they stopped, not understanding how to operate the
handle.

Carver turned away to search for another stairwell, one that
would take him to the upper floors of the building.

His eyes spotted the sign for the stairwell and he called out to
his people. When he had their attention, he moved out, leaving a
few behind to hold the lobby. The people staying behind knew to
only stay until it got too hard to stop the oncoming ghouls, then
they were to fall back to the bus and wait inside for the rest of them
to come back out. Then Carver would have Dax blow the building
and the war would be over forever.

With twenty people behind him, Carver dashed across the
lobby, avoiding bodies and crushed stone, then opened the stairwell door and ran upwards. Behind him, the heavy footsteps of his
people came to his ears. Once they reached the upper floors, his
people would fan out and begin systematically slaughtering the
enclave. The only rule was not to kill children. If they found any
children, they could bring them back with them. After all, if the
human race was to survive, children were needed; especially
babies.

He grinned while he climbed.

If Pearson didn't know he was here before, then he damn sure
knew he was here now. And when Carver found him, Pearson
would die slow and hard.

* * *

Paul was startled awake the moment the cement truck crashed
into the building. Though he didn't know what had happened, he
knew it couldn't be good.

As he struggled to wake up, his mind raced with the reason for
the building to shake like that.

Grenades, bombs and a dozen other ideas floated through his
head and none of them came out with a positive result.

A small flame appeared in the darkness and Francesca lit a
candle, bathing the room in a suffuse glow.

"What happened?" she asked groggily. Baby Shaun was sleeping soundly next to her and she blinked away sleep.

"Don't know, but whatever it is, it can't be good," Paul said as he began dressing. He only had his pants on and his tan skin reflected the candle light, showing his muscled torso. He was in excellent shape and had stayed that way even after ending up at the office complex. Playing handball on the main roof and jogging around its interior, plus lifting weights in the employee gym, he had made sure he stayed at the peak of physical conditioning. And that was why he had survived for as long as he had.

Strapping on his Colt and slinging the Winchester over his shoulder, he moved to Francesca who was sitting up, not moving.

"Francesca, listen to me and listen good. Get all your stuff together and you and the baby get up to the roof."

"The roof? But why?"

"There's no time to explain in detail. Whatever that explosion was it can't be good. Get to the copter, get it running, and wait there for me. If I don't come up and get you or if anything happens you don't like, take off and don't come back."

"What? Paul, no, I can't, not like this, it's just like back at the complex, when you..."

"No, Francesca it's not like at the complex, I promise. Now please, just go, and go fast before whatever's happening gets up here. And if you see anyone come onto the roof that shouldn't be there, you go."

She saw the angst in his face in the dim candlelight and nodded, knowing he was right. When Paul knew she would do as he requested, he gathered all the ammunition he could carry and headed for the door.

"Remember, if anything at all..." he began but she cut him off.

"Yes, Paul, I got it, I will," she said though her heart wasn't in it. But she had to think of baby Shaun now.

Paul opened the door, and with one last glance at Francesca, stepped into the dark hallway.

The instant he stepped into the hall, he heard the distant sound of gunfire coming from the floor below. Knowing if the people he had taken refuge with died then so too would the haven for him and Francesca, he charged off to join the fray, hoping he could help in some small way.

*   *   *

Francesca climbed the stairs to the roof, and when she was at the door, she stepped out into the moonlight, the cool breeze immediately drying the sweat on her face. Dust was in the air and she knew it was from whatever had happened to cause the building to shake. Stepping out onto the roof itself, she began walking, baby Shaun cradled in her arms. Her rifle was slung over her shoulder but her .45 was nowhere to be seen.

She was almost to the helicopter when two men stepped out from behind the aircraft. They had been inspecting it. Both held firearms, one a rifle, the other a handgun. Their faces were hidden in the shadows of the helicopter, but their posture and the way they aimed their weapons at her made their intentions clear.

"Well, well, well, look what we got here," one man said to the other. When he moved closer to Francesca, she could see the man needed braces and his face was streaked with dirt.

"Looks like we got ourselves one sweet piece of ass," the other replied as he licked his lips. If he hadn't been threatening her, she would have called him handsome, but as it was, she barely noticed his looks, only the rifle in his hands mattering.

"And will ya look at that," the first man said. "She got a baby with her. Didn't Carver say we need to bring all the kids to him?"

"That he did," the handsome man replied.

The man with the bad teeth grinned lecherously and rubbed his crotch with his free hand as he eyed Francesca.

"Well, I don't see why we can't have some fun with her before we take the rugrat to Carver," he said heavily.

"Works for me," the handsome man said.

The entire time the two men were talking, she never moved, but held baby Shaun in her arms protectively. The two men were moving closer to her, not worrying about her in the least. After all, she had her hands full with the baby and her rifle was slung uselessly over her shoulder. She was as helpless as a woman could be.

"I want first dibs," the crooked teeth man said as he stepped so close to Francesca she could smell his body odor.

Handsome man couldn't see Francesca for a second as his partner was now in his way, blocking his view, but he heard the gunshot a second later and didn't understand what was happening. Crooked teeth turned around then and faced his buddy and the man saw a bright red spot where crooked teeth's heart was located under his shirt.

Crooked Teeth swayed for a moment and then dropped to the roof, dead, his heart nothing but shredded meat.

Handsome man was in shock for only a second and then he raised his rifle to fire at Francesca, but she was already moving. As the man tried to squeeze the trigger on the rifle, she had already fired her own gun for the second time.

The bullet struck the man in the nose, obliterating his handsome features in a spray of blood. The back of his head exploded outward, the tuft of scalp riding on the wind to roll away across the helipad.

He slumped to the roof, dead.

Francesca sighed heavily and cradled baby Shaun as he began to cry, startled from the gunshots going off so close to him.

There were two small bullet holes in the bottom of the baby's blanket, and Francesca pulled her arm out, the smoking .45 still in her hand. She congratulated herself on her foresight for not wanting to take any chances.

She was through being a victim; those days were long gone.

The crooked toothed man began to stir again, his eyes opening once more. This time he didn't speak, as his brain wasn't functioning like before. Though his heart had stopped, the rest lived on after death and the newly revived ghoul tried to regain his footing.

Francesca took a step closer to the struggling body and shot the zombie point-blank in the forehead. The head snapped back and the body slumped to the roof, red blood spilling out; the plasma looking black in the moonlight.

With baby Shaun crying, she shook him and hugged him while she stepped over the prone corpses and moved to the helicopter. She remembered what Shaun had taught her and knew she needed to do a quick pre-flight test before the helicopter would be ready to fly, then all she could do was wait and hope Paul would be arriving soon.

Chapter 26

Frank was dreaming again, this time about how things were before the dead walked. The sun was high in the sky and he was walking in a golden field of daisies.

But all of a sudden, while he watched, the sky began to darken and lightning flashed, leaving silver streaks across his vision.

Thunder crackled overhead like dynamite was going off and he remembered a fond memory of sitting on his father's lap on the back porch of their house in Fairmont. Every time the thunder roared, his father would tell him the angels were bowling. And being young and naïve, he would nod, believing everything his father told him.

Then he felt the first rain drops fall on his face, followed by more thunder cracking and he closed his eyes to avoid being blinded by the flashes of lightning dancing across the sky.

And when he opened his eyes, he was back from the dream world and slammed back into reality.

The thunder was still cracking only it wasn't thunder.

It was something else.

A book sitting on a desk over his bedroll was knocked off to tumble onto his chest. That woke him up for real and he sat up, searching for the origination of the noise. He could feel the vibration through his body, coming from the floor below him and he knew something had happened, something bad.

Jumping up, he dressed in seconds and charged out into the hallway. Don was there, the man half dressed. He was about to bang on Frank's door to wake him.

"What the hell is going on?" Frank asked the war veteran.

"Don't know, but it shook the goddamn building to the core," Don replied. "Pieces of the damn ceiling fell on me and woke me up."

Frank ran to the closest window in the hallway, but all he saw outside was darkness.

"Shit, we need to find out what's happening and make sure everyone's okay."

Footsteps sounded from down the hall and both men looked up to see Marc racing for them at top speed.

The man slowed when he saw them and he pointed back to the stairwell.

"Frank, Don, oh, shit, you won't believe this, but a friggin' truck just crashed into the first floor lobby."

"What? How?" Don snapped impatiently.

Marc held up his hand for Don to stop talking "Wait, it gets worse. Carver's the guy who drove it. I was on the second floor when I heard the crash so I ran downstairs. I saw him climb out of the truck, and it gets worser still. The hole he made in the building....well, the zombies are coming inside. I don't know if they're anywhere but on the first floor, but all they have to do is go up the stairwells and they're up here with us."

"Shit, that crazy bastard!" Frank yelled. "What the hell does he think he's doing? He'll get us all killed!"

Marc shook his head, not having an answer.

"I think that's what he wants to do, Frank," Don said simply.

Frank bit his lip, trying to come up with what they should do next and then he grabbed Marc by the shoulders as ideas flooded his mind. They had to act fast before all was lost.

"Get to the others and tell them what's happened. Protect the kids and the rest need to be armed. We have to stop Carver and the zombies or everything we've built here is gonna be shit."

"Right," Marc said and took off down the hallway.

Frank turned and dashed back into his office, donning every weapon he had. His Glock was first, plus an old .22 rifle he used mainly for practice, plus a small Derringer and the nine inch Bowie knife used mostly for opening cans.

When he had everything he could carry, he nodded to Don to do the same.

"Get your weapons, Don, this is gonna get worse before it gets better."

Don took off at a run, his legs moving slowly despite the man's will to want to go faster.

Frank waited with his hand on his Glock. He wanted to find Carver now, not later, and he'd be damned if he'd let the man off with a warning. No, this was it. He had attacked him in his home. When he found Carver, he would make the man pay...in blood.

Don returned two minutes later, his automatic rifle in his hands and a sidearm strapped to his waist. He even had a few grenades strapped to his belt, courtesy of an abandoned military guard post they had found a few months back.

"Okay, let's go," Frank told him and headed for the stairwell door. Don said nothing but followed, the two men now on the hunt for the intruders of their home.

*   *   *

Paul was trapped in the second floor stairwell. There were five men and one woman and they were peppering his position from down the hall. Every time he tried to fire at them, he had to duck back or risk being shot.

He knew he needed to make a move or sooner or later they would be able to reach him. All they had to do is have two or three of the attackers keep him under cover while the others moved forward, then, when he tried to take a shot at them, they would have a perfect line on him.

He took small comfort in knowing he would probably never feel the bullet that killed him.

In a lull in the barrage of rounds he took a chance and sent off a few shots of his own. He was rewarded with a scream of pain and he saw a man go down, but he was quickly dragged out of the line of fire.

Paul grunted, knowing the shot had been dumb luck, but taking it anyway.

More rounds pockmarked the wall and doorframe where he hid and he was about to retreat and try to go downstairs when he heard the distinct sound of moaning.

Pulling away from the open door for an instant, he glanced down the stairs to see the first heads of a pack of zombies making their way to his position.

"Damn it," he muttered as he watched them stagger like drunks up the stairs, bumping off the walls like they were blind.

With nowhere else to go but up, he went back to the door, fired off a few more rounds and then backtracked, running up the stairs to the next floor.

Maybe he could help there as he couldn't stay where he was. Taking the steps two at a time, he climbed higher.

* * *

Fred Sherman watched the tall Mexican man disappear from view, and when the man didn't reappear after more than a minute, he decided it was worth the chance to attack and take him out.

He remembered the tall man from the warehouse and knew Carver would reward him well if he could take the guy out, so setting up covering fire, he told two of the others to make a run for the stairwell.

With bullets chewing up the doorframe, the two men dashed for the doorway, weapons up and ready to shoot the man when they reached the stairwell. But what they thought they would find, namely one lone gunman, was not what was there.

When the two men reached the open doorway they were greeted by a dozen zombies, all packed into the stairwell like sardines. The two men began firing, panicking, but all they did was chew up torsos and limbs that already felt no pain.

Sherman watched from across the hallway as his two men tried to run away, but just as they reached the hallway, they were dragged down and overwhelmed.

"Take those dead fucks out!" Sherman yelled as he and the others around him began firing at the ghouls. Then, before he or any of his men realized it, another ten zombies popped out from behind them, swarming into the hallway and knocking him and his men to the tile floor.

Sherman tried to fire at the dead faces, but there were too many, and as he felt the first cold hands and fingernails digging into his flesh, he knew he was about to die.

As he screamed in pain, he managed to reach down for his sidearm, pulling it up through the tangled mass of hands and arms. Getting the gun under his chin, he fired the weapon, the bullet entering his lower jaw, going up through the roof of his mouth and then rebounding off his skull to exit out the side of his cheek. It wasn't a killing shot and his world was agony as his pain receptors registered the trauma to his face and head.

He didn't have time for a second shot, however, and with his face a mangled mass of blood and meat, he screamed yet again as his insides were ripped out and fed on. His throat filled with blood and he began to choke, and with his pain-filled eyes literally watching as his beating heart was plucked from his chest, he wondered if he would be going to Heaven or Hell.

Then he fell into oblivion and his thoughts dissolved like mist on the morning shore.

*   *   *

On the first floor, near the stairwell door that led to the basement, the zombies still banged on the door fruitlessly.

One of the ghouls in front, who was a little more intelligent than the others, got lucky and managed to open the door, its dead hand actually working the latch.

With the door opened, the living dead swarmed into the stairwell, some going up to where Paul was moments ago, but more going downward, as down was easier for their dead legs than climbing.

One at a time they moved down to the lower lever, and when they reached the bottom, they moved to the only door there.

Unknown to Dax and the three men guarding him, the latch had been jury rigged with duct tape so the door wouldn't close and lock. This had been because the door had locked once and had trapped one of Frank's people down there for half a day. So Frank had decided to just leave it unlocked permanently.

The zombies struck the door and pushed it open easily and then moved in to the dark basement. Across the wide open space, they could see lights bobbing in the darkness.

With their dead brains following the light like a moth to a flame, they headed towards it.

*   *   *

Dax was just finishing setting the last cement pylon with dynamite, then fitting the blasting cap, the electrical wire trailing out across the floor to the junction box.

The junction box was connected with two lantern batteries, something he had designed himself.

Knowing it wouldn't be feasible to run the wire all the way out of the building, he had jury rigged a junction box with an electrical switch.

The detonator for the box was in his hand, a simple relay with one red switch. All he had to do was flick off the protective cover on the switch and one press of his thumb would send the signal to the junction box to release its current.

When the current reached the blasting caps, the fuses would ignite and the dynamite would be set off.

He thought about the epic power he had just strapped to the pylons of the building.

Each stick of dynamite contained 2.1 million Jules of energy. In everyday terms, one Jule would be enough energy to lift a small apple a meter into the air. So with more than thirty sticks of dynamite scattered across the foundation of the building, the amount of destructive energy would have this building collapsing like a deck of playing cards.

"Hey, hold that light closer, I can't see," Dax told one of the men with him. He thought his name was Adam or something.

The man did as he was told and Dax made sure the blasting cap was secure.

Then he took a step back to admire his work.

"Okay, let's get the hell out of here," Dax told the guard.

The other two men were across the basement, investigating some boxes of supplies and paperwork. The other rooms in the basement were full of old files and the boiler room, nothing that interested Dax.

No, he needed the main part of the lower level to do his work. When the middle pylons gave out, the sheer weight of the building over his head would sag like a sand castle after a bucket of water was poured over it.

He was looking forward to seeing his handwork.

As he stared at the guard, he noticed shadows moving behind the man, and then he heard the first moans of the undead.

"What the..?" he asked while trying to pierce the darkness. With only the flashlights to see by, it was all but impossible to make out the figures.

"What are you lookin' at, Dax?" the guard asked.

Then he flashed the light in Dax's face and saw where the armorer was looking. Spinning around with the flashlight, the tight, focused beam of light flashed directly into the face of the first zombie. The pale, dead visage glared back, the milky white eyes reflecting the light of the flashlight. The skin was taut, tight against the skull and the protruding forehead made the ghoul look like a caveman wearing modern clothing.

"Holy shit!" the guard yelled and tried to get his weapon up, but even as he tried, he was attacked, three bodies surrounding him and pulling him to the floor. The flashlight fell from his hand to roll across the floor and at the man's utterance of shock; the other two guards came running back.

With the flashlight on the floor, the two men couldn't see what was happening and they flashed their own beams around as they ran back to Dax.

When they were closer, they quickly found what was happening and their flashlights illuminated the feeding frenzy of the hapless guard.

"Jesus Christ! How the fuck did they get in here?" a guard yelled. In the darkness, Dax couldn't see who it was.

"Shoot 'em; shoot 'em for God's sake!" Dax screamed as he unslung his rifle and began firing at the walking corpses.

The two guards began doing the same and the lower level was filled with a cacophony of sound and flashes of light as the three men fired round after round at the attacking ghouls.

But with almost no visibility, most of the bullets went wide, missing completely, and with the muzzle flashes from their rifles giving away their positions, the zombies attacked, pulling each man to the ground with screams for help and cries to their chosen god.

One zombie charged straight at Dax and when it tried to grab him, Dax stuck the muzzle of his rifle into its chest. Squeezing the trigger and keeping the rifle on full auto, the rounds exited the muzzle of the rifle to shoot through the zombie, then continuing onward to enter other bodies of the undead.

When he was finished with his clip, there was a fist-sized hole in the ghoul's torso. But the zombie wasn't fazed, and it continued walking, the barrel of the rifle entering the hole to stick out the back of the ghoul. With Dax face to face with the undead visage, and his rifle trapped in the gore filled hole of the zombie's body, he was helpless.

As Dax stood transfixed, the zombie dove in and sunk its teeth onto his nose. Chomping down hard, the ghoul ripped it free of Dax's face, and the armorer screamed, blood already sliding back into his sinus cavity and causing him to choke. More shapes came out of the darkness, surrounding him, forcing him to the cold floor.

He felt hands ripping into his flesh and then warmness as his blood escaped its frail prison and soaked into his clothes.

As he screamed for mercy, his hand was still holding the detonator. With his last living thought, he flicked off the plastic protector cover and pressed the switch with a bloody thumb.

He had time for one more scream and then the world went white as the blasting caps did their job, detonating the dynamite and pulverizing the pylons, the foundation of the building dissolving in an instant.

As the thunderous blast roared through the lower level of the building, the outer edges began to crack, not able to withstand the pressure now being placed upon it.

With the ceiling falling in, the City County Building began to collapse.

If his head had still been attached to his body and if he had still had a body, Dax would have been proud.

Everything had gone off perfectly

* * *

Upon reaching the third floor, Paul charged into the hallway and immediately jumped back when bullets ricocheted off the wall only inches from his head.

Damn it, he was trapped again!

Whoever was attacking the building, they were everywhere and Paul was fast running out of ideas of what he could do to help Frank or the others in the enclave.

Bodies were strewn across the floor of the hallway and Paul recognized a few of the faces from earlier in the night. They were part of the enclave and had gone down fighting. He saw Jeff lying with half his torso missing, intestines spilled across the floor like a dumped plate of spaghetti.

Sending a few rounds at his adversaries, he jumped back into the hallway to avoid being shot. Down below and behind him, he could hear the dead moving up the stairwell and he knew he was out of options once again.

He didn't want to run out on Frank and the others, but for all he knew they were all dead and he was the only one left.

He was wrestling with the decision to get to the roof and just let Francesca fly them away when he felt the building shake like a bomb had gone off, this time the feeling of the building shaking was three times worse than when the cement truck had plowed into it, and he knew something very, very, bad was happening in the lower levels of the building.

The entire hallway shifted and Paul could only guess that Pittsburgh was actually suffering from a massive earthquake.

Though unlikely, he had no idea as to what could be happening, so after ducking back into the hallway, he shot the first three ghouls climbing up the stairs and then headed for the roof, taking the stairs three at a time.

His gut was screaming at him for running away, and if he knew for sure Frank was still alive along with Don and the others, he may very possibly have turned around and tried to help them. But he didn't know and Francesca needed him. A woman and a baby alone in this undead world was tantamount to suicide. If he left her alone, he might as well sign her and the baby's death sentence.

So in the end he knew the only choice he could make, though it grated him to the bone. While he charged up the stairs, the stairwell creaking as the building shifted, he thought back to only a few days ago at the office complex. He remembered the incident like it had happened only seconds ago.

Shaun had been trapped in the east stairwell with zombies everywhere and then the radio had gone dark. After a few gun shots there had been nothing. He had agonized over going back to try and help the man, but in the end knew it was fruitless.

And when Shaun had turned up as a zombie, his assumption had been proven correct. If he had tried to save his friend, all he would have accomplished was getting himself killed in the process, leaving Francesca all alone with a baby on the way.

With the ceiling falling in around him and the stairs shifting like the building was on a massive fault line, Paul raced up the stars, praying Francesca was still there waiting for him.

*　*　*

On the second floor lobby, amidst the paintings and wall art, Frank, Don, Dale and Lucy met Carver, O'Hara and ten other men and women.

The battle was hard and fast as each group attempted to slaughter the other.

All around them bodies were spread at odd angles, casualties of the ongoing conflict and spent shell casings littered the floor.

Dale was the next casualty.

He was across the lobby, hiding behind a pillar when he saw Lucy get hit in the arm when she tried to take a shot at the enemy. Fearing for his woman, he dashed out of cover and was immediately riddled with bullets from five different guns. Lucy shrieked in pain and loss when she saw her lover go down, and not thinking, she ran out to try and help him. She made it less than five steps before she was struck repeatedly in the upper back. She went down hard, falling only a foot from Dale's cooling corpse. Her left hand reached out when she fell and her fingers touched Dale's right hand, the two holding hands in death.

Frank saw the couple go down and he screamed, taking one of Don's grenades and tossing it towards the shooters. The grenade went off three seconds later and two bloody bodies soared through the air like they had been bounced on a trampoline. They landed in a heap of bloody limbs and one dead man had half a head.

Carver saw his men blown to hell and he fired back, spraying Frank's position with hot lead. Frank ducked down lower behind the oak desk he was using for cover, feeling the rounds fly over his head, and he cursed Carver's name.

Don was to his right, firing steadily to try and keep Carver's people from trying to outflank him. The lobby was big enough they could try, but he was letting them know if they did, it would cost them dearly.

Frank stared at the bodies of Lucy and Dale, and as he watched them, he saw the fingers on Dale's right hand began to twitch.

"Ah shit, no, not them," he said as he watched what was now an everyday occurrence. Next to Dale, Lucy began to move also, and in a matter of seconds both were sitting up as rounds peppered their bodies from Carver's people. Neither seemed to notice as they slowly stood up. Dale's right leg was at an odd angle, the muscles all but destroyed from bullets, but he was managing just fine.

Lucy was in better shape, only her upper body riddled with bullet holes. With both of them dripping blood from their wounds, they turned and began stumbling towards Frank and Don.

Carver held his fire, making the rest of his people do the same. He knew what was happening and he wanted to enjoy the show, knowing what Frank would have to do.

He would have to kill his own people or risk them attacking him.

"Shoot 'em, Frank, come on, man, shoot 'em in the head. You got no choice," Don told him as he sat by his side. He didn't know why the opposition had stopped firing at him, but he was using the time well. Changing out his spent clip, he slapped in a new one, sending a round into the chamber. Meanwhile, Dale and Lucy were only a few feet away, their slow, trudging steps seeming to take forever. Behind them a slim red trail could be seen as their wounds seeped blood.

"Shit, Don, that's Dale and Lucy," Frank said as he stared at the two new zombies.

"No, Frank, it's not. Dale and Lucy died a minute ago. Those are nothing but hollow shells. Now shoot them goddammit or I will!"

Don's voice was hard and he had never spoken to Frank like that before, but like everyone else, he was under pressure and the stress would get to any man. Sure, he had fought in the jungles of

Vietnam, but he had never fought zombies and even after six months of it, whenever he was face to face with one of the undead he felt a chill go down his back.

With tears in his eyes, Frank raised his Glock, lining up Dale's slack face in his sights. He waited until the dead young man was only two feet from him and then fired. The round struck the man in the forehead and the head snapped backward. The rest of the body followed and the corpse hit the ground hard, the skull smacking the tile floor hard. Lucy was next, and though she was dead, she was still beautiful. Her blonde tresses had fallen over her face to partly hide her slack-jawed look, but Frank knew she was as dead as Dale.

The bullet holes in her torso were proof of that.

With heartfelt sorrow, he waited while she moved around Dale's body and when she was only a foot away, so close he could see the irises of her dead eyes, he shot her in the face, sending her back to where ever she had come from only moments ago. She slumped to the floor and landed on top of Dale, the two young lovers together forever, and then Frank turned and looked over the desk he was behind to yell across the lobby.

"You bastard, you no good bastard! They were my friends! Why are you doing this? We could have worked together!" Frank called out.

"Fuck you, Pearson! You killed my woman. I'll see you die for that," Carver replied. Then he began firing again, sending bullet after bullet at Don and Frank. While they were shooting, the dead bodies scattered about the lobby began to rise. Both groups had people down and the dead now rose, all fighting on the same team.

In the middle of shooting at each other, Carver and Frank would have to shift their fire, shooting the ghouls down before they got too close. Once they were put down, the battle continued unabated, each trying to do in the other.

Don was the next one to die.

While Don was firing straight in front of him, trying to keep three of Carver's people in hiding, he never saw the zombie move up on him from behind. With the noise the rifle was making, he never heard the footsteps or the moans until he felt cold hands wrap around his face and teeth sink into the side of his neck. He screamed long and loud as his jugular was ripped out, his blood shooting out to bathe the face of the ghoul in a baptism of crimson. Frank turned abruptly, saw what was happening and shot the zombie in the side of the head, putting down Don's attacker. But Don was bleeding out and as Frank scooted next to his friend, Don handed him his rifle.

"You...know...what...you...have to...do," he gasped as he died with his eyes open. Frank could do nothing, his voice frozen in his throat. Don had been alive a second ago and now he was gone, like God had snapped his fingers.

Frank reached out carefully and took the last two grenades from Don's belt, then he moved as far away as he could from Don's body. Blood was spilling across the floor and was slowly moving to the left. There was a slight angle to the floor and no one would have known unless they chose to do a similar test.

Frank wasn't about to shoot his friend until he was absolutely sure he was coming back, so while he waited, he pulled the pin on a grenade, stuck his head over the desk, got his range, and tossed it at a group of three; two men and a woman.

The grenade soared across the lobby, bounced once on the floor and landed almost at the first man's feet. The man was O'Hara.

He yelled out a warning to the others and just as he finished yelling, the world went white and he was blown into a hundred gobbets of flesh and bone. His two companions fared little better. The first man taking the brunt of the blast, they were peppered with the bone shrapnel from O'Hara's decimated body and one man received a large piece of shattered rifle in the middle of his face.

Both dropped to the floor dead, their life's blood seeping from a dozen wounds, most of them mortal. The woman was luckier, at least in how she died. A piece of rifle sliced across her neck, taking her head from her shoulders like a scythe. The head tumbled to the floor, the eyes still lucid as the head gazed back at the decapitated corpse that was once her body. Then she died, her body slumping forward and spouting blood from the jagged stump of a neck like a water fountain gone mad.

Frank laughed out loud when he saw the three go down and he sent a few rounds at Carver's position. After Carver, there were four more of his people remaining and Frank knew how to even the odds even better.

He heard moaning behind him and he turned to see Marc and Ronny shambling towards him. Both were leaking blood from multiple bullet holes and were now obviously part of the undead team.

Cursing under his breath for the loss of more of his people, he shot both men in the head, then turned away while they dropped to the floor.

He spun back around and waited for four of Carver's people to pop up and fire a few times and then he risked it all and stood up, throwing the last grenade at them like a baseball. He had already pulled the pin and had counted to two before throwing it, and as the ordnance flew through the air, it exploded just above the four attacker's heads. The shrapnel sliced them into bloody hunks of flesh and all four dropped to the floor in pieces, dead.

Frank noticed movement to his right and saw Don was beginning to stir. There was a low gurgle coming from the man's mouth, the shredded jugular filling his throat with blood. Don tried to moan, but nothing but a bloody froth emerged.

Frank sighed heavily, and with a heart numb from loss, shot his friend in the head.

A black hole appeared right between Don's eyes and the body slumped to the floor, the hands dropping to his sides.

"Sorry, old friend," Frank said as he stared at the dead veteran.

A few sporadic rounds ricocheted off the desktop and Frank risked a peek from the side. All he saw was Carver. The man desperately trying to reload. A few more shots sounded and he knew Carver was putting down his own people after they had come back.

Reaching out, Frank picked up Don's rifle and waited for Carver to appear. Sure enough, he popped up and Frank sent a dozen rounds at the man, expending half a clip in seconds.

Carver dropped down and waited for Frank to stop shooting, then returned fire. Frank dropped down, as well, waited, and returned fire.

The men were at a standoff, neither able to gain ground on the other.

Carver hid behind a large leather chair, one of three in the lobby, and cursed his luck. He was so close to getting his revenge but the old bastard wouldn't go down.

That was when he knew he would have to take a chance if he wanted to end this.

Glancing around the lobby, he knew Frank was all alone. It was one against one now, and if he took the chance and won, it would soon only be him remaining. Frank fired again but after only a few short bursts of gunfire, he ducked down. In the echo of the lobby, Carver could hear the man changing clips. Deciding now or never, he jumped up and dashed across the lobby, knowing he had less than two seconds before Frank was reloaded and would bring the weapon to bear on him.

Frank heard the pounding footsteps and he turned to see what was happening when he was shocked to see Carver charging across the lobby directly towards him. Knowing he had no time, he tried to pop the fresh clip in, but he couldn't, his rushing only messing him up.

Carver yelled at the top of his lungs as he ran around the desk, the .38 aimed directly at Frank's face. Frank closed his eyes, expecting to feel searing pain and then nothing when all he heard was the dry click of an empty chamber.

Carver was empty. The man hadn't counted his shots.

Not waiting for a second chance, Frank jumped at Carver, wrapping his arms around the man's muscular legs. Both men went down in a tangle of limbs as each tried to beat the other one down, their growls of anger and hatred filling the lobby.

Carver kicked Frank away from him and the man rolled across the floor. Coming to his knees, Frank pulled his Bowie knife from its sheath, already preparing to go back in for more. Carver saw the knife and pulled one of his own, the blade flashing in the gloom.

It was still ten minutes until dawn and the lobby was bathed in darkness.

"I'll kill you, you bastard!" Frank snarled.

"You first, you fuck," Carver snarled. "You killed my woman and I'm gonna see you dead if it's the last thing I do!"

"I don't know what the fuck you're talking about, but you came in here, killed my people and attacked us without provocation! You're the one whose gonna die!"

Carver screamed a reply and charged at Frank, swinging his blade the same time Frank did.

Both men were not even trying to protect themselves, both only wanting revenge for past misdeeds. Carver reached Frank and plunged the knife into his ribs, slicing through his ribcage like it was marshmallow. Frank did the same, puncturing Carver's abdomen with seven of the nine inches of his knife. Both men grabbed each other necks with their free hands and stayed locked in a viselike grip. If either man removed their blade, the other would possibly bleed out in seconds from the mortal wounds. With their free hands straining to hold one another in place, they struggled back and forth, slipping and sliding in all the blood coating the floor.

From the stairwells, dozens of zombies began spilling into the lobby, coming up from the first floor. Neither man moved, not wanting to give in to the other.

The zombies began feeding on the supine and prone corpses littering the floor, ripping the bodies apart. Though the bodies were dead, they were still warm and it was good enough for the ravenous ghouls.

While Carver and Frank danced back and forth in the middle of the lobby with steel jammed in each others torsos, the zombies fed, ripping legs and arms from torsos and digging deep into body cavities, pulling out the warm, moist organs within. Lucy was devoured whole, her body ripped to a dozen pieces. The ghouls ate heartily, digging deep.

Dale was next, his head pulled from his shoulders as teeth chewed at his neck. Others bit down on his fingers, tearing them off to truly call the digits *finger food*.

Don's corpse was pushed to the floor where the ghouls promptly tore off his head, a zombie digging deep into his neck cavity to pull out the gobbets of meat within. His tongue was plucked from his mouth and chewed on like day old tripe, the eyes swallowed like hardboiled eggs, and his stomach torn open, his

intestines pulled out like greasy rope to be devoured by the undead.

O'Hara was easier to devour, the man already blown into bite-
sized chunks. Zombies leaned over and picked up the choicest bits,
popping the bloody chunks into their mouths like appetizers at a
buffet.

Attacker or defender, it was all just food to the walking dead.

In the middle of the lobby, Frank and Carver struggled over one
another for dominance.

It was while the two men fought back and forth, snarling into
each other's faces, and as they were becoming surrounded by the
undead, that everything changed for the worse.

There was a massive explosion from the floors under them, Dax
setting off the dynamite. The building began to shake and the floor
began to sag, but neither man would give ground, both locked in
mortal combat with the other.

There would be no winners here today, only losers.

With the building imploding around them, Carver twisted his
blade to the right, slicing deep into Frank's sternum.

Frank screamed in pain, spitting blood, and he returned the favor, pushing his knife to the hilt, then slicing upwards, gutting
Carver like a fish. Carver's intestines spilled out, steaming onto the
two men's boots to then become flattened under their feet. Bile and
excrement slathered the floor, adding to the pools of flesh and
blood.

Both men sagged on their feet and actually leaned against one
another, blood loss taking its toll.

They were now holding each other up, their hot breath caressing one another's ears.

"I'll see you in Hell, Carver," Frank hissed.

"You first," Carver snarled, and then the ceiling seemed to
groan in pain and collapsed, a thousand tons of cement and metal
raining down on the two men as the floor fell out beneath them,
sending them into the lower levels, burying them and every zombie
in the building forever.

* * *

Paul was at the top of the stairwell when the dynamite went off in the lower level of the building.

His feet went out from under him and it took all of his strength and balance not to tumble backwards down the stairs. The zombies following him were knocked over, falling head over heels in a massive ball of human arms and legs.

As for Paul, he pulled himself to his feet and charged up the remaining stairs, kicking the roof door open as he dashed onto the roof.

His Winchester rifle was in his hands and he aimed it at anything that looked dangerous.

With the building rumbling beneath him, he had no idea he had less than sixty seconds to reach Francesca before the entire roof collapsed inward, taking him and the helicopter with it.

He spotted the two prone bodies lying near the helicopter and then saw Francesca in the pilot's seat. The rotors were spinning so fast he could barely see them, only the slightest blur of the blades easy to detect.

And then the building shuddered in its death throes, a massive groan of stressed steel and concrete. Knowing whatever was happening was very, very bad, Paul began moving across the roof towards Francesca just as the roof began to cave in below his feet. Pieces began falling away; leaving gaping holes four feet long and Paul knew he had only seconds to reach the helicopter.

With the rifle in his hands, he began sprinting across the roof, jumping over the holes as the material fell apart behind him. It was like he was running on a building made of eggshells and each time his foot came down another piece fell away.

He glanced at Francesca once as he made his mad dash to the helicopter and her face was filled with worry. The rotors were spinning at top speed and blew the dust rising from the roof away, and Paul put on a burst of speed, already halfway to her.

More than half the roof was gone now, large black holes left in their wake. Paul knew if he missed even one footstep, he would plunge to his death into the building below. Massive sounds of crashing filtered up to him and penetrated the sounds of the helicopter's engine.

"Go, Francesca! Go! Before the whole damn thing falls in!" Paul yelled to her, waving for her to take off.

Behind him, a few zombies stumbled onto the roof, but as they made their way out, they fell into the openings, tumbling away to bounce off girders and jagged pieces of the building.

"Goddamn it, Francesca, go!" he yelled, the anger in his voice apparent because she hadn't left yet.

Though she didn't want to leave Paul behind, Francesca did as she was told and slowly began to raise the helicopter into the air. No sooner had the landing skids touched off the helipad than it began to crumble beneath her, the cracks spreading until small holes appeared, which were growing larger with each passing second.

Paul was jumping from one piece to another, slowly trying to reach the helipad when he felt himself losing his balance. With no choice, he dropped the Winchester and used his arms as a counterweight, and leaped for the last remaining piece of rooftop between himself and the helicopter.

As he landed on the remaining roof piece, he felt it shift under his weight and knew he wasn't going to make it.

The helicopter was a few feet in front of him, hovering in the air, and with his last attempt, he lunged for the landing skid, the roof falling away into the rising dust cloud of smoke and debris.

"Go, damn it, go!" Paul yelled as his feet dropped out from under him and he found himself hanging from the landing skid four stories up. He managed to glance down and saw nothing but a billowing smoke cloud which was growing and rising with every second.

In the pilot's seat, Francesca was struggling to hold the helicopter steady. Paul jumping onto the skid had shifted the weight, and she was now fighting the controls. She was a novice and this was far beyond what Shaun had taught her as they had practiced over the main roof of the office complex.

And with baby Shaun in her arm, she only had one hand to use and her feet pushed on the pedals as she did her best to right the helicopter. The aircraft swung back and forth and the tail rotor swung from side to side as it began to slide out of control. The rising air current from the imploding building caught the rotors, the helicopter losing what air it could find as it began to spin.

"Oh my God, Paul! I'm losing it, I can't control it!" Francesca yelled.

The baby was crying now and all Paul could do was hold on tight and hope he could keep his tenuous grip. If he let go now, he would fall to his death, there was no doubt about it. And with the helicopter spinning out of control, the centrifugal force prevented him for even attempting to climb into the rear seat.

And then the dust and smoke rose up into the air and consumed the fragile helicopter, swallowing it like some massive grey monster.

The sound of the rotor wash became lost in the explosion as the gray and white aircraft disappeared from view.

Chapter 27

Only seconds had passed since the building imploded, steel and concrete collapsing and crushing everything within its walls. The smoke rose into the air, a massive pillar of soot and dust that stained the sky a dark gray.

At first there was nothing but smoke, but then another sound slowly made itself known, echoing after the initial explosion.

At the perimeter of the smoke cloud, spinning rotors sliced through air, quickly followed by a helicopter appearing, the aircraft breaking out of the billowing smoke and soaring away from the collapsed building.

Paul was still hanging onto the landing skid, spitting soot from his mouth and blinking his eyes clear of dirt and dust, and when Francesca cleared the gray and black cloud, she managed to hold the helicopter steady for a few precious seconds.

With a groan of pain, Paul reached up, and slowly, agonizingly, he pulled himself up, his shoulders screaming from hanging for so long.

The helicopter bucked once and he almost lost his grip.

"Sorry!" Francesca called out, her voice barely audible over the howling wind.

Grumbling to himself, Paul tried again.

He had to let go with one hand to reach up to the door latch, and if he missed, it was very possible he would lose his grip and fall to his death.

But he had no choice, so with a deep breath, he reached up and managed a finger hold on the latch.

With numb fingers, he strained to get the rear door open, but eventually he succeeded, and with one last growl of pain, pulled himself into the helicopter and dropped onto the floor, breathing heavily now that he was safe. His shoulder and arms felt like he'd been bench pressing a car and he struggled to move further inside the aircraft when all his body wanted to do was rest.

He was covered from head to toe in a thin film of ash, the dust coating every inch and crevice of his clothing and body. As he rolled to the side, ash fell out of his ear and he knew he needed to get up and close the helicopter door. His feet were still sticking out and the wind was howling inside, causing baby Shaun to cry.

He realized he'd lost his rifle, as he hadn't thought about it when he'd tossed the Winchester away. He had only reacted; knowing to hesitate would be to die.

It didn't matter, it was irrelevant now. And there were other firearms in the storage compartment of the helicopter; both he and Shaun had made sure of that. It was just lucky they hadn't been at the enclave long enough to consider unpacking their supplies. They still had everything they had loaded onto the helicopter at the office complex, minus one Winchester rifle and a few boxes of ammunition.

All in all, they were in pretty good shape.

And they were still alive; which was more than could be said for Frank and his people. Paul didn't know what had happened down there in that collapsed building, but he was glad he, Francesca, and the baby weren't buried in it.

Climbing onto the rear seat, he reached out and closed the door which was flapping in the wind. As the door sealed shut, ceasing the howling wind, he realized Francesca was talking to him.

"What did you say?" he asked.

"I said, thank God you're all right, Paul. I didn't think you were going to make it," she said as she gently cradled the baby with one arm, trying to get him to stop crying. It was hard to fly the helicopter with only one hand but she kept reaching for the control stick and then letting it go as the other hand held the throttle. This was only for seconds but it became a balancing act as she hugged her baby and flew the aircraft.

"Is he okay?" Paul asked, wondering about baby Shaun.

"He's fine, just scared."

He nodded, satisfied with her answer.

Leaning back in his seat, he glanced out the window of the helicopter at the rubble below, the building nothing but crushed stone and jagged spires of twisted metal and glass. Fires were burning here and there in the debris and already he could see the stumbling forms of walking corpses.

Zombies crawled around in the debris and glass, most feeding on severed limbs they carried in their hands. Rotten teeth bit deep, devouring the limbs like they were turkey legs, the added dust and dirt nothing for them to worry about.

A few pale-blue faces gazed up at the smoke-filled sky to watch the helicopter hovering over the wreckage, a few actually reaching up to it, their hands filled with pieces of meat and slippery, moist organs.

After a minute or so, Paul looked away.

Francesca hadn't moved, not knowing where to go, and he knew they were burning fuel just hovering over the destroyed building.

"How much fuel do we have left now?" Paul asked while he wiped his face clean of soot and ash.

"Not too much, just a little more than when we left the office complex," Francesca said as she rocked baby Shaun with the crook of her arm while her hand held the throttle. It was awkward but it would suffice until he fell asleep in her lap.

He nodded curtly, a slight grin creasing his dirty face.

"Okay then, go on, get going and let's see what's out there," he said.

She merely nodded and banked the helicopter north, in the direction Richard and Shaun had wanted to go; the rotors reflecting the sun's rays like long mirrors.

It was the dawning of a new day, the rising sun filling them with hope, and as the helicopter disappeared into the horizon and the welcoming arms of another day, both of them realized that hope was all they needed.

VISIONS OF THE DEAD
A ZOMBIE STORY

by Anthony & Joseph Giangregorio

Jake Roberts felt like he was the luckiest man alive.

He had a great family, a beautiful girlfriend, who was soon to be his wife, and a job, that might not have been the best, but it paid the bills.

At least until the dead began to walk.

Now Jake is fighting to survive in a dead world while searching for his lost love, Melissa, knowing she's out there somewhere.

But the past isn't dead, and as he struggles for an uncertain future, the past threatens to consume him.

With the present a constant battle between the living and the dead, Jake finds himself slipping in and out of the past, the visions of how it all happened haunting him.

But Jake knows Melissa is out there somewhere and he'll find her or die trying. In a world of the living dead, you can never escape your past.

DEAD MOURNING: A ZOMBIE HORROR STORY
by Anthony Giangregorio

Carl Jenkins was having a run of bad luck. Fresh out of jail, his probation tenuous, he'd lost every job he'd taken since being released. So now was his last chance, only one more job to prevent him from going back to prison. Assigned to work in a funeral home, he accidentally loses a shipment of embalming fluid. With nothing to lose, he substitutes it with a batch of chemicals from a nearby factory.

The results don't go as planned, though. While his screw-up goes unnoticed, his machinations revive the cadavers in the funeral home, unleashing an evil on the world that it has not seen before. Not wanting to become a snack for the rampaging dead, he flees the city, joining up with other survivors. An old, dilapidated zoo becomes their haven, while the dead wait outside the walls, hungry and patient.

But Carl is optimistic, after all, he's still alive, right? Perhaps his luck has changed and help will arrive to save them all?

Unfortunately, unknown to him and the other survivors, a serial killer has fallen into their group, trapped inside the zoo with them.

With the undead army clamoring outside the walls and a murderer within, it'll be a miracle if any of them live to see the next sunrise.

On second thought, maybe Carl would've been better off if he'd just gone back to jail.

ROAD KILL: A ZOMBIE TALE
by Anthony Giangregorio
ORDER UP!

In the summer of 2008, a rogue comet entered earth's orbit for 72 hours. During this time, a strange amber glow suffused the sky.

But something else happened; something in the comet's tail had an adverse affect on dead tissue and the result was the reanimation of every dead animal carcass on the planet.

A handful of survivors hole up in a diner in the backwoods of New Hampshire while the undead creatures of the night hunt for human prey.

There's a new blue plate special at DJ's Diner and Truck Stop, and it's you!

DEAD WORLDS: Undead Stories
A Zombie Anthology Volume 2
Edited by Anthony Giangregorio

Welcome to a world where the dead walk and want nothing more than to feast on the living. The stories contained in this, the second volume of the Dead Worlds series, are filled with action, gore, and buckets and buckets of blood; plus a heaping side of entrails for those with a little extra hunger.

The stories contained within this volume are scribed by both the desiccated cadavers of seasoned veterans to the genre as well as fresh-faced corpses, each printed here for the first time; and all of them ready to dig in and please the most discerning reader.

So slap on a bib and prepare to get bloody, because you're about to read the best zombie stories this side of Hell!

THE DARK
by Anthony Giangregorio
DARKNESS FALLS

The darkness came without warning.

First New York, then the rest of United States, and then the world became enveloped in a perpetual night without end.

With no sunlight, eventually the planet will wither and die, bringing on a new Ice Age. But that isn't problem for the human race, for humanity will be dead long before that happens.

There is something in the dark, creatures only seen in nightmares, and they are on the prowl. Evolution has changed and man is no longer the dominant species. When we are children, we're told not to fear the dark, that what we believe to exist in the shadows is false.

Unfortunately, that is no longer true.

SOULEATER

by Anthony Giangregorio

Twenty years ago, Jason Lawson witnessed the brutal death of his father by something only seen in nightmares, something so horrible he'd blocked it from his mind.

Now twenty years later the creature is back, this time for his son.

Jason won't let that happen.

He'll travel to the demon's world, struggling every second to rescue his son from its clutches.

But what he doesn't know is that the portal will only be open for a finite time and if he doesn't return with his son before it closes, then he'll be trapped in the demon's dimension forever.

SEE HOW IT ALL BEGAN IN THE NEW DOUBLE-SIZED 460 PAGE SPECIAL EDITION!

DEADWATER: EXPANDED EDITION

by Anthony Giangregorio

Through a series of tragic mishaps, a small town's water supply is contaminated with a deadly bacterium that transforms the town's population into flesh eating ghouls.

Without warning, Henry Watson finds himself thrown into a living hell where the living dead walk and want nothing more than to feed on the living.

Now Henry's trying to escape the undead town before he becomes the next victim.

With the military on one side, shooting civilians on sight, and a horde of bloodthirsty zombies on the other, Henry must try to battle his way to freedom.

With a small group of survivors, including a beautiful secretary and a wise-cracking janitor to aid him, the ragtag group will do their best to stay alive and escape the city codenamed: **Deadwater.**

DEAD END: A ZOMBIE NOVEL

by Anthony Giangregorio

THE DEAD WALK!

Newspapers everywhere proclaim the dead have returned to feast on the living!

A small group of survivors hole up in a cellar, afraid to brave the masses of animated corpses, but when food runs out, they have no choice but to venture out into a world gone mad.

What they will discover, however, is that the fall of civilization has brought out the worst in their fellow man.

Cannibals, psychotic preachers and rapists are just some of the atrocities they must face.

In a world turned upside down, it is life that has hit a Dead End.

DEAD TOWN: A DEADWATER STORY BOOK 8
By Anthony Giangregorio
WORLD OF THE DEAD

The world is a very different place now. The dead walk the land and humans hide in small towns with walls of stone and debris for protection, constantly keeping the living dead at bay. Social law is gone and right and wrong is defined by the size of your gun.

UNWELCOME VISITORS

Henry Watson and his band of warrior survivalists become guests in a fortified town in Michigan. But when the kidnapping of one of the companions goes bad and men die, the group finds themselves on the wrong side of the law, and a town out for blood.

Trapped in a hotel, surrounded on all sides, it will be up to Henry to save the day with a gamble that may not only take his life, but that of his friends as well.

In a dead world, when justice is not enough, there is always vengeance.

FAMILY OF THE DEAD
A Zombie Anthology
by Anthony, Joseph and Domenic Giangregorio

Clawing their way out of the wet, dark earth, these tales of terror will fill you with the deep seated fear we all have of death and what comes next.

But if that wasn't bad enough to chill your soul, these undead tales are penned by an entire family of corpses. The zombie master himself, Anthony Giangregorio, leads his two young ghouls, his sons Domenic and Joseph Giangregorio, on a journey of terror inducing stories that will keep you up long into the night.

As you read these works of the undead, don't be alarmed by that bump outside the window.

After all, it's probably just a stray tree branch...or is it?

END OF DAYS: AN APOCALYPTIC ANTHOLOGY
VOLUMES 1 AND 2

Our world is a fragile place.

Meteors, famine, floods, nuclear war, solar flares, and hundreds of other calamities can plunge our small blue planet into turmoil in an instant.

What would you do if tomorrow the sun went super nova or the world was swallowed by water, submerging the world into the cold darkness of the ocean?

This anthology explores some of those scenarios and plunges you into total annihilation.

But remember, it's only a book, and tomorrow will come as it always does.

Or will it?

DEADFALL

by Anthony Giangregorio

It's Halloween in the small suburban town of Wakefield, Mass.

While parents take their children trick or treating and others throw costume parties, a swarm of meteorites enter the earth's atmosphere and crash to earth.

Inside are small parasitic worms, no larger than maggots.

The worms quickly infect the corpses at a local cemetery and so begins the rise of the undead.

The walking dead soon get the upper hand, with no one believing the truth.

That the dead now walk.

Will a small group of survivors live through the zombie apocalypse?

Or will they, too, succumb to the Deadfall.

DARK PLACES

By Anthony Giangregorio

A cave-in inside the Boston subway unleashes something that should have stayed buried forever.

Three boys sneak out to a haunted junkyard after dark and find more than they gambled on.

In a world where everyone over twelve has died from a mysterious illness, one young boy tries to carry on.

A mysterious man in black tries his hand at a game of chance at a local carnival, to interesting results.

God, Allah, and Buddha play a friendly game of poker with the fate of the Earth resting in the balance.

Ever have one of those days where everything that can go wrong, does? Well, so did Byron, and no one should have a day like this!

Thad had an imaginary friend named Charlie when he was a child. Charlie would make him do bad things. Now Thad is all grown up and guess who's coming for a visit?

These and other short stories, all filled with frozen moments of dread and wonder, will keep you captivated long into the night.

Just be sure to watch out when you turn off the light!

BOOK OF THE DEAD

Edited by Anthony Giangregorio

This is the most faithful, truest zombie anthology ever written, and we invite you along for the ride. Every single story in this book is filled with slack-jawed, eyes glazed, slow moving, shambling zombies set in a world where the dead have risen and only want to eat the flesh of the living. In these pages, the rules are sacrosanct. There is no deviation from what a zombie should be or how they came about.

The Dead Walk.

There is no reason, though rumors and suppositions fill the radio and television stations. But the only thing that is fact is that the walking dead are here and they will not go away. So prepare yourself for the ultimate homage to the master of zombie legend.

And remember... Aim for the head!

CLAN OF THE BIGFOOT

BY ANTHONY GIANGREGORIO

LIVING DEAD PRESS.COM

VICTORY OF THE DEAD

ANTHONY GIANGREGORIO

ZOMBIES, MONSTERS, CREATURES OF THE NIGHT

OPEN CASKET PRESS

OPEN CASKET PRESS.COM

THE NEW NAME IN HORROR

CREATURE FEATURE
A MONSTER ANTHOLOGY
EDITED BY
ANTHONY GIANGREGORIO